From Hell to Health:

Rick Thomson's Story

TR

FROM HELL TO HEALTH:
RICK THOMSON'S STORY

iUniverse books may be ordered through booksellers or by contacting:

iUniverse LLC
1663 Liberty Drive
Bloomington, IN 47403
www.iuniverse.com
1-800-Authors (1-800-288-4677)

ISBN: 978-1-4917-4451-2 (sc)
ISBN: 978-1-4917-4452-9 (hc)
ISBN: 978-1-4917-4453-6 (e)

Library of Congress Control Number: 2014914639

Printed in the United States of America.

iUniverse rev. date: 08/25/2014

CREDITS

Elements from Every Man's Battle Workshop weekend incorporated into Adventure 15. For more information about this helpful workshop, visit their website www.newlife.com/emb.

The highly embellished story of Walta' Duffy in the chapter entitled "Fun Time" was a fusion of stories originally told by Jeff Owen and the late Phil Kuchinsky.

The "Progression of an Idol" from Peacemaker Ministries incorporated into Adventure 19 used by permission. For comprehensive information about their ministry and resources, visit their website at www.peacemaker.net.

DEDICATION

A personal paraphrase of Matthew 13:54-55 would read, "How did he amount to anything—he's just the son of a son of a logger."

Without a foundation in Jesus Christ and effective discipleship mentoring, it's amazing how much baggage someone can accumulate during the first 20 years of life and not even realize it. Being seen but not heard was a family virtue that communicated to me I had no value. Anger was viewed as a production virtue in the logging industry, but others suffered because of the violent grip it held on me. Unknown generational sins were deep influences that moved me down dark paths. Relationships were always disposable if they got in the way of production or personal preferences. I entered adulthood with very few relational skills and large amounts of internal frustration that I didn't know how to handle. Others didn't seem to know how to help either—until God stepped in. He adopted me into His family, became my Heavenly Dad, and led me on a series of adventures (Philippians 1:6) so that His glory would shine through His redemptive plan for my life (Ephesians 2:10).

This story is dedicated to my Heavenly Dad—my greatest Hero and Mentor.

TESTIMONIALS

"*From Hell to Health: Rick Thomson's Story* will help you learn biblical discipleship principles and practically apply them to your daily life. We learned these principles many years ago by diving straight into God's Word verse by verse, with TR showing us how to grow in our Christian walk. We were told to put our 'hard hats, chaps, and steel-toed boots' on because it wasn't going to be easy. He was right, it wasn't; yet it was very rewarding. We consistently use these principles over and over again. Reading this book reminded us that relationships truly are the hardest part of the discipleship process; yet, as you'll see in this story, they can be the most edifying and important aspects of a Christian's growth." *–Jon and Ginny Ingerson (first couple discipled by TR), Jon, artist and pastoral ministry leader; Ginny, composition coordinator and ministry leader*

"No single person has had a greater influence on my walk with God than TR—from the first time when we sat down in his living room and he asked if Christ was the only way to God, and then proceeded to explain why He was. TR encouraged us to not just take his word for it but to study and chase the truth. He encouraged discussion of Scripture and increased our learning by having us take the responsibility to teach others what we had learned. I am so glad that I had someone show me what authentic Christianity is supposed to be like, not just a box to check." *–Ben Cross, owner of Bunkhouse Trailer Sales and ministry leader*

"TR's investment in my life has led me to leading a Life Group and preaching part time. I believe this is due directly to experiencing the gospel being lived out through this discipleship process in a real way." *–Glenn Marker, railroad engineer, Life Group leader, and pastoral supply leader*

"The Lord has blessed TR with the ability to disciple and train others. I just completed the Discipleship Development & Team-Building Training course for leaders. The personal discovery process used to develop spiritual maturity was great. It was a process that truly brought clarity and confidence to my beliefs." *–Kevin Burton, CPA and serving leader*

"From Hell to Health: Rick Thomson's Story is deep, impactful, and full of the 'survivor' everyone wants to emulate." *–Dianne O'Brian, RN, pastor's wife, ministry leader, and co-author of* I Can't Do It All: Breaking Free From the Lies That Control Us

"What I like most about *From Hell to Health: Rick Thomson's Story* is that I know the author has 'been there and done that'! He has experienced the incredible highs and lows of life, but through it all has allowed God to prune him and make him into the leader he is today." *–Charlie Grenade, marriage counselor and author of* DELIGHT: True Satisfaction . . . God's Way

"I'm 37, married 12 years, and the father of two boys, ages 5 and 11. I grew up in church but ran from God at age 17. My walk and life really changed when I began to be discipled by TR who was real and taught me about accountability. We did life together with other couples for a year and began to see how much hurt, baggage, and damage we had received and dealt out. It has been a five-year process of dealing with my issues and failing and getting back up again. I almost lost my marriage and my sanity; but through relationships with men who helped keep me accountable, I am in the best place spiritually I have ever been. I can see clearly what God wants for me, and I can see others struggling through the same things I did. I have begun to take other men and disciple them, taking them through the steps I went through and giving them love and grace, alongside exhortation and real accountability. This is a process and a sacrifice, but well worth it. We all have to come to the place where we realize that we need to be saved and grow to maturity; until then, we are just playing church." *—Jeremiah Gardner, owner of Gardner Road Kustoms, winner of 2006 Dupont Hot Hues Award, and disciple maker*

"God wants His kids to grow and be healthy. He desires His kids to know Him and to trust Him. His plans for us are great and wonderful. Every Christian has an extreme potential to live richly and effectively. God has given TR the ability to spiritually develop people through the progressive stages of maturity, so that they can grow and in turn mentor others. I was a spiritual infant when I met TR; but after seeing and engaging in the process of spiritual development, I can see God changing and maturing me. God is sanctifying me, and He is using TR greatly in that process." *—Jason Muhr, plumber and spiritual mentor*

"Being a Christian for a long time and still struggling in my walk with Christ was very frustrating. Going through discipleship with TR helped unlock areas in my life that led me to freedom and peace." *—Frank McMillen, farmer and ministry leader*

ACKNOWLEDGEMENTS

This story is the collective result of a variety of people and resources that have directly or indirectly influenced my life as I've journeyed through my spiritual development. The following acknowledgements are thorough; but if I had the misfortune of not acknowledging someone, please accept my humble apology.

First, I acknowledge that my work ethics and drive came from my father. Growing up, I didn't understand or appreciate what a blessing that would be throughout my adult years. I greatly underestimated the value of that gift.

Thanks, Mom, for always desiring the best for your children. My creativity and perfectionist tendencies were a gift from you.

To Marie's parents, Dad (Robert) and Mom (Marilyn) Patterson, I could never repay you for your unconditional acceptance and the gift of your daughter's love. She was the first person who put up with all the crap I dished out, and she never quit showing me love in languages that meant something to me. Only twice in the 16 years of our marriage did she ever lose her temper with me; only a saint could hold that kind of record! My accomplishments in life and ministry are largely because of her faithful partnership at the beginning of my journey. At 36 years of age, she had touched more people than the average person does in a lifetime. Remembering those who came to know Jesus on the day of her funeral is one of my biggest comforts. She had the distinct testimony of a life well lived in spite of its shortness.

To my older children—Jesse, Hannah, and Leah—thank you for being a part of my slow and painful growth. One of my greatest regrets in life is that I was unprepared to effectively disciple you through your childhood. One of my greatest joys is watching God redeem the brokenness of the past I created. Thank you also for the nine wonderful grandchildren you have blessed me with (Lane, Ellie, Madelyn, Quirt, Mya, Bearett, Marie, Harley, and Wyatt.)

In addition to many fistfights and heated arguments, my brother Wade provided more meaningful memories and support during my childhood and early adult years than anyone else.

To Wade, Donna, Dwight, Elisabeth, Sarah, and John—your individual lives have been windows for me to look through and learn courage and faith. Thank you for walking tall. Let's cross the finish line, having done our best.

A special recognition to Elisabeth for the inspiring way she lived out her stewardship of a brain tumor, with its increased complications, and completed her life's story during 2013. All the way to the end, she touched others with the love of Jesus!

Jim Ingram, Jonathan Chapman, and Dave Graybeal, you skillfully mentored me in several aspects of the construction field with complete Christian integrity. You lived what you declared as Christians. Thank you for setting high benchmarks professionally and spiritually for me to measure up to and for graciously putting up with my struggles in moving toward those benchmarks.

Thanks to all of you at Wentworth Baptist Church. You were the perfect partners for my first pastorate. The images of your faces and picture-perfect New England church will live forever in my mind. Even more important are the faith lessons we experienced together!

Pastor Clouse, Pastor Chamberlain, Pastor and Althea Hymer, and Pastor and Pattie Cardin, you were my life link to sanity after the death of Marie. You helped to prevent me from going over the edge of self-destruction and provided the advice and tangible help I needed to get back into the race again.

To Michael Deblois, I owe my discovery of the godly gift of Dee Martelle. Your willingness to help me get into twenty-first century technology surfaced a Proverbs 31 woman truly more valuable than all the wealth of the world.

I want to thank you, Dad (LeRoy) Martelle, for not shooting me when I called and asked for your daughter's hand in marriage only two weeks after meeting you. Your wisdom and trust in your daughter's judgment will never be forgotten. Thank you, Mom (Alice) Martelle, for the amazing way you mentored your daughter. The healthy example of a meaningful marriage you both set for Dee has helped us in our marriage. God bless you!

Pastor Dave and Dawn Lind, to you I owe a debt of gratitude for the years you invested in Dee's life and for the short, intense investments you have made in mine. Your counsel and influence have made a profound impact on our marriage and ministry. Your turn-around testimony greatly inspires me; you fought the darkness and won! THANK YOU!

God only knows where I'd be without you, Dee (A☺)! You ought to be awarded some kind of medal. I took your rich, fulfilled life and added way more enhancement than you thought was possible (or necessary at times). Between ending your nursing career, adding a ready-made family with three teenagers to the mix, having a premature baby born in our bedroom because I didn't believe you were in labor, having another premature baby costing us over $33,000 without insurance, and then moving to SD, OR, MT, AK, and NE, all in five years; we found out what we were made of. You were also the one that believed in this project, put our limited resources on the line, and helped make editing changes to the text, all to make this dream become a living reality. You are a great teammate!

In our travels, we met Pastor Rich and Dianne O'Brian. Pastor Rich, you are my spiritual father. You were the first pastor that identified with my past and gave me hope for my future. Dianne, your advice to "get off the farm" still rings in my ears. I think this story is the beginning result of our conversation. Thank you both so much!

Dieter Rademaker, your advice has been a benchmark for improving both my verbal and written communication. May God bless you for your willingness to invest in my life.

I owe many wonderful memories and much spiritual growth to those of you in Palmer, Talkeetna, and Cantwell, Alaska. You enriched my life in a variety of ways.

Some of my best snapshots of Alaska were because of Don and Caleb Holum. Thanks to you and your families for being friends beyond employment. Special thanks, Don, for introducing me to Enterprise; it is a truly beautiful place.

To Larry and Barbara Magnuson I am indebted for unpacking my past and for helping me develop a better spiritual paradigm. Your counsel was timely and has provided a solid compass for moving forward spiritually and professionally.

For those of you I had the privilege of doing life with at Mitchell Berean Church, you turbocharged my spiritual growth, leadership development, and team-building skills! Ben and Leslie, Glenn and Myrt, Greg and Kay, Brad and Kay, Robert and Lynn, Randy and Shery, Ron and Deb, Jeff and Jill, Gary and Gwen, Vickie, Jeff and Carrie, Jim and Fawn, Frank and Sheri, Jason and Cassandra, Jeremiah and Alesha, Russell and Holly, Levi and Amber, and Matt, thank you for spiritually partnering with me. To the "A-Team"

(Jason, Jeremiah, Jack, Glenn, Ben, Russell, and Larry), and the "Pastoral Supply Team" (Kevin, Glenn, and Jack)—you guys are the hope of the future; I couldn't be more proud of you.

Thanks to all my friends who provided valuable feedback in preparing this project for publishing. Special thanks to my "Ghost Editor" for her editing expertise that she willingly performed in the middle of an already full life. I am in awe of your gift!

CONTENTS

INTRODUCTION

In this real-to-life story, you will be exposed to five phases of spiritual development: *Lost, Infant, Child, Teen,* and *Adult.* Though brief sketches of the beginning phases are presented, this book is specifically designed to help followers of Jesus through the challenges of spiritual *Teen* development. The five phases are more fully developed in *5 Phases of Spiritual Development.* And, you will walk through the Adult phase of spiritual development in *From Hell to Health: Peter McCormick's Story.*

Without a relationship with God through Jesus Christ, this book will make very little sense to you. If you are *Lost,* God paid the highest price so that you could experience life at its best—a two-way relationship with Him. I would recommend that you read the Gospel of John in the New Testament of a Bible and find someone you know who is an authentic follower of Jesus to answer any questions you might have.

If you have already moved through the *Lost* phase and have accepted the finished work of Jesus, you are a child of God. Now you are working through the spiritual development process.

This spiritual development process is taught in the New Testament and also very clearly pictured in the Old Testament through God's activity with the nation of Israel. In Exodus, we see God save His people from bondage (being *Lost*) and then guide them through the security needs and messiness of spiritual *Infancy.*

At Mount Sinai, God gave them knowledge. He also provided the opportunity to practice that knowledge in a safe environment as they developed character and served Him and others through their *Childhood* development. After two years, God knew they should be ready for the *Teen* phase of testing out their new identity on the battlefield of spiritual conquest. Thirty-eight years later they finally caught up with God's spiritual development plan. In the books of Joshua, Judges, and First Samuel, we read of typical teenage decisions and the consequences that followed. Finally, God's people reached spiritual *Adulthood* under the leadership of King David and several succeeding relatives. The management of spiritual *Adulthood* can be seen through the rest of the Old Testament.

Many of the discipleship materials that are available deal with the *Infant* and *Child* phases of spiritual development and often create the illusion that discipleship is a fairly short process that can be learned academically. However, the challenging emotional and relational aspects that are needed to reach spiritual maturity are usually not adequately addressed. *From Hell to Health: Rick Thomson's Story* is designed to deal with the *Teen* phase of spiritual development. Spiritual *Teen* issues are presented in a mentored setting for readers to better understand what the process looks like.

The content and the concepts in this book will stretch many. Our Western culture is one of comfort, entitlement, and safety. Few are pushed to discover their full potential. Any bad that comes to the surface is quickly blamed on others. And, we want huge rewards for minimal effort. The Christian community is no exception. We hide behind a false concept of love where we believe nothing negative should happen to anyone.

Skillful and successful athletes, military personnel, and others in demanding professions all have common denominators—discipline and self-awareness. By engaging difficulty, many learn who they are and how they respond to increasing pressure. Many know how to acknowledge and control their emotions. Many know their limits and yet do not use them to avoid unpleasant challenges. Many know how to read people and make necessary adjustments to expectations. They often desire the best for others.

If you long for more than you are currently experiencing as a follower of Jesus, and you are willing to push through the hardships of God's spiritual development process, you will find this book a refreshing challenge.

I have used the medium of storytelling to communicate the concepts of spiritual *Teen* development because there is little in life more powerful than a well-told story. Jesus consistently and effectively used parables to communicate important truths. Many modern-day story resources have left meaningful impressions on my mind. After creating several discipleship workbooks of my own, I felt that taking truth and putting it into story form would provide additional clarity.

This story is a work of fictitious reality. Any resemblance to real life was intentional; but all names, places of origin, and exact details were changed to protect both the guilty and the innocent.

This story is not sanitized. Without being overly crude, I have added elements of real-life struggles. I want to reach people who can identify with the messier side of life, so some readers may find portions of this book to be offensive. If this story were a movie, it would probably be rated PG-13 for mild language, violence, sexual references, and thematic elements.

My hope for this Discipleship Development Adventure is to provide answers to some crucial questions that many followers of Jesus wrestle with.

> ➤ Who is God?
> ➤ Does God really care about me?

- Can I completely trust God?
- Does God have a specific purpose for my life?
- How can I discover/realize the full potential of my life?
- What does the discipleship process look like?
- Can I be free from the bondage I am in?
- Why does God make things so hard at times?
- How can I overcome negative past experiences and move forward into a productive future?
- How can I build relationships with a high level of trust?
- How does a disciple of Jesus reach spiritual maturity?
- How do disciples effectively disciple others?

THE
NEED FOR
DISCIPLESHIP

RICK THOMSON

It was a beautiful spring day in Wallowa County, Oregon, as 28-year-old Rick Thomson drove his pickup in the direction of Hell's Canyon. The sun was shining on snow-capped mountains. Rivers were flowing with crystal-clear water. Cattle dotted the landscape, grazing on fresh, green grass. The sky was the bluest of blues, making the gentle wisps of white clouds stand out crisp and clear on nature's canvas. But the contrast between what Rick was seeing with his eyes and what he felt in his soul couldn't have been greater.

He knew he was driving faster than he should; but with hands clenched on the steering wheel and a sick feeling in the pit of his stomach, he barreled down the winding canyon road to Imnaha and up the other side toward Hat Point, not sure if the snow had melted enough for him to make it all the way. With reckless abandon, he rammed through lingering drifts and skidded to a stop at his favorite overlook with a spray of gravel. Slamming the truck door with enough force to break the sound barrier, he briskly walked to a place where he came to pray when he wanted clarity.

Today, he wasn't looking for clarity. He needed reality—reality that God existed, reality that He really cared, and most of all, reality that his life had a purpose. His turmoil had started Sunday and built all week. A church in La Grande was having him speak each Sunday while they searched for a pastor. Although many expressed appreciation for his speaking, no one seemed to consider that he was capable of more than that. This week, after the service, he had been informed that they had found a "real" pastor; he wouldn't be needed anymore.

Throughout the rest of the week, Rick had become more and more aggravated by those who lived with a fulfilled sense of purpose. His brother Waylon seemed to have always known that he was born to be a logger. Jim, the owner of the local hardware store, constantly had a smile on his face and never seemed to tire of helping people. A waitress at his favorite café had a knack for making each customer feel like the most important person in the world; several senior citizens would only eat there when she was working. *For crying out loud,* Rick thought, *even the school janitor seems more fulfilled than I am.*

It was obvious that a particular occupation wasn't the key to having a sense of purpose. Maybe he was like the canyon in front of him—full of rugged potential but with a negative label stuck on him. Or, maybe his background would always define what he was allowed to do. His upbringing had produced no confidence that he was good enough to change his circumstances. He had never felt capable of pleasing his parents; so maybe he couldn't please God, either. Slowly, the thought was growing within him that God didn't think he was good enough to be used in a significant way.

"Am I, God? Am I good enough?" he yelled aloud.

His mind started to drift back in time, and a wry grin appeared on his face as he thought of his friend Peter McCormick. At age 31, Pete (or "Dr. Peter McCormick" as Rick liked to tease since Peter had earned his doctorate) was on his second successful pastorate. *(Little did either of them know that a third was just around the corner.)*

The two men had similar backgrounds and, though Peter was a few years older than Rick, they had been best friends during Peter's teenage years, growing up in one of the most beautiful places on earth—Enterprise, Oregon.

Peter's dad, John, was a coal miner from West Virginia, who had sensed God's call on his life and left the mines as a young man. Without any formal training, he had gone into pastoral ministry. Consistent with his desire to reach the breed of rough men he was familiar with, John accepted several pastorates in the West and eventually brought his family to Enterprise.

John was hardworking but easy-going, with wrinkles around his eyes that seemed to smile when he was talking with you. Even when Peter got into trouble, his dad had the unique ability to deal with each issue separately and to place the relationship he had with his son above any trouble Peter might get himself into. Rick found himself at Peter's house every chance he could get.

Rick's heritage was in Wallowa County and the timber company his grandfather had started. Eventually his grandfather passed the logging side of the business to Rick's father Ray, while the saw mill and trucking side went to an uncle.

Ray was a hard-bitten man with a troubled childhood and an excessive, no-nonsense approach to seemingly everything. Rick learned at an early age that displeasing his father would usually result in a fist to the head or a boot to his south end and a steady stream of colorful vocabulary not found in a dictionary but clearly understood by any who heard it. Rick grew up feeling that his behavior was the basis for whether or not he was appreciated and loved, a sense he eventually transferred to his relationship with God.

Over time, Peter's dad built a relationship with Rick's father and eventually led both Ray and his wife to the Lord. Rick's life took on a brand new vibrancy with his whole family at church every time the doors were open. He discovered the reality of Jesus all around him—a reality so deep that the church problems he later experienced never completely diminished it.

Looking back, Rick wished with everything in him that the effects of his family's newfound faith would have lasted. But, when Peter's mom was killed in a car accident, his dad decided to move the family back near relatives in West Virginia.

Rick begged Pete not to go, but there was no changing the plans Peter's dad had made. Just before leaving, Peter had looked at Rick and promised, "If there is any way I can move back here, I will."

Rick had never felt accepted by his father, and now he began to feel abandoned by Pete, by God, and by the church family that had been an anchor of stability for him. He began to wonder if there was anyone he could trust. With no mentor to disciple Rick through the spiritual development process, he began to experience every spiritual malady possible.

After Peter's dad left, the church board began to search for a new pastor and eventually called Andrew Richards. At first Pastor Andrew seemed to be a good fit for the culture of the area. His preaching was evangelistic and bold (something respected especially among the men), although a little too negative and focused on do's and don'ts. Many in the community came to know Jesus as Savior and, within just a couple of years, the church added an addition to handle the growth. During the building project, several character flaws surfaced in Pastor Andrew which resulted in a full-blown church war, with Rick's father right in the middle. It was an unwelcome and unwanted experience for a town built around family and community values, and it changed the dynamics of Rick's future far more dramatically than his friend moving away.

Rick's father left the church, disillusioned and embittered toward pastors in general. During the ensuing years, he made several attempts to get plugged into churches without much success. The only other pastor that Rick's father warmed up to was Pastor Vance Taylor whose first pastorate was at one of the churches in Wallowa. The family experienced a few years of relative spiritual stability under Pastor Vance's influence; but when he moved on to another ministry, Ray never completely trusted another pastor, even though he never stopped attending church.

Ray slowly returned to his hard-bitten ways. Over a period of years, he began a secret life of sin that would eventually surface to wreak more damage than Rick would have ever thought possible in a family that claimed to follow Jesus. Meanwhile, Rick was left to deal with the confusion and frustration of his spiritual immaturity.

Though he worked for his father, Rick distanced himself emotionally and began a few vices of his own in an effort to escape the emotional pain he was feeling. Though his vices gave him temporary relief, he was flooded with tremendous guilt. Free time became a dreaded enemy, either taking him down the road of his vices or of numb recovery. On one hunting trip, as he sat alone in a deer stand, the guilt and shame were so strong that he slowly pointed the rifle towards his body, only to become even more disgusted with himself for not having the guts to pull the trigger.

Because he was socially challenged, the only manageable relief Rick found was in the hard work of the woods, where at the end of a typical day, he had the satisfaction of seeing what he had been able to produce. That seemed to be the one thing his father somewhat valued in him. Rick's brother Waylon added a sense of camaraderie when he joined the family business after high school.

Out of desperation to break the spell of insignificance, Rick applied to a Bible college; but, after being accepted, he decided not to attend. Somehow, as he thought back over pastors he had been exposed to, their head knowledge and educational degrees couldn't make up for their lack of character and emotional immaturity. Pastor

Vance had been the exception. Rick wanted to be an exception also, and he wasn't convinced that college was the solution.

But that is all water over the dam, he thought, as he came back to the present. *Here I am still confused and frustrated more than a decade later. Will I ever be able to find and live out my purpose in life? Why am I so messed up? Maybe I'm not even a Christian anymore.*

At moments like this, he seemed to hear a quiet voice say to him, **"I have great plans for you!"**

God, is that You speaking to me? If You are, help me figure things out!

Looking out over the expanse of Hell's Canyon, Rick continued to question and cuss internally, while God smiled lovingly from Heaven, knowing what He had planned for this son of His. It would be awhile before Rick would heal from his inner turmoil and find true purpose in life.

Little did he know that God was preparing to send that healing through his friend, Peter McCormick. But first, God wanted to guide Rick through spiritual development challenges so that he would be prepared to help many others struggling with the same issues. It was also a good thing Rick didn't realize that Satan and the demons of Hell would try with all their might to destroy him.

PETER MCCORMICK

Tall, smart, dark, and handsome would have been an accurate description of Peter McCormick. He had wavy black hair, the appealing looks of his father, and the height and studious personality of his mother.

During the years of Rick's struggle, Peter earned his bachelor degree at a conservative Christian college on the East Coast where he married the girl of his dreams and started a family—first a boy and then a girl. He began to pastor a small local church. Under Peter's pastoral leadership, the church experienced solid growth; people were saved and grew in their faith.

Moving to the Midwest, Peter earned his master's and doctoral degrees in discipleship and leadership development. He served as the successful lead pastor of a large contemporary church. This church had a totally different philosophy of ministry and structure than his first pastorate. Here, Peter was able to live out his passion of investing in the development of potential young leaders; he began mentoring them to reach their personal goals and visions. God blessed his family with another baby girl.

On the surface, Peter's life looked perfect. But Peter had dealt with the death of his mother, his dad's unhealthy grieving process, the glories and limits of a traditional church culture, the mixture of freedom and complacency in a contemporary church, and the frustration of how to ideally and practically create a church culture to achieve lasting health and growth.

While Rick was dealing with personal spiritual development issues, Peter was dealing with the mechanics of discipleship, leadership development, and team building.

Though Peter deeply appreciated his academic training and the doors it had opened for him, he became increasingly frustrated by what he called "church politics" and his lack of training in addressing those issues. He received practical advice from seasoned pastors, business journals, and his own personal trial-and-error experiences. **He knew that God designed the church to be a healthy and growing entity, so he was determined to discover how to make that the norm rather than the exception.**

Then the opportunity for which he had hoped and prayed came. Peter found a struggling church in Kennewick, Washington, close to where he had grown up, that was looking for an *Equipping Pastor*. After several interviews with the church, he knew that this was the best place to live out the philosophy of ministry that God had been forging in his life. Peter hoped that Rick would become an important part of this ministry.

God was getting ready to ignite the fuse to plans He had for both Peter and Rick. There was going to be some heat while the fuse burned, but the fireworks display would be well worth it.

RECONNECTION

It was Saturday morning, and Rick was in the bathroom getting ready to start his day. As he looked into the mirror, sometimes he was okay with his rather long and rugged-looking face; other times, he felt like God would have done better giving his features to a mule. In his opinion, the mustache and chin whiskers helped to improve his appearance, though his family strongly objected to anything less than military smoothness. His deep-set eyes could be intimidating without their occasional smile wrinkles when he found something humorous. He had just finished combing his thick brown hair when the telephone rang.

"Guess who?" questioned the voice on the other end.

"Well, if it isn't the honorable Dr. Peter McCormick," Rick laughed, recognizing the voice of his friend.

"Guess what?"

"With the highly professional line of questioning I'm getting here, it sounds like one of us is in trouble."

"Not yet, but it's a distinct possibility now that I'm moving back reasonably close to your neck of the woods."

Rick felt his heart begin to race. "Are you kidding?"

"Everything was finalized yesterday. I wanted you to be the first to know."

"Are you moving back to Enterprise?" Rick questioned hopefully.

"Reasonably close by Western standards. A church in Kennewick has asked me to be their pastor. If you can handle the drive, Lisa and I would love to have you spend some time with us after we get settled."

"It's not the drive that I'm worried about," Rick answered more seriously than he had intended.

"Then what *are* you worried about, tough guy?"

Rick suddenly wished he had simply accepted the invitation instead of cracking open the door to an area of personal turmoil. "It's just that I have been trying for several years to figure out my purpose in life. I don't want anything to happen to our friendship, but I can't help envying how things have turned out for you. And besides, are you sure Lisa will want to put up with me? I might be a corrupting influence on you and your kids."

"Rick, one of the reasons I took this job was to be closer to you. I told Lisa when we got married that if God ever provided us with the opportunity to move back out West, I wanted to be close enough to reconnect with you in a meaningful way. **As a couple, we've been praying for over a year that God would provide this opportunity**.

"Besides, if you still eat like you used to, you'll at least get fattened up while you're with us. Lisa's the best cook in the world!"

"That sounds good! Hey, do you need a hand moving?"

"Thanks, but we've got a moving company lined up to help minimize the stress. For some reason, Lisa felt I was a little unreasonable during our last move. She politely, but firmly, refused to go through a similar experience this time. Maybe it was throwing an unlabeled box of her favorite clothes into the dumpster that tipped her over the edge," Peter chuckled.

Hearing the humor in his friend's voice helped Rick relax. "Having never been married, I wouldn't know for sure; but it does sound like you may have figured it out. Let me know when you're settled and ready for me to come over."

A few weeks later, Rick found himself making the drive to Kennewick. After finding the address Peter had sent, he slowly walked up to the door and nervously knocked.

When Peter opened the door, Rick's envy grew. Memories of the times he had with Peter's parents as a kid flooded his mind. Nothing had really changed except the faces; instead of Peter's dad and mom it was Peter and Lisa, but the warmth and security he felt were the same. Inside he was choking up. This might be harder than he had thought it would be, but the smells of food coming from the kitchen helped provide some equilibrium. Soon he was sitting around the dining room table and proving that one of the ways to a man's heart is through his stomach.

CATCHING UP/
HEALTH PROBES

After supper, Peter showed Rick the house, ending up in the den. Rick quickly scanned the room, taking in his friend's framed academic achievements combined with pictures that let him know Peter had not forgotten his roots. He was lost in warm memories when Peter's voice brought him back to the present.

"So, Rick," Peter probed, wanting to hear about the years they had been apart, "tell me about your efforts to discover God's purpose for your life."

Relieved, but still cautious, Rick answered, "Well, let's see. After you left, the church board hired a guy named Pastor Andrew who ended up splitting the church, and then we bounced around to several other churches. I spent most of my weekday hours after high school working in the woods. Then a pastor over in Wallowa helped me discover that I was gifted to teach, and I started to sense that God wanted to use me in full-time ministry. To be honest, though, I've never been overly impressed with the educational process used to develop ministry leaders, so I chose not to go to college. But, without credentials, it's hard to find a church that will take me seriously."

Rick stood up, nervously pacing back and forth, before continuing. "My father's no help, either. Once, when I was foolish enough to share my dream of being in ministry, he told me, 'Son, you don't have what it takes to be a pastor.' You know, I can't remember a single time he has supported me. Mom has tried, but my father always makes sure that he undoes any effort she makes. He is a master at making me feel—well, useless. To this day, I don't know if he was motivated by bitterness over what happened with Pastor Andrew, or if he just didn't want to lose one of his work crew. Either way, it worked. I caved in and just kept working for him. Fortunately for me, Waylon got so pissed off with father's hard-ass, self-centered ways that he went into business for himself, and then I went to work for Waylon."

Peter was surprised. "Waylon's in business for himself?"

Rick grinned, mild humor shining in his eyes, before growing serious. "Yeah. Who'd have ever thought I'd be working for my younger brother! Between work, some damnable vices I can't seem to shake, and an occasional speaking opportunity, that's pretty much been life for me since you left. It almost seems as if God Himself has it in for me; and, in some ways, I can't blame Him. In the grand scheme of things, I'm just a backwards cog in the machine of life."

Rick sat back down, a frown forming on his face. "So is my purpose to spend the majority of my life working at an unfulfilling job so that I can afford to occasionally do what God seems to have gifted me to do?"

Peter shook his head. "I don't think so. **I think you are allowing the problems of your past to get in the way of knowing God and how He works.**"

Peter paused, and then asked, "Rick, have you ever been discipled?"

"Never. It seems like after you're saved, you're just expected to figure things out by going to church. That sure hasn't cut it for me."

With a look of understanding, Peter responded, "Christians can be discipled in a variety of ways. However, I can tell you from experience that the discipleship process should be more relational—focusing on transparency and accountability—than the method typically found in traditional American churches, and more intentional than the average contemporary church culture.

"This Sunday, you're going to hear me teaching a series on spiritual development. If you think you can handle hearing some of the same content twice, I'll share the basic points with you tonight."

Rick exhaled with a huff. "I can handle it, but you need to be warned; I've been accused of being unteachable."

"Why?"

"I chose not to go to college."

"That's it?"

"I think there was more to it than that, but nothing more was mentioned."

"Interesting; how did you handle that?"

"At first I was pissed off; actually, that's putting it mildly. After I cooled off and could think, I concluded that the statement was made more from believing that I was a pain in the—aaah rear end than from really understanding my beliefs. I mean, David didn't go to boot camp or officer's training, but he kicked some serious butt when he took Goliath down. Before the battle, though, Saul tried to tell him that he needed to learn how to fight the *normal* way. David just believed God could use his simple way of doing things to get the job done."

"Well, I'll make up my own mind as to whether or not you are teachable."

ONE-ON-ONE DISCIPLESHIP

SPIRITUAL DEVELOPMENT OVERVIEW

At that moment, Lisa came in with a couple of glasses and a pitcher of iced tea. As they drank, Peter suggested, "Before we get started, Rick, let's move down closer to my desk. I've got some teaching tools there that will help me to communicate."

As they moved toward the other end of the den, Rick found himself taking in the pine wainscoting and beautiful walnut bookcases and desk. He noticed that Peter had organized this end of the den so that it had a warm feel to it, but there was also a whiteboard and charts that hinted this would be more than a casual conversation.

"Most of what I am about to share with you came from my first pastorate. I worked hard to develop a practical discipleship process that made sense to the average Christian. I do want you to know, however, that this is not a formula. **Spiritual development is a very fluid process that can regularly change based upon the choices people make**.

"Also, please do me a favor as I go through this. If I start to get too preachy, let me know. I sometimes can get pretty intense because I know the power this has to help people see life from God's perspective."

"Sweet! This is the first time I've ever had permission to tell a pastor off." Rick noticed that his comment brought a grin to his friend's face.

Peter pointed to a chart that looked similar to a physical development poster found in a doctor's office. "What is the normal process for a baby to become an adult?"

"I'm no expert, but I'd say he needs food and someone to change his diaper. Then there's school and, eventually, if he has any drive at all, some kind of job, followed by marriage and a family."

"If I labeled each phase of the development process you just described as moving from *Infant* to *Child* to *Teen* to *Adult*, would that make sense to you?

"Sure."

"Biblically and practically, the spiritual development process is quite similar to physical development."

"I can see the connection," Rick replied.

"Good. That will help us as we go through the individual phases. To begin with, spiritual *Infants* need *Food, Filthy Messes* cleaned up, resources to *Fight* harmful influences, a sense of *Family* security, and *Fun*. They also need help determining if their *Fussiness* is over a want or a need. *Infancy* can be the messiest phase; but if it is handled well, it should be the shortest and safest of the phases."

Rick quickly questioned, "So if I have messiness in my life, does that mean I'm still a spiritual *Infant?*"

"Not necessarily. Spiritual *Infancy* is generally messy. But when a follower of Jesus is plagued by a particular brand of messiness, then there is probably an emotional and relational root of dysfunction driving the messiness."

"What phase deals with those types of issues?"

"The *Teen* phase, which is the toughest phase of all. It's just like moving from physical adolescence to adulthood."

"So what's the *Childhood* phase like?" Rick asked.

"It's the knowledge phase."

"Bible knowledge?"

"That's part of it; but in addition to biblical *Content*, it also involves *Change Choices*, *Character* development, and *Caring* for others while discovering personal *Capabilities*."

Rick wore a puzzled frown. "So, when someone has gone through the *Infant*, *Child*, and *Teen* phases and has moved into the *Adult* phase, does that mean that he is done growing spiritually?"

"Rick, let me answer your question with a question: since becoming a physical adult, have you stopped learning things?"

"Heck, no!"

"Do you think that, if you are still alive 50 years from now, you will still be learning things?"

"If I want to."

"Exactly! Being an *Adult* doesn't end spiritual growth, but it does mean that you are processing things like an *Adult* instead of like an *Infant*, *Child*, or *Teen*. It also means that you are reproducing yourself in the lives of others. You are not only receiving spiritual benefits, you are actively and skillfully investing in the spiritual well-being of others."

"That makes sense," Rick responded thoughtfully.

"So, where do you think you may be in the spiritual development process?" Peter probed.

"Whew, I'm not sure! Maybe ending the *Child* phase."

"That's a pretty good guess. What I'd like to do right now, if you are up for it, is to go over the *Teen* phase in detail to help you get an idea of what lies ahead of you."

To ward off his internal uneasiness, Rick joked, "Okey dokey!"

TEEN OVERVIEW

"I've tried to organize the *Teen* content in a way that's easy to explain and remember. To get a big picture of the *Teen* phase of spiritual development, the number combination 3-4-5 can be a helpful memory hook."

That's easy enough to remember, Rick thought.

Peter began to explain the numbers, "First, there are *three* key spiritual *Teen* development components:

- *Paradigm*
- *Past*
- *Potential*

"Next, there are *four* key *Paradigm* questions:

- What do you believe about God?
- What do you believe about Satan?
- What does Satan believe about you?
- What does God believe about you?

"And lastly, there are *five Potential* building blocks:

- Practices
- Partnership

- Personal Wiring
- Passions (Spiritual Gifts)
- Perseverance

"Before I begin explaining some of these concepts, let's see if I am communicating clearly. What are the three key components in the spiritual development of *Teens?*"

Rick jokingly mocked, "That's easy, Dr. McCormick! The three key spiritual development components are *Pair-a-dime, Past,* and *Potential.* And, by the way, what's a cott'n-pickin' pair-a-dime? Those $100 words are over my head. It sounds like someone just found two dimes in a parking lot."

Peter chuckled as he wrote the spiritual *Teen* development components on the whiteboard. "Cute! And just in case you aren't aware, here's how you spell paradigm: p-a-r-a-d-i-g-m."

"Oops."

"Let's see now.... A paradigm is a particular structure, pattern, or example of how things can, or should, be—like a business plan or a blueprint. Here's a practical explanation from your world of logging. You're working for Waylon now, right?"

"Yeah."

"Does Waylon run his logging business the same as your father?"

"Heck, no!"

"What's different?" Peter probed.

Rubbing his fingers together, Rick answered, "Well, for one thing, he pays me more."

"Why?" Peter pressed.

"Because one of his gripes with our Old Man was that we didn't get part of the business profits. Using your word, our father's paradigm was that his boys existed to make him money. Waylon believes in sharing profits with those who make the profits possible."

"Anything else?" Peter continued to press.

Pushing his hat further back on his head, Rick thoughtfully answered, "Well, I'd have to say that Waylon isn't afraid of new ideas. Our father believed that his system was the *ONLY* way of doing things. He'd go into orbit when one of us would even suggest something new. Waylon, on the other hand, is always looking for innovative ways to make things easier, faster, and more profitable. He's recognized that the timber industry is changing quickly, with the very real possibility that logging will become a challenging way to make a living in Wallowa County. To keep ahead of business changes, Waylon has already diversified into ranching, and he's even mentioned starting a rustic furniture company to join the small-business atmosphere of Enterprise."

"Are you beginning to see just from the example of your father and brother that **a person's thoughts and beliefs are the example, the framework, the pattern—the *Paradigm*—for the way he or she views and interacts with life?**"

"Yeah; that actually is making a lot of sense."

"It also means that the better you know someone else's paradigm, the better you can choose the degree to which you want to be associated with her or him. In the context of logging, if I mention the name of Waylon Thomson or Ray Thomson, you automatically know what you think and believe about each of them. And, based upon what you think and believe, you chose to be identified with and work for Waylon."

Rick nodded in agreement.

"While we're on the *Paradigm* component, I'd like to help you visualize the differences between God's and Satan's *Paradigms*, and then explain how you can choose to let the *Past* and *Potential* components of your life story be identified with God's *Paradigm*. Let's draw a diagram that you can help me complete."

Rick watched as Peter uncapped his marker and moved to the center of the whiteboard to draw a large box divided into four sections by a cross that extended above and below the box.

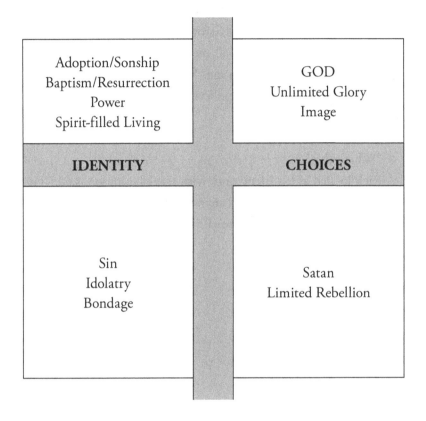

Peter gave the marker to Rick and directed, "I want you to write some words, which I call 'faith-anchors,' in each of the four sections surrounding the cross. In the upper right section, write the words *GOD*, *Unlimited Glory*, and *Image*. Then write *Satan* and *Limited Rebellion* in the lower right section. Now, in the lower left section, I want you to write several words that represent concepts derived from Satan's influence: *Sin*, *Idolatry*, and *Bondage*. Lastly, but very important, are the redemptive God-concepts, represented in the upper left section by the following words: *Adoption/Sonship, Baptism/Resurrection Power, and Spirit-filled Living.* On the left cross member I want you to write the word **IDENTITY** and on the right cross member write the word **CHOICES**."

Rick studied the chart as he wrote.

"Now, I realize you know all the facts that I'm about to share with you, but please bear with me. Many followers of Jesus know the facts, yet most miss the application; they fail to anchor their faith on the facts."

"Pete, I have a confession."

"What's that?"

Rick looked at his friend and, with some hesitation, said, "I'm not sure if I even believe in God anymore; I'm not even sure whether He cares about people in a personal way."

GOD, OR NO GOD

Leaning forward and looking Rick in the eyes to show how much he cared, Peter said, "That's okay. Sometimes life circumstances can make belief in the unseen God a challenging exercise. Many Christians, even spiritual leaders I know, have doubted the existence of God. It was their doubt that made them search for answers. Integrity compels me to admit that some of them abandoned their faith. But most people who struggle with doubt find that, in their quest for truth, their faith becomes unshakeable. **Faith must have a rational basis as its anchor point.**"

"Really?"

"Really."

"Wow! I thought you might flip or start chewing me out."

"Not my style. Besides, one of Jesus' disciples was dubbed 'Doubting Thomas.' Jesus didn't get upset with Thomas's crisis of faith. He simply provided the facts Thomas needed to move on. I think that, as we go through the *Paradigm* components, you'll begin to get answers to some of your doubts."

"I hope so. I'm sick and tired of what's going on inside me."

"Would you say that you doubt the existence of God because of a lack of evidence to support His existence, or because your life circumstances unfolded differently than you feel they would have if God were real and cared?"

"To be honest, it's probably the second reason."

"Sometimes it's helpful, when you are struggling with God concepts, to go back to what you know is true. What rational anchor points do you have when it comes to your faith in God?"

"I'm not sure I ever thought about it."

Peter pressed, "Do you have any credible evidence to support the existence of God?"

"Yeah, I think I do. The origin of our physical universe has to be explained somehow."

Peter nodded in agreement. "That's a great starting point."

"I just can't see how Eastern religions, mythology, or tribal beliefs offer credible explanations of origin. Atheism offers a lot of reactionary noise. Modern science presents *Random Chance* as the answer, but to believe that random forces had pre-existing resources and the power to be responsible for everything we see defies common sense. It violates too many mathematical and natural laws. When I think of the intricate details involved in the design of things like wildlife, photosynthesis, the human body, tidal changes, or the solar system, I realize it takes less faith to believe in an *Intelligent Designer* than other theories of origin."

Rick paused for a moment before adding, "I think getting rid of God is more about people not wanting accountability than anything else; if He's the Creator, then everyone has to answer to Him."

Peter sat quietly, knowing that silence would best help his friend to process his answers.

Rick continued, "Also, when I take God out of the picture, what is the meaning of life? What kind of fulfillment does alcohol, drugs, sex, or possessions provide? Every accomplishment or experience needs a greater one to take its place. Possessions need insurance to protect them, and faith in an insurance company is not very reassuring for me. Then there are those who think they are the cock of the walk until someone or something comes along and knocks them over. To top it all off, without God, most people struggle with the thought of dying."

For clarification, Peter responded, "What I'm hearing you say is that God's existence is real to you because of His creative abilities and the purpose He has behind His creation?"

"I'd say so. Creation is the only rational explanation for the existence of what I see around me; and even I am smart enough to realize that when something is created, it is always created with a purpose."

Peter looked at Rick quizzically and asked, "Those sound like very convincing anchor points; so where are you stuck?"

With a pained expression, Rick asked, "Why doesn't God use His creative powers to prevent all the crap that goes on in the world?"

"You are dealing with what I call a 'Tension Point.'"

"What do you mean?"

"Between the God presented in the Bible and real life there are seemingly contradictory practices and principles that create varying degrees of tension. Sometimes it involves contrasts within the character of God such as grace versus justice or holiness versus forgiveness. God is very clear about the roles and responsibilities He has for people—in marriage, government, or church life. But, what you see in real life doesn't match His ideal. That's when it is fairly easy to wonder *why*. I mean, if God has an ideal, then *why* doesn't He do more to protect it?

"The tension point in your question lies between seeing life with your finite limitations, and being unable to understand God's infinite and perfect wisdom."

With eyes blazing and his fist clenched, Rick exploded, "Don't give me that bullshit! I hate the mind games people play when it comes to the tough questions about God."

Peter calmly asked, "Then what answers have you come up with?"

Trying to get a grip on his emotions, Rick replied, "I don't have any that make sense."

Gently Peter pressed, "May I share some answers that help me manage tension points?"

With head and shoulders sagging, Rick replied, "Sure." Inside he was cussing himself for venting his frustration to one of the only friends he'd ever had. He didn't want to ruin things now that Peter was back in his life.

Peter spoke with assurance, almost as if he had read Rick's mind. "Rick, you need to feel comfortable being yourself with me. I've discipled a bunch of guys over the years, and you need to know that you're not going to do or say anything that will scare, shock, or upset me."

Rick relaxed a little. "Really?"

"You can count on it." Peter looked warmly at his friend. "Tension points are really a gift from God. In the middle of the tension, faith has an opportunity to grow. **As you wrestle with tension points, you learn a little more about God, about others, and about yourself**. As you gain knowledge, you have an opportunity to grow your faith to higher levels than you thought possible. You'll never figure everything out in this life. Any person, Christian or not, who claims to have all the answers is lying through his teeth.

"Test what I'm telling you and see if it is true. What have you learned about God, others, or yourself through 'all the crap' you have experienced?"

Rick slowly answered, "Well, I guess I'd have to say that God is more patient than I've given Him credit for. If I were Him, I'd have shot a bolt of lightning down and toasted a lot of people, myself included."

What else would God's patience towards problem people imply about His character?"

Rick hesitated, "That He believes the best about people?"

"Yes. He has a purpose for their lives greater than the mess they create. You see, God is using tension points to develop spiritual muscles of faith in your life. But you've become so focused on the tension that you're missing the point.

"I think, as we go through the *Paradigm* and *Past* spiritual development components, you will discover even more answers for your inner tension. My hunch is that some of your past experiences are clouding the paradigm you need in order to make sense of your life story. Right now, your pain is clouding reality."

Quietly, Rick replied, "Maybe."

"Let's keep going with the chart. I think it will give you the help you're looking for."

PARADIGM OPTIONS

Almost as if he were preaching a sermon, Peter shared a very old story that he never tired of telling. "God's intended *Paradigm* for Adam and Eve, the first created couple, was that their relationship with Him would display His glory in innovative ways as they took care of His creation. As they walked and talked with Him, they learned more about His image and their identity with that image.

"But, along came another *Paradigm* option presented to them through Satan's subtle temptation. He offered a deceptive substitute for God's glorious image by getting them to doubt God's attributes, diminishing the penalty of violating God's instructions, and directing their desires towards personal fulfillment. Faced with a choice between these two paradigms, Eve and Adam chose Satan's substitutes, causing them to experience sin and its consequences. The epic battle between God and Satan, good and evil, now had human participants."

Rick nodded as Peter continued. "Fortunately for all of us, God's attributes went to work on the behalf of humanity, and He provided payment for sin—the death of an innocent Life to pay for the guilty. Ultimately, God sent Himself as the Son Jesus to enter life on earth and become the perfect sacrifice for sin. Jesus' final words on the cross guaranteed forgiveness to every person for every sin forever if they would accept His substitutionary death by faith. The penalty for sin had been paid. The visual reminder we have of that sacrifice is represented by the bread and cup of His Last Supper.

"Three days later, Jesus physically rose from the dead to prove that He, as God, was the source for breaking sin's power. Sin was not only paid for, it no longer had the power to permanently enslave people. Only those choosing to remain in sin's grip would experience its destructive power. The visual reminder we have of this resurrection power is baptism, where our sinful identity is buried, while our original identity is restored. Our identity with Jesus' resurrection gives us the opportunity to once again represent, through our life story, the glory of God's image."

Making sure that he still had Rick's attention, Peter stated, "Up to this point, I doubt I've shared any information that would be new to you."

"No; but believe it or not, I always enjoy being reminded of the Gospel story. In spite of all my negative experiences, I've never gotten over those initial memories of Jesus coming into people's lives when your dad was the pastor in Enterprise."

Peter spoke with increased excitement and conviction. "So, here is the application that most Christians do not consistently grasp. Facts are not enough to change people's lives. Faith is what releases God's power to make those facts become a living reality."

Grabbing a marker, Peter moved back to the whiteboard. "Let me draw a picture to show you what this looks like. And no laughing; I'm not an artist."

Out of the corner of his eye, Peter saw a grin on Rick's face.

"I'll start by drawing a body made up of a head, a heart, and a pair of legs. The head represents what you think, the heart represents what you believe, and the legs represent your choices and actions. It's like a chain reaction. What people think in their minds, eventually leads to what they believe in their hearts. Heart beliefs always translate into action with corresponding results.

"Your life choices reveal the *Paradigm* you believe. Your beliefs rest on the facts you have allowed to influence your mind."

Peter was studying Rick's face, trying to read whether or not this was making sense. "Why would what you think and believe about God and His thoughts of you be the most important thing about you?"

Rick's forehead wrinkled. "I guess if my thoughts were accurate, my life would reflect that accuracy. If there were distortion, my life would reflect that as well."

"You're exactly right. When a follower of Jesus anchors his thoughts and beliefs to truth, then his life reflects that truth; that is a natural result of a biblical, God-centered *Paradigm*. The opposite is also a paradigm reality; thoughts and beliefs based on distortion and lies result in bondages of varying kinds and degrees called idolatry. **Your *Paradigm* is the pivotal point in your growth because it helps you interpret your *Past* and influences the *Potential* of your life; it is the basis for all the decisions you make.** Is this making sense?"

"I think so. You are telling me that if someone gets the *Paradigm* part wrong, it has a negative impact on everything else."

"Yes. And, if they have a God-centered *Paradigm*, it has a healthy, positive impact."

"So, how does someone get an accurate view of God?"

"Creation, God's Word, and authentic followers of Jesus are all windows to discover His character and makeup. But, it will be choosing to act on those discoveries in everyday life that will solidify your view of God."

"I don't see those realities in very many people who claim to be Christians, myself included."

"So what needs to change?"

"I'm not sure."

"Do you know your rights and resources as a child of God?"

"I know I am a child of God, but I'm not sure I've thought about anything beyond that."

"Do you know how to have the resurrection power of Jesus flow through your life?"

"Not really."

Hoping to stimulate some mental images for Rick, Peter explained, "*Paradigm* truth is kind of like those pictures you've seen of a cross spanning a fiery chasm. On one side are those people in bondage to Satan. On the other side of the chasm are those who have accepted what God has done for them through Jesus and are choosing to live out their redemptive potential."

"What about those who say they are Christians but don't show it in their lives?"

"Though I believe it is impossible for someone who has become a child of God to lose that relationship and go to Hell, I do believe that it is possible for some of God's kids to experience spiritual malnutrition—to allow their *Past* to keep them stuck at the base of the cross in an unhealthy spiritual state. In that condition, it can be impossible for a person looking on from the outside to discern whether or not such people are followers of Jesus or not. Sadly, many Christians seem content with a fire insurance policy that keeps them from walking over the cliff; experientially, they spend much of their time on Satan's turf. Like Lot in the book of Genesis, their *Paradigm* prevents them from living out a life story of redemptive *Potential*."

"What about those who say they can live any way they want because they invited Jesus into their heart?"

"Do you think the Bible supports that kind of thinking?"

Rick fidgeted in his seat a little. "Probably not. So, how about me? I say I'm a follower of Jesus, but I sure don't live it out the way you just described."

Peter was noticing a subtle change in Rick's body language. Something was happening inside him, and Peter began to wonder, *Should I keep going or give him a break?*

He was close enough to completing the *Paradigm* applications that would help Rick with his *Past* that he decided to keep going. Later he would wonder if he made the right decision.

PARADIGM STORIES

Breathing a quiet prayer, Peter continued working through the *Paradigm* components he felt Rick especially needed for his spiritual development.

"In your opinion, Rick, what makes a good story? Or, maybe a better way to ask the question would be, 'What are some of the best stories you have been exposed to?'"

"You mean in the Bible?"

"It doesn't matter. The Bible is an incredible collection of narratives, but there are also great stories in other venues. You can tell me your favorite Bible story, book, or movie; they're all stories."

"Well, one of my favorite movies is *The Power of One* about an English boy growing up in South Africa. He experienced one tragedy or injustice after another. Eventually, through friendships with a South African nanny, an elderly German scientist, and a black prisoner, he learned skills that helped him fight the injustices around him. The story ended with the idea that his influence would grow in the future."

"Okay, tell me what makes that one of your favorite movies."

"Well, I guess it's the solid friendships that he has and the help they give him."

"Do you think the movie would be meaningful to you if it just focused on his friendships?"

"Yeah; that's why I like it so much. Real friendships are hard to come by. When someone has real friends, he has something valuable."

"I think you're missing the point, Rick."

"What do you mean?"

"Why were the friendships so valuable to this boy?"

"Because they helped him—ooohh, I think I can see where you're going. They helped him deal with the problems, or tension points as you call them, that he was experiencing. Is that what you're looking for?"

"You got it. One crucial component of a great story is the way a leading character deals with the negative elements of his circumstances. When a lead character uses a healthy *Paradigm* to navigate through believable problems, he becomes a hero. The greater the problems he faces and overcomes, the greater the hero he becomes. It's only when he makes destructive choices and moves to the side of evil without recovering that he is viewed in a negative light."

"Pete, what does this have to do with my life?"

"When I asked you to tell me about your experiences of figuring out your purpose in life, what did you focus on?"

"I told you about all the problems I've gone through."

"The first sin committed in the Garden of Eden was to doubt the goodness of God, and that was in a perfect environment. So, in our fallen world where people do very damaging things to each other, Satan loves to use those wounds to distort God's image and hold people in bondage to idols that substitute God. Often those idols are in the form of harmful coping, defense, and escape mechanisms like the vices you have alluded to. Your *Paradigm* determines how you handle your *Past*.

"Now here's the application to all of this, Rick. Which side of this *Paradigm* diagram do you identify with? Are you going to let your problems (with your father, your vices, your negative church experiences, and your failed efforts to find your purpose in life), define your life story on the Satan and Sin side? Or, are you going to let God help you solve those problems through the power of His Holy Spirit?"

Rick sat with arms crossed, listening.

As an afterthought, Peter added, "The best spiritual leaders I know are men and women who, like Jacob in the Bible, walk with a limp. They have found that the wounds and scars of their lives serve as a valuable factor in their ability to understand God better and glorify Him through their life stories. The worst spiritual leaders I know are those who take their wounds and scars, and either make others pay for their perceived injustices, or fearfully protect themselves from further pain. Their life stories are filled with bitterness, complacency, illegitimate pain reducers, insecurity, jealousy, or power struggles. They build sinful idols that ultimately demand sacrifices at the expense of God's glory and the people they serve. Their ministries are marked by spiritual carnage.

"Here's the bottom line. **Do you believe that God can use your negative life experiences to tell a better story, a story that will glorify Himself through you?**"

With his face instantly as red as heated steel, Rick's words sizzled. "Damn it, Pete! That is easy for you to say. What problems have you had to face? You had a great dad and mom, you have titled educational credentials, and you have had successful experiences as a pastor. You've got a wonderful wife and family of your own. It seems like your life story lacks the problems you are telling me I should be so happy about. Can't you at least feel a little sympathy for what I've gone through?"

Before Peter could respond, Rick bolted out of the den, slamming the door behind him.

Earlier in his ministry Peter would have viewed the sudden turn of events as a total failure, but he had dealt with enough people to know what God could do when a raw nerve was hit. He was hoping that this would be one of those times that would produce a teachable moment in Rick. Peter sighed. *I guess I'll know in the morning.*

Lisa poked her head into the den and asked, "Everything all right?"

"I hope so. Rick's just never had anyone help him process the negative experiences of his life. I pushed hard enough that I hit a raw nerve, and he over-reacted. He also thinks that my life has been a piece of cake."

Lisa raised her eyebrows at that comment. A wave of encouragement washed over Peter knowing that, more than anyone else, she knew the hardships he had been through.

"Let's pray for Rick to experience healing from his past," Lisa suggested. Another wave, this time of gratitude, flooded Peter's soul as he knelt beside the incredible wife God had given him.

HEAVEN'S PERSPECTIVE

As Peter and Lisa prayed, God sent some angels to surround Rick with protection against the gathering demons determined to keep him in spiritual bondage. God also invited many other angels to gather and watch with awe as His glory burst through the life of another human being the next morning.

In the meantime, the angels had a thoroughly enjoyable night retelling stories of other people they had seen find victory from problematic experiences. The angels remembered how a *Paradigm* adjustment released these people to live out their redemptive *Potential* and bring God glory through their life stories.

They also discussed how fortunate humans were. Each angel shuddered when he remembered the permanent consequences that Satan brought on himself and those who followed him when he tried to overthrow God. Each of them knew former angels, now demons that they battled, who were no longer among their number. Yet humans, no matter how sinful, had the opportunity to turn back to a God-centered *Paradigm* and experience His loving forgiveness and restoration. If only they knew how fortunate they were.

PARADIGM ADJUSTMENT

The next morning, Rick sheepishly entered the dining room where Lisa was setting a mound of bacon and eggs on the table next to a platter of pancakes. She asked, "Hungry?"

"Always."

"Want to go fishing today?" Peter asked. "I thought we could take our boat down to the river and see if you are still as good as you used to be."

"I didn't bring any of my gear, and I don't have an out-of-state license."

"I've got gear you can use and I was also hoping that you'd be up to buying a license that was good for the rest of the year. We're hoping that this isn't just a once-in-a-while kind of connection."

"Sure; I can do that!" Rick wasn't sure if he was just relieved that he would have a safe place to talk with Peter about the night before, or if Peter really wanted to spend time with him. Either way, it would be worth the price of the license.

Shortly after launching the boat, Rick decided to get things out in the open. He had never learned to deal with suspense very well. "I guess I didn't stay long enough for you to answer my question last night, did I?"

"Which one?"

"I asked more than one?"

"You asked what problems I've had to deal with; then you asked why I wouldn't sympathize with you. Which one would you like me to answer first?"

"I guess the sympathy one. I thought that, of all the people I know, you would have been the most understanding."

"I empathize with you, Rick; but I do not have sympathy for you, or anyone else for that matter, in the way they typically want it. **God uses conflict, problems, pain, testing, and trouble to help people grow spiritually.** As I listened to your life story, I could understand and relate to your pain; but I can also see that **you have a powerful opportunity to take your life story and make it a glory story for God.** Sympathy keeps people stuck in their pain."

"How can you understand and relate to my pain?"

"Do you know why we left Enterprise?"

"Yeah; your dad accepted an invitation to pastor a church back in West Virginia so that he could be closer to his family and have help taking care of you and your sisters."

"That's partially right. Do you really know what life was like for me after leaving Enterprise?"

"No, I guess I don't. I mean, we've kept in loose contact over the years, but we haven't really talked about deep personal stuff."

"Well, after Mom died, Dad lost it. For several years, I not only lost my mom; I also lost my dad. His early life was a lot like yours. So when he and Mom got together, she became his best friend. Life without her was unimaginable. Nothing had prepared him to live alone. Losing Mom took him back to wounds and scars from his *Past* that he had never fully dealt with. He began drinking, and in a matter of months, he resigned from the pastorate. He took a job in one of the coal mines where he used to work before he went into the ministry. There were no friends to support him. Family members helped with my sisters and me, but they were hesitant to get involved in his pain. Church people felt embarrassed or helpless; they tactfully avoided him. So he shut himself off emotionally from everyone. Though Dad kept a roof over our heads, food on the table, and clothes on our backs, my sisters and I were pretty much left to figure out everything else for ourselves. His free time was spent in a workshop behind the house, sitting in a rocking chair, listening to country music, and drinking."

Rick's eyes opened wide in disbelief as he compared what he was hearing with what he knew of Peter's dad.

Peter continued, "After high school graduation, I made preparations to go to college. I didn't want to let Dad's misery drown me; so I left home, but with quite a bit of bitterness of my own. Who knows? I may have wallowed in self-pity the rest of my life if it hadn't been for a very dear couple.

"My freshman year, I met a retired pastor and his wife who took a liking to me. Brian O'Reilly was, as he liked to put it, a well-seasoned man and proud of his Irish heritage. He possessed a love for Jesus that you don't see in very many people. Brian and his wife Donna began to invite me over to their home. Looking back, I can see that they mentored me through my pain. They eventually helped me know how to interact with Dad. As I healed, God began to use me to help emotionally and spiritually restore my dad back to the place where he could be in the ministry again.

"Looking back, I think they helped me understand that I could choose to look either through the lens of my pain or through the lens of God's glory (encompassing His complete attributes and abilities). They helped me see that the lens I chose would powerfully color and influence how I interpreted life. They gave me a living example of people who looked through the lens of God's glory. That's how I discovered the *Paradigm* principles.

"Brian and Donna were instrumental in helping me get my first pastoral opportunity. One of their friends was a member of a nearby traditional church that was without a pastor at the time. In a matter of months, I found myself a full-time pastor as well as a full-time student."

Peter's face shadowed as he continued. "Sometime, I'll tell you of all the challenges that I had to face in that church as a nineteen-year-old kid. A couple of elderly deacons did their best to convince me that pastoral ministry was an assignment from Hell, instead of a privilege from Heaven."

Rick began to look at the floor of the boat in embarrassment at he listened to his friend's story.

"Since the time I entered ministry, I've experienced more pressures and problems than I could describe to you in one weekend. And I wish for a moment, Rick, that you could hear the stories of pain and suffering from the lives of many that I've counseled over the years. I've seen effects of physical abuse so grotesque they would make you sick to your stomach. Lisa and I have had the agonizing privilege of helping young girls and women recover from traumatic sexual abuse. I've listened to stories from wives whose husbands left them for some short-sighted affair; from children feeling abandoned after the divorce of their parents. Others have told me of being ostracized by peers because of the color of their skin or some cultural standard beyond their control. Addictions, betrayal, debt, disabilities, PTSD, suicide…**there is no limit to the ways that dysfunction and pain can wound and scar people,** and it's hard to measure who suffers more than someone else.

"So, my friend, I hope you are beginning to realize that you are part of a large group of people branded by pain. It really doesn't make any difference what specific brand of pain you have suffered.

It's enough to know you aren't the only one. I really do understand and empathize with your pain."

Rick sat there trying to absorb all that his friend had shared.

Peter continued, "I believe God brought me back into your life to help stimulate your faith and trust in His ability to restore you to your redemptive *Potential* in spite of, or in light of, your pain. That *Potential* starts with an accurate *Paradigm* of what God believes about you. I pray that you will eventually understand your adopted position in God's family. He adopted you into His family with the same rights as His Son Jesus. He wants to glorify Himself through your life story."

Rick's face lit up like a light bulb. He had allowed the problems of his *Past* to distort his image of God; he was living in the bondage of a false *Paradigm*. He had transferred images of his earthly father onto God. For the first time in his spiritual development, he realized that he had a Dad he could trust, a perfect Dad Who had already proved His love through the pain He had allowed His Son Jesus to experience.

Through eyes clouded with tears, he looked up into the sky and silently whispered, *Dad, please forgive me for the narrow view I've had of You because of my pain. Please help me to live life through Your Paradigm. I choose to believe what You believe about me.*

And for a brief moment, he thought he could see his Dad's face in the clouds. There was also that faint but familiar Voice saying, "I've been telling you for some time now that I have great plans for you; I really mean it."

Rick was quietly humbled. He'd had no idea of all that Pete had gone through since leaving Enterprise. He had not considered the pain of others. Now, because of Pete, Rick was beginning to believe that God really did care about him and have great plans for his life story.

The rest of the day was just a blur for Rick. As he lay down in bed that night, weary from the emotions of the last twenty-four hours, he realized that he was on the edge of the biggest adventure of his life.

As his Heavenly Dad watched Rick rapidly drift off to sleep, He smiled a knowing smile. The angels did, too; it had been quite a day for them as well.

THE CHURCH FAMILY

Sunday morning, Rick piled into the family van with the McCormick family and headed to church. It was obvious that, though Peter and Lisa had been here only a short period of time, they were well liked.

The atmosphere was unlike anything Rick had experienced before. There was a sense of genuine friendliness, combined with some unexplainable reservation. He felt a strong sense of spiritual passion, shadowed by unseen pain.

The conversations he overheard, ranging anywhere from sin struggles to asking for advice about dealing with a negative boss, were definitely more transparent than in any other church he had seen. Occasionally he would see people praying for each other. Out of the corner of his eye, he saw a lady quickly slip some money into the coat pocket of someone who looked like a single mom.

Several people asked if he would be visiting again and extended an invitation for him to share a meal with them. He made a mental note not to let those invitations fall through the cracks.

A boy he guessed to be about ten asked Rick if he was saved. After telling him "yes," Rick was asked to share how it happened. Then, the boy shared with Rick how he had gotten saved a couple of years earlier.

During the worship time, there were periods of spontaneous prayers, or someone standing to share what God had been doing for them. One teen stood and simply read a Bible verse, his hand raised upward in praise.

As the worship time came to a close, several people walked up to Peter and his family and began to praise God for bringing the McCormicks to their church family. They prayed for God to give Peter wisdom and courage. They prayed for the family to adjust well to their community. They prayed for the Spirit of God to fill Peter as he shared the Word of God with them. **And there seemed to be a holy pause as if everyone was actually expecting God to speak to them**.

Rick sat there taking it all in. He looked forward to being able to ask Pete some questions about what he was sensing. But right now, it was time to listen to the message.

PARADIGM REVIEW & INTRO TO THE PAST

Peter was using leading characters from the Bible as examples for this spiritual development series.

"Last week, the life stories of several leading characters from First Samuel helped us discover the importance of the key spiritual development component called *Your Paradigm.*

"I introduced you to Eli and his sons, along with a miracle boy named Samuel. Eli's sons clearly lived on Satan's side of the *Paradigm* choices, while Samuel lived on God's side. Eli himself went back and forth between the two *Paradigm* choices.

"Before we begin today's story, tell me how many of you remember the four *Paradigm* questions I asked last week?"

Voices from all over the room began to repeat the questions as the Tech Team projected them onto the screens.

A woman in the front row gave the first question. "What do you believe about God?"

A group of teenagers gave the next two questions. "What do you believe about Satan?" "What does Satan believe about you?"

The last question came from a casually dressed, but sharp-looking, middle-aged man. "What does God believe about you?"

At this point, Peter had the Tech Team show the head, heart, and feet picture that he had drawn for Rick. He asked, "Remember how the thoughts and beliefs of each of last week's Bible characters led to the choices that they made?

"Look at your own thoughts and beliefs in relation to the four *Paradigm* questions. What kind of choices did you make this past week?"

Rick sat there in amazement as he listened to people sharing their real life experiences. Who'd have thought you could actually talk during a church service! He connected with some of their stories at a deep level. All of the stories were transparent and motivational encounters with a living God Who was helping them develop a God-centered *Paradigm*. For a moment, Rick was lost in memories of his own encounter with God just the day before.

Peter brought him back to the present. "This week I want to use the life stories of Cain and Abel to help us discover the importance of another key spiritual development component of the *Teen* phase called *Your Past*."

"Cain and Abel were born into a family affected by the poor choices that their parents had made. How would you like to be born into a family where your parents started out in a perfect environment but failed to respect the one restriction God had given them? How would you feel when this caused you to suffer for the rest of your life?"

Rick watched as heads were shaking indicating either that they wouldn't want to be placed in that situation, or that they felt like they were living out a similar scenario. As he thought of his own upbringing, feelings of anger and confusion surged through him.

Peter reminded everyone, "**A person's responses to his or her Past make a difference in the outcome of his or her life story,**" as evidenced by the outcome of Cain's and Abel's life stories. It was Abel's faith that enabled him to move away from the negative consequences incurred by his father Adam and take ownership of his own life. His choice to leave the *Past* behind cost him his physical life, but his life story is still being used by God to help point others toward a meaningful relationship with God. Cain's life, on the other hand, is a warning about the destruction produced by someone who is unwilling to deal with the negative elements of his *Past*. God passionately tried to help Cain avoid repeating the same choices his parents made. But Cain refused, and that choice resulted in massive moral and human destruction."

Well-chosen images were being projected in front of everyone as Peter made his points. Now a picture of a path leading up to a high wall appeared. In the wall were two doors labeled "God-centered Responses" and "Satanic Responses." On the other side of the "God-centered Responses," the path continued toward a destination titled your "*Your Potential*." The door labeled "Satanic Responses" led to a dark room with no exit.

After a short pause, Peter continued. "When it comes to your *Past,* there are two typical responses. You either use a God-centered *Paradigm* to deal with your *Past* and move forward, or you develop satanic response patterns (also termed coping/defense/escape mechanisms). God-centered responses will lead you towards your full *Potential.* Satanic responses are a dead-end street.

"As we close this week's presentation, I would like to suggest two life application actions for those of you who are needing or wanting to troubleshoot your *Past.*

"First, evaluate any negative relational impressions and responses you may have developed from the family environment you grew up in. Are any of you wrestling with issues of abandonment, abuse, unrealistic expectations, or unhealthy restrictions? What type of emotions do thoughts of your father and mother, biological or figurative, invoke in you—positive or negative? This week, some of you may need to face parental issues from your *Past*."

Rick cringed at the thought.

"Secondly, evaluate any ongoing negative affects you may be experiencing from traumatic events outside your childhood family environment. Some of you may have been introduced to harmful addictions or experiences that had nothing to do with your parental figures. Maybe you are laboring under the burden of shame from what someone has done to you or introduced you to. Others of you may have been exposed to horrific graphic experiences where the scenes play over and over in your mind, driving you to the edge of your sanity. Maybe you made a decision that caused someone else to suffer, and you can't find the freedom to forgive yourself. Maybe your *Potential* is being limited by the unjust views and power plays of others from your *Past*."

How in the world does he know how to push all the pain buttons in a person's life? Rick began to feel waves of nausea as he thought of his own *Past*.

"The crippling power of the *Past* lies in unforgiveness and secrecy. As long as you choose to focus on past violations instead of forgiving others and moving on, you will remain stuck. As long as your *Past* remains a secret, it will continue to cripple and haunt you. **Dealing with your *Past* does not minimize or remove its pain. It simply gives you God's hope and help in dealing with your *Past* and moving towards your *Potential*.**"

Peter concluded his talk. "There is an epic battle raging between good and evil, between God and Satan. The way you deal with your *Past* is a key component in this battle. If you want to experience the spiritual health and growth God desires for you, then you can't bypass it. Will you deal with your *Past*? If you want to do that right now, Lisa and I would love to talk with you before you leave."

Will you deal with your Past? Rick sat there haunted by the question. In one short weekend, he had experienced more help and hope than he had found in all the years since Pete had left Enterprise. But, as he watched people around him making their way to Peter and Lisa to pray and find relief from their *Past*, Rick wondered if what he was learning this weekend would make a practical difference in his life. The Satan side of the *Paradigm* screamed, *This is not for you!* The God side thundered back, *You're My son, and I will live out My glory through the story of your life!*

Somehow Rick knew he was going to have to share all of his *Past* with Pete if he was ever going to be free to move towards his *Potential*, but doubt and fear gripped him by the throat. He could feel the epic battle Pete had referred to. Dark forces were surrounding him, using all the effective weapons in their arsenal. Immobilized for the moment, Rick just sat there cursing himself.

RICK'S PAST

The ride back to the house was unusually quiet. The meal was even more unusual; Rick ate hardly anything.

Peter and Lisa went into teamwork mode. Lisa took the kids to their rooms for a nap and then began busying herself with the meal cleanup. Peter invited Rick into the den. They sat there quietly for several minutes before Peter broke the silence. "You okay?"

"Yeah," Rick lied. Then with his head bowed and his body shaking, he sobbed, "No...no; I'm not okay; I'm a damn mess."

"What's going on?"

"I'm in that satanic, dead-end, dark room you talked about at church. I can feel Satan's forces all around me, wanting to keep me from dealing with my *Past*."

"Unforgiveness or secrecy?"

After a pause, Rick replied, "Both." He sat there wrestling with whether or not to open the closet door of his *Past*. Finally he began, "I hate my father. There were a few years before I went to work for Waylon that, if I'd had the courage and opportunity, I'd have beaten him to a bloody pulp. Every time I have to interact with him, or something comes up that reminds me of the way he has treated me, my mind starts playing what I call 'The Shit Tapes.' I can tell you every crappy offense he has ever committed against me." After a pause, he added, "And as much as I hate him, I hate myself even more."

"Is that the secrecy part?" Peter gently asked.

Ricked slowly looked up and nodded, "Yes."

"Do you trust me enough to get that part of your *Past* out in the open?"

"The few times I've tried haven't gone well."

"What do you mean?"

Rick quivered. A cold chill was running up his back as he remembered that dark night. "The first time I tried getting help, I had a church leader take what I shared with him and tell my father. That was the night he took me to the workshop and started beating the hell out of me with a broom handle. After it broke, he pulled off his belt and started hitting me with the buckle end until I tried to crawl under a work bench. He reached down and grabbed me by the shirt, pulled me to my feet, shoved me into a corner, and started punching me as hard as he could. Between bouts of punching, he would laugh at me, saying, 'Did you really think you could get away from me?' Then he'd remember why he had brought me to the workshop in the first place and shout in my face, 'I'll show you what I think of perverts.' Then he'd start beating me again. After I almost passed out, he ended the nightmare by looking at me and flatly stating that he would send me to a reform institution if he ever heard of me doing the same thing again."

As Rick looked up, he could see tears in his friend's eyes. Feeling awkward over Pete's display of emotion, he kept talking to release his own nervousness.

"Several years later, I tried talking to a guest speaker that Pastor Vance Taylor had invited for a week-long series of meetings. He agreed that I had a problem, but his only solution was trying to console me with the fact that a lot of guys had similar problems. No advice. No help. I walked away swearing I would never ask for help again."

"I'm beginning to see why," Peter whispered.

"As I listened to you speak this morning, I could see very clearly that I'm imprisoned by my *Past*. But daring to hope that things can change is risky for me."

Very carefully, Peter asked, "Rick, how many 'bad' people in the Bible who found the courage to go to Jesus and ask for help ever had the experience of not being helped by Him?"

Avoiding Peter's eyes, Rick mumbled, "I can't think of anyone as screwed up as me going to Jesus for help. Most of them were just diseased or wanted someone to be raised from the dead."

"How about the guy who was severely demon-possessed? He was so screwed up that he spent his time hanging out in graveyards, cutting himself, and terrorizing people. Every time someone tried to control him by cuffing and chaining him up, he would break free and return to his destructive lifestyle. It was Jesus' power that broke the hold of his *Past* and restored him to his God-given *Potential*."

With his face in his hands, Rick said, "I feel demon-possessed."

"Forces of evil can have a direct influence on all people," Peter responded, "but biblically, I don't believe they can possess a child of God. That technicality does not minimize the oppression that you can feel, though. I've grown to realize that experiencing demonic oppression is powerful evidence that I am on the right track."

Rick looked up. "That's because you don't screw up."

"Everyone screws up from time to time. Have you ever considered Jesus' disciple Peter? He screwed up a lot. Even though he was one of Jesus' closest disciples, Jesus called him 'Satan' on one occasion because of Peter's misguided comment. Peter also used an intense string of profanity to deny that he had any association with Jesus on the night of Jesus' trial. Have you ever failed as badly as that?"

"In case you haven't noticed, I also struggle with profanity."

Pete chuckled, "I hadn't noticed."

Thankful for tension release, Rick shot back, "Liar."

"Rick, have you ever thought about the various women Jesus dealt with who were promiscuous at best and whores at worst? Did Jesus focus on their *Past* or on their *Potential?*"

With a hopeful look, Rick answered, "Their *Potential.*"

"Why?" Peter probed.

Rick sat there thinking hard. "Does this have any connection with the *Paradigm* component that you have been sharing with me this weekend?"

"Yes," Peter coached.

"We-e-ell the-e-en, I guess the reason would be the question in the upper left box of your chart—"What does God believe about you?'"

"Exactly!"

Rick agonized, "How am I supposed to believe that Jesus will forgive and help me, when so many others have either beaten the crap out of me or ignored me?"

"Please tell me, why did Jesus become a human?"

"To prove what God believes about us?"

Peter carefully asked, "So, do you think you're ready to break the power of sin's secrecy and accept God's forgiveness?"

Again, Rick began to feel the tension between the forces of darkness and light. He knew he was at a crossroad, and he had a pretty good idea that the choice he was about to make would determine his entire future.

Nervous sweat began to trickle down Rick's side as he opened up. "Shortly after you left Enterprise, I felt totally abandoned. One weekend, someone who you know but I don't need to name, took me camping. That night, he started talking about all the sexual escapades he'd had, and then he started masturbating. At the time, I didn't know what in the heck he was doing; but as I watched, it was intriguing. After he jerked off, he told me to try it. I did, but nothing happened.

"After that weekend, I began experimenting with myself, and eventually I ejaculated. As a 12-year-old, the adrenalin rush of that first experience hooked me. The frequency and intensity of this newfound habit began to control me with increasing strength.

"The following year, I went on a lumber delivery run with my uncle; in a truck stop bathroom, I found a magazine. That unlocked a whole new world of addiction, ultimately leading to the sexual experience my father beat me for."

Staring at the floor, Rick continued, "Sometimes I get scared by the depth of my sexual exploration. So far I haven't pursued those mental explorations, and I pray to God that I don't. But I'm sick and tired of feeling helpless to break the sexual addictions I already possess."

Briefly looking up, Rick continued, "You know what's really crazy? My father's beating didn't stop my addiction. Nothing has had the ability to break its power. A couple of times, I've tried alcohol and drugs to numb my feelings of shame. I know others get hooked on those substances; but for some reason, my experiences with alcohol were sickening. And the one time I tried drugs, they made me feel so weird that I got too scared to use them anymore.

"I've tried suicide, but I didn't have enough guts to pull it off. Besides, it seemed like too permanent of a solution with no real benefits. I've heard Christians say, 'I don't know how people could possibly get to the point of wanting to take their own lives.' When I hear comments like that, my mind bounces between two extremes— *It sure would be nice not to know*, and *You narrow-minded idiot*."

Rick looked up with a sheepish grin. "So how's that for opening up the door to my *Past?*"

Peter nodded with approval. "Outside of the issues with your father, do you think that your sexual struggles are moral problems? Could they perhaps be stimulated by unnecessary feelings of guilt from misguided religious leaders?"

"N-no-o. I've heard and read the comments of people in the sex industry who try to remove any negative stigma or restrictions on their activities. I can understand some of their reasoning when I look at the abusive and ignorant way my father and others have handled sexual conduct they believe to be wrong. But I also know that the guilt and shame I experience from my sexual activities haven't come just from the religious extremists. Something inside lets me know that sex is a powerful gift designed by God to increase intimacy in marriage. Using that gift to gratify myself only produces a hollow emptiness and an unquenchable thirst for more. But I'm not married yet. I haven't been able to break the power of the habits I've unleashed, so I just stay caught in the vicious cycles of my addiction. Add profanity and a temper equal to my father's to the mix, and my *Past* looks like one of those billboard pictures of someone on crack."

"Rick, I've got some good news for you! If you can answer 'yes' to a few questions, you can be free from the power and effects of your *Past*."

Rick asked suspiciously, "What questions?"

"First, are you at rock bottom?"

"What do you mean?"

"Do you believe that you can change on your own?"

"Absolutely not! I can't tell you how many times I've tried to quit, or the variety of methods I've used. The results have always been the same—failure."

"My next question is this: 'What kind of help do you want?'"

"I want to be free from my *Past* and its addictions."

"Why?"

"That should be obvious. Who wants to live in that kind bondage?"

"Please don't take this wrong, Rick; but again, I think your answer is a little short-sighted. Were you created to be addiction-free or for a higher purpose?"

"Are we back to the *Paradigm* thing again?"

Peter nodded.

"Wow! We don't get very far from that, do we?"

"It's pretty hard to get away from something that is central to the character and purpose of God's existence."

"I guess you're right! So that means that **my reason for wanting help with my *Past* has to be to glorify God through the life choices that I make.**"

The warm glow on Peter's face was all Rick needed to realize that he had found the correct answer.

Rick hesitated, "Any other questions?"

"Just one," Peter replied. "Are you willing to do the hard work of changing your habitual response patterns?"

"I don't understand what you're asking."

"For years you have been making choices based on mental associations and emotional triggers. Are you willing to learn different response patterns? Saying 'yes' and living 'yes' are two different matters altogether."

Tension started building again in Rick. This was more than a decision to disclose his *Past*. This decision would limit or unleash *Potential* in his life story, and the longer he waited to make this decision, the harder it would become. Dropping down on his knees, he began pouring out his heart to the Dad he was beginning to know and trust.

Peter got down on the floor beside his friend and put his hand on his shoulder.

As Rick prayed, Heaven's armies began to clear enemy forces away from this precious son of God. Something happened at that moment that took Rick back to the day he had asked Jesus to save his soul and give him the gift of eternal life. He was determined not to lose the returning joy he was experiencing. He knew it wasn't going to be easy; but for the first time in his life, he felt like he had real hope and help.

POTENTIAL: H.E.R. PRACTICES

When Peter and Rick emerged from the den, Lisa looked into Rick's face and commented, "You look like a new man!"

A sense of peace had washed over Rick, removing many of the hardened lines etched into his face.

As the three of them sat down in the living room, Rick watched Peter slip his arm around Lisa and give her a quick hug. Reading between the lines, he realized something of the connectedness and gratitude that had just passed between them.

Rick longed for that kind of connection. As meaningful as the weekend had been, he was going back to a lonely reality in a matter of hours. That realization stimulated another question.

"I'm beginning to understand the *Paradigm* thing as it relates to my *Past*, but how does it relate to my *Potential?* I mean, if I'm going to learn how to overcome my *Past*, I can't just stand still, can I? Shouldn't I be trying to move forward? I think I remember hearing somewhere that **if I take something negative out of my life, I need to add something positive to replace the negative, or the negative will come back.**"

"*The Replacement Principle*," Peter interjected. With a pleased look on his face, he asked, "Got your Bible handy?"

"Yeah. It's right here."

"Turn to the first chapter of Second Peter and read the first eleven verses; then tell me if you see any practical answers to that question."

Rick read slowly, his mind trying to process what he was reading.

"Well, the first four verses talk about what you showed me this weekend."

"In what way?"

"Verses three and four talk about God's glory and how that is the source of all the good things available to help me live out my *Potential*. The implication is that, if I am tapping into the glory of God through knowing Him and His promises, I have the ability to reach *Potential*."

"Good observation! Do you see any practical ways to live out your God-given *Potential* in the rest of the verses?

"It looks like there's a list of things here that I'm supposed to be doing."

"What are those things connected with?"

"I'm not sure."

"According to the first part of verse five, would they be tied to the promises of God based on His glory?"

"Yeah, now I can see it."

"According to the second half of verse five down through verse seven, how many specific things are you supposed to be doing—things that have the promise of God's glory to help you accomplish your God-given *Potential?*"

"Seven."

"To help unpack these seven specific things, I want to give you two tools that have helped me a lot as I study the Bible. The first is a microscope, which you just used. It helps you see all the little details (in this passage, seven). The next is a telescope that lets you see the big picture. The telescope takes some getting used to because of its various settings. You can use the largest setting to ask how the passage you're studying relates to the entire Bible. The next setting asks how the passage you're studying relates to the individual book of the Bible that you are studying—in this case, Second Peter. And the last telescopic setting is the weakest; it asks how the passage you're studying relates to itself.

"Using the weakest telescopic setting, do you see any ways you could group the seven microscopic parts of this passage into larger groupings?"

Rick was amazed at how simple Pete made things seem. "It looks like the last three involve relationships: God, Christians, and people in general."

Lisa quietly interjected, "Rick, you may have the spiritual gift of teaching. You made that connection pretty fast."

Rick beamed with pleasure. "I've been told that before."

Peter continued, "Do you see any other telescopic connections?"

"Well, it looks to me like the first two involve actions—things you do; the second two affect how you feel."

"I agree with Lisa and the pastor you told me about Friday night; it looks like you do have the spiritual gift of teaching. I frequently teach this passage to new believers, and I don't think anyone has described it to me any better than you just did. The first two items are *Habits*; the second two involve *Emotions*, and the last three deal with *Relationships*.

"You will find that, as you remove negative habits and replace them with positive habits, the redemptive *Potential* of your story will more and more reflect the glory of God. There will be challenging battles over removing the sinful habits that have gripped your life, along with battles to begin spiritual habits that fuel your life with the power of God's resources; but the promises of God are available to help you experience victory."

"I have some real work to do."

"As challenging as it is to deal with the habits in your life, dealing with your emotional reactions takes the challenge to the most intense levels humans experience. You can somewhat plan your habitual *actions*, but it's almost impossible to forecast your *reactions*, especially when your emotions are involved. Emotions are powerful influences on the human soul. As you told me story of your past, I heard a lot of emotional pain."

Rick nodded. He had displayed his emotions quite visibly over the past couple of days.

"Finally, God wants you to take your habitual and emotional growth and apply it to every relationship in your life.

"**I like to summarize these *Potential Practices* with the *H.E.R.* acronym:**

- *Habits*
- *Emotions*
- *Relationships*

As Peter was finishing his explanation, the doorbell rang, and Lisa got up to see who was there. With the *H.E.R.* acronym in his head, Rick looked up and saw—not *H.E.R.*, but *her!*

UNEXPECTED
OPPORTUNITY

"Hello, Miriam! Come in," Lisa invited.

With more adrenalin running through his veins than the time he rolled his brother's skidder over, Rick stared in awkward wonder. Miriam was not like anyone else he had ever seen—that is until her sister Penny followed her inside!

Where have they been hiding? Rick thought. He knew he would have noticed if Miriam and Penny had been at church.

"How's your grandmother doing?" Lisa asked.

Rick gathered, through further conversation, that their grandmother's health was failing and that the family took turns watching her, so that she would not need to be placed in a nursing home.

Lisa introduced Miriam and Penny to Rick and, before he realized it, the day was gone. A quick glance at his watch told him that, if he was going to be worth anything at work the next day, he needed to head back to Enterprise. Regretfully, he said his "goodbyes," grabbed his duffle bag, and headed for the door. Peter and Lisa followed him outside.

"Hey, Rick, before you leave, we've got an offer for you to think about. Would you be interested in moving to Kennewick? I believe, with you living here, that we could really help you with your discipleship development. Plus, there are ministry opportunities here that could help you discover your God-given *Potential*. "There is a local contractor in our church family who is always looking for hard-working guys that he can train as carpenters. I think you'd be a really good fit for his company."

Then with a twinkle in his eyes that reminded Rick of Pete's dad, Peter added, "There would also be chances to get to know Penny and Miriam better—if that interests you."

Lisa's gentle voice helped to ease Rick's chaotic thoughts. "Why don't you ask God what He thinks about the idea and get back to us when you know."

As his mind raced a thousand miles an hour, bouncing between all the positive benefits of moving, the challenges of telling his brother and father, and the unknowns of learning a new trade, Rick already knew his answer would be "yes." But he was so overwhelmed that he just hit Peter on the shoulder and said, "I'll let you know"; then added, "soon." And just like that, he walked to his pickup and was gone.

Lisa looked at her husband. "That was a little weird."

"What?"

"The way he left. No goodbye, no thank you, no excitement; just 'I'll let you know'. You didn't think that was a little strange?"

"Not really, Honey. How much did you get to hear of his story this weekend?"

"Not much. I'm sure he loves Jesus and respects you, but there is a side to him that I don't know how to read yet. It was obvious that he had some unresolved issues. Sometimes he reminds me of a dog that has been beaten, but not to the point that he has turned mean; just very protective of himself with his tail between his legs. He wags it a little when you speak to him, like he's glad you noticed him; but he doesn't feel comfortable with letting you get too close."

"What did I remind you of when we first met?"

Lisa's gaze flitted to Peter's face. "Is Rick struggling like you were?"

"Worse, Honey. His father is nothing like mine. Dad was a fun-loving man before he met Jesus. After meeting Jesus, he was a caring and thoughtful man, both to his family and to those in his church. He had one significant negative turn in his life that he had to work through. Rick's father, on the other hand, is a man deeply scarred by his *Past*. His brief positive encounter with Jesus was ripped away by someone in ministry. He's a hard man that has taken his struggles out on those nearest to him. Your description of Rick is closer to the truth than you realize. We really need to pray for him this week. Leaving the family business could be a little like trying to leave a gang after having been initiated into it."

Sweetly, Lisa responded, "Then let's go inside and pray."

"How someone like me ended up with someone as wonderful as you continues to be one of life's greatest mysteries."

Arms wrapped around each other, **they headed for the house and knelt down to pray for God to go to work** on Rick's behalf. In heaven, angels were getting their work orders for the week; they were going to be busy. And again God smiled at the thought of what He had in store for these two friends that He had reconnected.

TRANSITION

The next day, Rick decided not to say anything to his family about the offer Pete had made. He wanted to process his weekend's experience in his mind before dealing with what his father and Waylon would say.

Tuesday morning went well; but by afternoon he knew that, like it or not, he was going to have to lay his cards on the table. He had already determined that he was not going to fold like he did the first time he shared the dreams of his heart and met opposition.

No sooner had he worked out a plan in his mind to break the news after work, and then he heard a loud explosion. Too late, he saw that he had punctured one of his tires. Jumping off the skidder in a rage and cussing the air blue with profanity, he walked back to the wood yard to get his pickup and tools to remove the tire. *At least the twitch road is smooth enough for the pickup*, he thought. For the next hour, he worked as quickly as he could to get the tire off the skidder and loaded into his pickup so that he could get to the tire shop before it closed.

He arrived just before closing, which didn't make the tire guys any too happy. Rick told them to suck it up and bill him for their aggravation, and they only too willingly obliged.

As he headed back, he was glad that it was late spring so that he would have enough daylight to get the tire back on. By the time he got the skidder back to the wood yard and fueled up, everyone was in bed. He'd just have to wait until tomorrow to break his news.

Wednesday morning, Rick could feel his aggravation starting to get the best of him. *This is ridiculous*, he thought to himself. *Didn't I learn from Second Peter that God has promised His help for any need I have? So what do I need? And **what is the promise I need to help me glorify God in this situation?***

As if guided by an Unseen Hand, he reached for the Bible laying on his nightstand. He turned to Proverbs 3:5-6, a passage he had underlined and memorized as a kid.

Though they were familiar verses to Rick, it seemed as if he were reading them for the first time. He began to break the passage up into separate thoughts and figure out their meaning using his newly discovered microscope and telescope tools. *First, God wants me to trust him completely. To be able to trust God completely, I have to stop trusting myself and my personal resources. That's probably the reason I have been so miserable—I'm trying to figure things out on my own. Last of all, if I put all my cards on the table, God is going to guide me and work things out.*

"Well, God, that's clear enough. Please help me to apply those truths today."

As peace filled his inner being, his confidence began to grow; he actually began looking forward to discovering how God would work things out.

That night after supper, Rick broke the news. "This weekend Pete asked me to consider moving to Kennewick. He knows someone in his church that could train me as a carpenter for his construction company." He decided to keep the rest of the details—Peter's offer to mentor him…and the two sisters he couldn't get out of his head—to himself for now.

Waylon simply looked at him and asked, "When?"

"I don't want to put you in a bind, but I don't want to miss this opportunity either."

"How about staying on til the end of the month? That should give me enough time to find either a buyer for the skidder or some numbskull to replace you."

Rick knew that was Waylon's backhanded way of being supportive. He countered, "You're going to have a hard time finding anyone to replace me. You'd better plan on selling."

Ray got up from the table and went to the living room to sit in his recliner and thumb through some hunting magazines without saying a word. Rick didn't know whether to be relieved at not having to explain himself or hurt at the seeming indifference. What Pete had shared with him this past weekend about *Past* problems and *Paradigm* choices allowed Rick to accept the first option.

THE MOVE

The next month flew by. Rick called Peter to let him know about his decision and to make arrangements to meet Gary Ingerson, the contractor Peter had mentioned. Rick felt an immediate connection with Gary.

The search for housing was more challenging. Rick knew that he wanted to be close to Pete and Lisa, the church, and Penny and Miriam; but there didn't seem to be much available. Lisa was the one who discovered the best lead. She knew an elderly couple from church that had a small apartment available and could use some help with chores that they could no longer do. After meeting Harry and Ellen, there was no doubt that this was what God wanted for all three of them.

Lisa also arranged for Penny and Miriam to come over for a meal the weekend before Rick actually moved. His dilemma over which one of these ladies he liked the most and how to pursue a relationship with her was about to be resolved.

Miriam offered to drive to Enterprise on Saturday to help him move, and Penny agreed to join her. He knew he didn't have enough stuff to warrant them making the trip, but he could see no harm in taking advantage of this chance to get to know them better. *Besides,* he thought, *the drive to Enterprise is beautiful enough that, if I pay for their gas, it should be a win-win situation for them and for me.*

What he didn't count on was Waylon overhearing him give them directions over the phone. When Waylon realized that two young ladies were coming to help his older brother move, he suddenly felt inspired to join the moving team.

Saturday morning found Waylon and Miriam hitting it off. By the end of the loading process, Waylon had made the decision that he could spend the rest of the weekend in Kennewick. As Waylon and Miriam were getting into her car, Rick asked if Penny would like to ride with him. She answered with a sweet smile and headed toward the pickup. Rick remembered his manners and raced to open the door for her.

They quickly found that they had a fair amount to talk about. **Rick was able to tell the story of his life in a way that was truthful but not as wounded as when he had shared it with Peter.** He did skip the part about his personal vices.

"How about you?" Rick asked.

"I had a fairly healthy childhood and early adult experience. My parents came from challenging backgrounds, but somehow they managed to create an environment for us where we felt loved and where problems were resolved."

"What do you do for work?"

"I knew early in life that I wanted a career so that I would always have something to fall back on, whatever circumstances I found myself in. After taking a few career assessments, I chose the field of accounting and I've been happily employed at the same firm since graduating from college. They seem to be reasonably pleased with me; I keep getting raises, and they invest significantly into my retirement plan."

Rick felt a little out-classed; but they were just pulling into Kennewick, so he didn't have time to dwell on it. Besides, she had the face of an angel!

STRETCHING TOWARD POTENTIAL

The next couple of weeks found Rick trying to learn every possible aspect of the construction world. He seemed to take naturally to the work. Evenings and weekends were split between time with Peter and Lisa and dates with Penny.

On a couple of occasions, Peter and Lisa helped Rick see the progress he was making in practicing the *Past* and *Paradigm* principles he had learned. Peter even convinced Rick to try to make things right with his father. Attempting to give Rick a big-picture perspective, Peter said, "At the very least, it will demonstrate to your Heavenly Dad that you are willing to forgive your earthly dad."

At first, Rick resisted. "Pete, I don't want to sound like I'm making excuses; but in the past, I haven't done too well communicating with my father. I'm not sure that I'm going to measure up to your expectations."

"You need to know that my only expectation for you is that you keep trying and don't quit. As long as you are choosing to move forward, I'm willing to keep investing in your future. And for the record, Lisa and I have seen some incredible growth in you in the short time you've been here."

Rick wasn't used to hearing positive feedback. It made him feel wonderful and weird at the same time. Fortunately, Peter moved on. "Besides, there is a scary principle called *The Law of Bitterness.*"

"Which is…?"

"What you focus on is what you become. When you focus on the negative aspects of someone who has hurt you, you slowly turn into the exact same kind of person."

Rick was shocked. "You're kidding, aren't you?"

"I am very serious. When you spend all your time thinking negative thoughts about a specific person or occurrence, those thoughts start to affect your heart and the choices you make. *The Law of Bitterness* has to be exchanged for *The Principle of Replacement* which you already know. Instead of thinking that you *don't* want to be like your father, start asking yourself who you *do* want to be like."

"That will be…a challenging exercise," Rick tried to put a good face on his response as that familiar sick feeling washed over him.

"Taking steps to deal with your dad will help you learn how to deal with other people. Lisa and I are putting together a Discipleship Team that will be starting up after Labor Day. We think that the best context for advanced discipleship is in a Christian community where the Spirit can use other authentic followers of Jesus to help each other learn how to become intentionally transparent and accountable to the spiritual development process."

"Transparent and accountable?" Rick wasn't sure he liked the sound of that. "Am I going to have to share my *Past* with people I don't even know?"

"*Intentionally* transparent and accountable. Do you trust me yet, Rick?"

"Yeah. I trust *YOU.* Why isn't that enough?"

Peter looked like he had access to an amazing secret. "I've got some good news for you."

"Okay?"

"I'm not going to let you build an unhealthy dependency on me."

Rick struggled with confusion, hurt, and rejection. What's that supposed to mean?"

Putting a hand on Rick's shoulder, Peter explained, "I'm going to let you go back and think of all the conversations we've had over the past couple of months. The next time we get together, see if you can answer that question. When you can, you will have discovered more good news."

"Really? You're not going to tell me?"

"Not tonight. You have incredible analytical skills, and I want to see how well you exercise them."

Rick glared at Pete in disbelief. "First, you want me to try to make things right with my father. Now you want me to open up to people I don't even know. Isn't there a limit to how much someone should have to stretch?"

As he stared into his friend's face, Rick saw those familiar smile wrinkles around his eyes. "Rick, can't you see that each phase of spiritual development requires change…some very stretching and challenging change?"

"Seeing it and wanting to admit that I *need* it are two different things."

"Then, without pushing for admission, I'll simply remind you that **the *Infant, Child, Teen,* and *Adult* phases each have unique challenges, characteristics, needs, and opportunities. They also become a fairly accurate diagnostic tool to figure out where someone is in the spiritual development process.** With that in mind, when does a person begin to transition towards independence from his parents?"

"I guess it would be during the *Teen* years."

"And when does a person gain enough life experience to begin to know what kind of potential he or she has for a vocational direction?"

"Again, I'd say during the *Teen* years."

"Which phase requires a lot of emotional, physiological, and social change?"

With a sheepish smile, Rick answered, "*Teen* again!"

"Bingo! Rick, you have a lot of Bible knowledge, and you know how to navigate the playground rules of the average church culture. But I'd bet a brand new pickup against yours that you don't like to think about getting stretched in the areas of conflict resolution or emotional control. I'd make that same bet against you having very many friends that you trust over ninety percent and against you being willing to place yourself in a position of vulnerability and transparency."

"You'd win your bet," Rick agreed.

"Most leaders ride on their skill set until they run into conflict, and then their lack of maturity comes back to haunt them and cause harm to others. I want to guide you through the *Teen* phase so that you can emerge into the mature *Adult* God wants you to be."

"How long does the entire process of moving from *Infant* to *Adult* take?"

"Second Corinthians 3:18 teaches that maturity is ongoing, constantly moving us toward Christ-likeness. But from studying the discipleship efforts of Jesus and the Apostle Paul, it seems that a healthy and willing follower of Jesus could develop from *Infant* to *Adult* in approximately three to five years. Believers who don't have biblical discipleship care at the time of their spiritual birth have a slower growth process that depends on a number of variables. I would say from practical experience that, if a believer is resourced, and if he has no stubbornness or trauma issues, it should take no more than five years. Without discipleship, spiritual development rarely happens; sadly, there are thousands of believers running around in spiritual diapers, totally dependent on others to care for them."

"Well, one thing's for certain—if it wasn't for the help you and Lisa have given me, I'd be stuck between *Child* and *Teen* the rest of my life."

Rick left Peter and Lisa's home that night with mixed feelings about these new steps in his spiritual development process.

POTENTIAL BEGINNINGS & HOPE

The following week, Rick decided to head home for the weekend to visit his parents. When he invited Penny to come along, it took only one night of sisterly interaction and a couple of phone calls between Miriam and Waylon to find all three of them on their way to Enterprise Saturday.

Rick thoroughly enjoyed the trip. It seemed like all of them had known each other for years. It was also obvious that Miriam was smitten with the *Love Bug*. Rick chuckled to himself as he answered a lot of questions about Waylon.

When they arrived, Rick decided to put off talking with his father. He didn't want the weekend to be spoiled by turmoil if things didn't go well. Instead, the two couples enjoyed a relaxing afternoon at the lake.

But as Rick got back into the truck to head back to his parent's house, he realized, *It's now or never!*

"Are you nervous?" Penny sympathized.

"More than I'd like to admit."

"Let's pray." It was comforting for Rick to discover that Penny had the same response to problems that he had seen in Peter's wife Lisa.

As they began to talk to God, Rick felt God give him a sense of courage and grace that convinced him everything was going to be all right. He couldn't help glancing sideways at the woman sitting next to him and realizing what a wonderful gift their growing friendship was. He expressed gratitude to God for bringing Penny into his life.

At home, Rick headed into the living room where his father was sitting in the recliner. It was difficult to open his heart to his father and allow himself to be vulnerable to criticism and rejection once again. Ray answered Rick's pleas for understanding and reconciliation with cold distain and accusations. At the end of the discussion, Rick felt that he hadn't made any progress. Although things went about like he had expected, Rick couldn't ever remember the feelings of settled peace and joy he was experiencing simply from following through with what he knew was right. He was confused about how to develop a meaningful relationship with his father but encouraged to realize that he no longer felt imprisoned.

As they prepared to head back to Kennewick, Rick, Penny, Waylon, and Miriam all agreed that they had had a great weekend. After dropping Penny and Miriam off, Rick headed to Peter and Lisa's to share how things had gone. He knew now why Peter wanted him involved with the Discipleship Team, and he had some questions to ask.

THE UNEXPECTED

As Lisa served milk and pie, she asked, "How did things go this weekend?"

"Pretty much like I expected, but I felt like a huge weight lifted off me; I feel free."

"We're so glad. We've been praying for you all weekend."

"Thanks! It's hard to believe that, after all the years I've spent trying to follow Jesus on my own, I've gained more ground this past couple of months than ever before."

"Are you ready to take that help to the next level we talked about?" Peter asked.

"I've given that a lot of thought. I'm a little self-conscious about my lack of social skills, and it's not very easy for me to trust people. But talking with my father this weekend provided a reality check. I remembered what he was like when he first accepted Jesus. That's very different from what he has become. I'm still frustrated over how that happened, but I'm absolutely sure that I don't want the same thing for my life."

Lisa responded, "Are you familiar with Satan's two major objectives?"

You could almost see the wheels spinning in Rick's brain. "Off the top of my head, I would guess that one is *wanting to take as many people as he can to Hell.*"

"Yes," Lisa agreed. "The other is *preventing those who become children of God from being effective in their Christian walks.* Satan knows the *Potential* of a sold out Christian, so he does everything in his power to destroy it. Frequently, he uses the failure of other Christians, especially spiritual leaders, as a means of damaging that *Potential*."

"That's exactly what happened to my father. I remember him telling me once that I needed to attend church to avoid getting sucked back into the world, but never to get involved with leadership because I would get burned."

At this point, Peter interjected, "Your father is not the only Christian who feels that way. That's why we want to help you learn how to effectively interact with other believers. That process may be challenging, but we know that, once you experience authentic Christian community, you will never be the same."

"One of the reasons I stopped by tonight is to answer your question why I believe you want me to be a part of this group you are starting. I need to learn how to interact with other followers of Jesus in a healthy way. If I can't or won't do that, I'm still in bondage to my *Past*. Another reason is that I need to have more than one important spiritual person in my life. Then, if something happens to one person, all of my supposed progress would not be in jeopardy."

"I was fairly confident you would discover the answer, Rick. Remember this—as you begin interacting with and helping people spiritually, be sure you point people to a healthy, God-centered *Paradigm* instead of to yourself."

"Who will be in this group you've been talking about?"

Peter responded with practiced patience. "I'll answer that question in a few minutes. First, I think it would help you to know the purpose and function of the Discipleship Team. It's going to take two years to build and train the team. We will take a year to unpack the three key components of spiritual *Teen* development: *Paradigm, Past, and Potential*. The second year, we will form two smaller teams and begin practicing the leadership and team-building principles of the *Adult* phase: *Syncronized Purpose*, *Strategic Planning*, and *Systems of Effective Communication*. At the end of this training experience, one team will multiply itself here in Kennewick and become a model of an equipping church culture. The other team will take this model and reproduce it in a brand new community. Within five years, we hope this process will become a multiplying model that will produce future leaders and new churches, and also influence other churches to take a fresh look at what it means to be healthy and growing."

"You mean you don't plan on being here for more than five years?"

"Not in my current role."

"How will the church handle a plan like that? Who would ever be able to replace you?"

"One question at a time, Tiger! The church knew before I came what my plans were. As a church, they have been through some tough circumstances with abusive, complacent, or misaligned leaders. They were looking specifically for someone who would equip them to be able to take ownership for the entire ministry of the church."

"Wow! I've never heard of such a thing."

"Even though Ephesians 4:11-16 explains it as God's plan for the church, it doesn't happen very often."

"What if this doesn't work?"

"I believe that **if you pursue the heart of God and base your practices on the principles of His Word, you cannot fail with the overall mission. You may make mistakes along the way, but those become teachable moments to help discover a better way of living out God's principles.**"

As Rick was processing what he was hearing, Peter rocked his world with more *Potential* than he had ever dared to dream possible. "And as for the answer to your question about who would replace me—possibly you."

MOVING FORWARD

Rick stood there in stunned amazement. "How could I ever replace you?"

"We'd have a lot of work to do before you're ready. But Lisa and I have been watching your ability to learn and your gift mix. We believe you are a good match for leading this church into a healthy, growing future. Others in the church family have been watching you, too. Your boss is one of them. He tells me you are picking up construction faster than anyone else he has ever trained. He also says that you are a born leader."

"Really?" Rick asked in pleasant surprise.

"Why's that so hard for you to believe? You said that you felt called by God to a life of ministry, and that would require leadership ability, wouldn't it? **When God calls someone to a task, He also gifts and wires them specifically for that purpose so that they will thrive and succeed in their work.**"

"Yeah, but after all these years of rejection and failure, I guess I just figured it would never happen," Rick replied with a look of wonder.

"Well, it hasn't happened yet," Peter cautioned, "but the process is beginning. We're going to let you in on some inside information. Lisa and I have been working on a discipleship, leadership, and team-building program for several years. It is designed to equip lay leaders to a standard of excellence in administrative and relational skills that exceeds typical institutional systems of higher education. We have benefited greatly from our degreed studies, but we have also become convinced that there are some major deficiencies in higher education that need to be addressed."

"What do you think of being part of an experiment?" Lisa asked.

Rick looked like a kid in a candy store. "This isn't an experiment; it's the opportunity I've been looking for!"

Peter held Rick's gaze. "Okay then; let's see what happens with an ordinary guy who is committed to letting God work in and through him."

Lisa broadened Rick's perspective. "I hope you also realize that many others we have approached about this venture are struggling just like you. A few of them are chafing at the bit to get started, but most are dealing with self-doubt and fears. As God walks you through this process, you could also be a help to them."

Rick sat there in amazed disbelief. *Was this really happening to him?* Another thought hit him with exciting possibilities, and just as quickly, he was second-guessing himself. "Would it be okay to include Penny in this process, or would that not be a good thing?"

Peter chuckled. "Thanks for bringing up the subject. We were hoping that she would become a vital part of the Team. We just don't want to create a situation that would place either one of you in circumstances you aren't ready for, or don't believe are right for you."

"Becoming part of the Discipleship Team seems to be an opportunity consistent with where I've wanted to go with my life. I'm not sure if that's true for Penny."

"What would your expectations be regarding her decision about whether to become part of the Team?" Lisa asked.

"I think it's kind of like Pete's desire to invest in my life without me becoming dependent on him. I would want her to join this team because it is right for her, not just because we're dating and I did; but I really would like it if she did join."

Peter nodded in agreement. "Then let's ask her if she is interested in joining the Team based on a desire for spiritual development. The relational dynamics between the two of you will be up to you to figure out."

During the week, Peter and Lisa approached Penny about their desire to have her join the Team. Rick saved his discussion with Penny about his desire for Friday night.

WHAT WILL SHE SAY?

Rick had seen a few girls in the past who had interested him; but as time passed, things surfaced that would not allow him to entertain serious thoughts about an ongoing relationship. Penny was different. Though he wasn't sure how far things would progress, he had seen enough to know that he wanted to pursue a sincere relationship with her.

Monday night, he called to ask Penny for a date Friday night. After she agreed, he asked if could talk with Miriam.

"Why?" Penny asked.

"I will let you know Friday night," Rick teased.

Reluctantly, Penny handed the phone to her sister and was intrigued when she heard Miriam say, "I'll have to step into another room to answer that question."

"So what did he want?" Penny asked, after Miriam hung up.

"You'll find out Friday night."

"You two are having way too much fun at the expense of my curiosity," Penny fumed playfully. Rick had piqued her curiosity, and she enjoyed it.

"Waylon told me, not too long ago, that the most predictable quality of a woman is her curiosity. Maybe he was right!" They looked at each other and laughed. Then they began talking about Rick and Waylon, their favorite topics of discussion lately. Little did they know that, at that same moment, the two brothers were talking about them.

The week dragged by, and Friday night came none too soon for Penny; but Rick was busy trying to think of all the ways he could say what he wanted to say. After work on Friday, he stopped to pick up some flowers, and then hurried to his apartment to get cleaned up. Six o'clock found him at Penny's home, flowers in hand. After a short exchange with her family, they headed out for a memorable evening.

"Is this what you and Miriam talked about on Monday?" Penny asked, as they drove into the parking lot of her favorite restaurant.

"I wanted to surprise you with something special." The smile on her face let Rick know that he had succeeded.

After a pleasant meal, he looked across the table and, with some effort, said, "I want to—what I mean is…wow—I didn't think it would be this hard."

Penny just sat there with an unreadable face.

Turning red, Rick tried again. "I've practiced a thousand different ways this week to say what I want to say to you tonight, and nothing sounded good. I was kind of hoping that something intelligent would pop out of my mouth when the time came, but obviously that isn't working any better for me than practicing a script."

Eventually Rick found the words he was looking for. "Peter and Lisa have asked me to join a Discipleship Team that they are putting together. They also want this opportunity to be a means of training me for ministry. Looking into the future can be challenging, I know, but I was hoping that you would be interested in going through this process with me. You are the finest, godliest woman I have ever met, and I would love to have your permission to pursue a serious relationship with you."

Rick sat there anxiously waiting for some kind of a response. He waited. And then he waited some more. *What is she thinking?* he wondered.

"Rick...I...believe...that I....

Rick leaned forward a little.

"...that...I...would...

If she's trying to make me nervous, it's working!

"...I would like that very much," she finished with a smile.

Rick's face was a mixture of relief and concern. *This Discipleship Team is either going to be a piece of cake compared to this, or I'm in way over my head.* He was going to find out that he was right on both accounts.

GROUP
DISCIPLESHIP

THE TEAM

Peter and Lisa experimented with recruiting techniques to see which ones would produce the highest level of commitment and long-term impact. They asked several potential Discipleship Team members to complete an application process, the premise being that repetition would help deeply embed the training principles. Peter invited a few of the more relationally-oriented people to join the Team after a series of intense discussions. A couple of others were simply asked if they would like to join.

After years of preparation and revision, it was exciting to be ready to move the first group through the spiritual *Teen* development process. Peter and Lisa decided to have a get-together on Sunday evening to begin connecting everyone together and laying out their expectations for the Team.

Rick brought Penny. When they arrived, Rick's boss Gary Ingerson and his wife Kim were already there. Kim was a stay-at-home mom, busy with homeschooling their five children and doing the bookwork for Gary's construction business.

Burt and Betty Larson and Maggie Davis had also arrived. Burt, a lawyer working for a small firm in Pasco, was a tall, good-looking guy with a professional but winning way. His wife Betty was a bit of a socialite. She was involved in Tri-City politics and stood a good chance of becoming Pasco's next mayor. Both of them were driven individuals, sometimes caught up in the pressure of their careers.

Maggie was a third-grade teacher in her mid-thirties. Passionate and quite proficient at her vocation, she was loved by students and parents alike. During her childhood and early adult years, she actively participated in a liturgical church. Then in college, a friend introduced her to a campus ministry where she had a real encounter with Jesus; her life hadn't been the same since.

A few minutes later, Kevin and Misty Jordan, Garret Johnson, and Jared and Ruth Williams walked in. Rick worked with Kevin at Gary's construction company but didn't know his wife at all. He learned that Misty worked for Human Services as a case worker. In contrast to Kevin who was pretty laid back, Misty seemed like she was on a mission to right every wrong in the world.

Rick was surprised to find out that he was vaguely familiar with Garret, a gifted bronze artisan with a down-to-earth attitude. He had heard his name spoken with respect from some of the artists in Joseph, the town just south of Enterprise whose *Bronze Artwalk* on Main Street proudly displayed several of Garret's large bronze art pieces. Rick found Garret easy to talk with, and he felt comfortable being around him.

Jared Williams was a good-natured, rugged character with a vise-like handshake. He was a self-employed truck driver, doing as much local hauling as he could. Occasionally, he found himself taking long-distance runs to keep the money coming in. He articulated his philosophy of distance to Rick. "Anything under a thousand miles is a day; anything over a thousand miles is a long day." Under his breath, he added, "I don't think that's the same standard the D.O.T. uses."

Jared's wife Ruth was a homemaker with a small but growing web business. A few years ago, she had been diagnosed with an inoperable brain tumor. Ruth had spent a considerable amount of time traveling to specialists in Portland for experimental drug treatments. Her typically positive attitude and visible faith in God to control the circumstances of her life made her an inspiration to many people. She had learned that every day is a gift from God and was determined to make the most of those gifts.

Rick's head was swimming with information. He knew all of these faces from Sunday worship services, and he knew most of the names. The problem was going to be making the right connection between names and personal information. Fortunately Penny knew everyone. He made a mental note to have her straighten him out on anything he missed tonight.

The last couples to arrive were the Maxwells and the Rogers. Instantly, Rick was uneasy with the Maxwells. He tried to set his feelings aside as he asked what they did for work. Ted shared that he worked for the State Corrections Department. His wife Jan was a cashier at a local department store. Outwardly they were engaging enough; but there was just something that didn't feel right. Rick knew Peter well enough to know that, if they were here, they had potential. So why did he feel so unsettled?

Today the Rogers arrived in one vehicle, but, Vickie informed Rick that, due to Vern's frequent inability to be punctual, she often drove her own car to, in her own words, "minimize marital stress." Vern worked as a salesman for a local car dealership, and Vickie was a dental hygienist. They both had a sense of humor that was infectious, evidenced by how many people were gathering around to listen to them relate episodes from their recent vacation. Vern referred to himself as a "Landlocked Salmon." He originally "come" from the state of Maine, and nearly everyone made good-natured fun of his accent. The one area of his life that he would outwardly laugh about, while feeling totally defeated on the inside, was his significant weight problem.

The Freemonts, Sam and Michelle, were away on vacation. Peter reminded Rick what they looked like and shared that Sam was a radio station D.J., while his wife Michelle worked for a day-care center. Later Rick learned that Sam and Michelle had personal baggage which was negatively affecting their marriage. This was balanced by the fact that their backgrounds allowed them to identify with a broad spectrum of humanity.

As Rick looked around the room, he wondered what was in store for each of them during the upcoming year. ***Will I develop real relationships with this group of people,*** *or will they be added to my list of those who have become untrustworthy?*

TEAM EXPECTATIONS

After everyone had had a chance to eat and relax a little, Peter and Lisa began to share their expectations for the Team. In past ministries, their discipleship expectations were based on personal growth goals; so they had used a soft-start method before sharing what those expectations would be. Knowing that their expectations for this group were based on leadership goals, they decided to use an up-front approach to help stimulate either buy-in or a safe, but necessary, exit.

"You're all well aware of the goals we have for this Discipleship Team. We believe that should be enough to help you realize the importance of committing to the five expectations we have. There will be no hard feelings at all if you choose not join this venture."

"Here are our five Team expectations:

1. *Trust*
2. *Tactics*
3. *Talent*
4. *Teamwork*
5. *Two-way Talking*

"*Trust* has to be number one because, without trust, no joint venture will succeed. Trust impacts commitment. A lack of commitment indicates a lack of trust and will be addressed. Failure is not a breach of trust, if it is coupled with ownership. Blame-shifting and excuses are not acceptable traits."

"What exactly are we committing to?" Misty asked.

"Spiritual *Teen* development is a commitment to study biblical principles about emotional, relational, and spiritual maturity, and then apply what you learn with each other."

"That's too vague for me. I'm a 'feet on the ground' type of person. Can you give us specifics like homework, memorization, weekly meetings—those types of things? When I get home, how will I need to adjust my schedule and habits to make room for this process so that I can be successful?"

"It's not quite that simple, Misty. Some of this process is cut and dry. There will be a personal commitment to study 25 workbook sessions involving *Paradigm, Past,* and *Potential* issues on your own. We will meet as a Team each week to share study discoveries. Sometimes there will be verses to memorize.

"But, people are not made from a mold; aren't you thankful for that? We are not 'cookie cutter' beings. So, equally important is the seemingly nebulous personal commitment for each of us to engage in transparent accountability. The spiritual *Teen* development process goes far beyond a typical educational experience—study/test/pass or fail. We will each be responsible to make life changes based on the spiritual, relational, and emotional maturity principles we study—changes that are specific, changes that each member of the Team can see and verify as they watch us grow. Once you identify a change that you need to work on, you will make yourself accountable to the Team. This is the part of the process that can't be spelled out ahead of time.

"Lisa and I could teach this exact same spiritual *Teen* development process twenty times and, though the material and the end result would be similar, the journey would look different each time. One time, we may have a group where the majority comes from an addictive *Past*. Another time, we may have a group suffering from PTSD. The ratio of extroverts to introverts makes a vast difference in group dynamics and would have a distinct effect on the way we navigated through this process. Abuse, adultery, divorce, infertility issues, stubborn pride, unemployment—all of those issues and more impact the spiritual Teen development process."

"Thanks, Peter. That gives me a better feel for what's coming," Misty responded.

"We're not going to have to do 'touchy-feely' exercises, are we?" Burt asked.

"We'll be doing things like having everyone open up their homes to host our Team meetings."

"Why?" Jan asked.

"Very little builds community as well as letting people into the most personal spaces of your life. When you can let others share your kitchen, refrigerator, and bathroom, among other things, you've crossed a significant boundary needed to build trust."

When everyone seemed to grasp the commitment issues Peter moved on. "Our next expectation is *Tactical* agreement. This speaks of having a unified purpose and plan to live out New Testament Christianity. Our values and vision must be clear and unequivocally bought into. Our processes must be equal to our desired goals. We will not take short-cuts.

"Which leads us to *Talent*. In nearly every arena of life, skills matter. Yet strangely enough, the Christian community is often characterized by lackadaisical indifference. We will expect each of you on this Team to strive for excellence, without excellence becoming the ultimate goal. New Testament Christianity will always remain our ultimate goal."

"How will you help us to develop *Talent?*" Vern questioned.

"You will be exposed to a wide variety of resources," Peter reassured. "Some will be team-oriented; others will be personalized."

"Maybe I shouldn't even mention this, but how do you know that we are all a good relational fit for each other?" Misty asked.

"I don't. *Teamwork* can be a discretionary expectation which makes it the most challenging aspect of all. Sometimes a person can be trustworthy, agreeable on the tactical values and vision, and quite talented in their individual performance. The problem is whether or not he or she truly wants to be a team player on *this* team. We'll work through any team mismatches together as we go."

Peter was reading body language as he spoke, looking for any signs of discomfort. From his vantage point, he was pleased at the overall responses he was seeing.

"Last of all, and possibly the most important of all, is *Two-way Talking*. We will listen to each other instead of reacting negatively, especially in the areas of feedback and navigating through change. We will be honest and not lie, even by silent omission. We will intentionally strive to build each other up and not tear anyone down. And whenever offenses do occur, we will lovingly confront them, sincerely confess our own wrongs, willingly forgive the offenses of others, and biblically forget them.

"Anyone here who can embrace these five expectations wholeheartedly is welcome on the Team. I know that sometimes there are personal limitations that make it unwise to commit to such a venture as this. If you have concerns with anything we have shared tonight, please talk with Lisa and me before our first Team meeting which, by the way, will be the Sunday afternoon following Labor Day."

When Peter finished, there was an air of excitement. Each Team member understood that this was going to be a worthwhile venture.

Quite possibly, it was the team expectations that helped them see the importance of what lay ahead.

Those who showed up for that first meeting would be stating their commitment to the Team. *Will everyone show up?* Peter wondered. *Will those who choose to commit endure through the entire process?* Time would give him those answers.

FEEDBACK ON THE TEAM

The next night, Rick and Penny brought pizza to Peter and Lisa's. After everyone had finished eating, Peter kicked things off. "So, what do you two think of last night?"

Penny volunteered, "The positive response to the expectations you laid out surprised me. I thought there would be some resistance, but from where I was sitting, I didn't see any."

"I remember," Lisa reminisced, "a few times where open resistance would have been a pleasant experience compared to the undercover practices that eventually surfaced. **Only immature Christians fail to rise to the kind of expectations we laid out** last night. What we have found over the years is that, if people are reasonably aligned regarding what is important, and if we lay out our expectations clearly and show biblical reasons for them, people will be excited to become part of something significant."

"I can relate to that," Rick replied. "Gary has been very clear about what he wants from me on the jobsite. What helps is that he always ties his expectations to the impact that they have on his customers. He also consistently rewards us when we meet or exceed his expectations. He is one of the most firm yet grateful people I've ever met. It makes me feel that what I do is important, and that drives me to give my best."

"In the workplace Gary is living out the same principles we will be using as a Discipleship Team," Peter agreed. "I'm excited to see that God knew exactly what he was doing by having you work for him. You will be experiencing the spiritual development process in two different team contexts."

"Why so many people?" Penny wondered.

Lisa explained, "Eventually we want to divide this group into two smaller teams—a home-base team that becomes an equipping model and a church-planting team in a new location. The large group will make things more challenging on the front end; but, after weighing our options, we felt that there would be a common thread to both teams if we started out together."

"What were your people observations from last night?" Peter asked.

Penny responded, "Having known everyone in our church family for several years, I could see why you asked those who were here last night to be part of this Team. I'm looking forward to building stronger relationships with everyone."

Rick added before asking a question that had been troubling him since the night before. "Surprisingly, from where I was just a short time ago, I'm really looking forward to being part of this Team. I still need to meet the Freemonts, but everyone else was fairly nice. Betty seemed a little self-absorbed, and Vickie could talk the ears off an elephant, but no one's perfect. The one question I have is about the Maxwells. Are you sure they want to be part of this process?"

Rick noticed Peter and Lisa glance at each other before Peter asked, "Why?"

"I'm aware that you know everyone better than I do. There's just something in Ted that reminds me of a warning light on a dashboard, and something even more subtle about Jan that I haven't been able to put my finger on yet."

"What are you basing those 'somethings' on?" Peter asked.

"Man, that's challenging. They seem very sincere and dedicated on the surface. Another part of Ted seems kind of like a porcupine; if he were to ever get riled, you would either need to back off or get hurt. Jan is even harder to figure. For now, I would have to say that she reminds me of people that I've met who were pleasantly stubborn. As long as things go their way, they're wonderful people. When things don't go their way, they just politely lock up."

"So, just a gut feeling—nothing really concrete?"

"Yeah."

"Interesting. I haven't sensed that in either one of them, but neither do I discount your perspective. We haven't been here much longer than you have. What do you think Penny?"

"I'm remembering some background that might weigh in on this. Ted has survived a horrible first marriage and a not-so-pleasant experience with one of our former pastors."

"What kind of *Paradigm* does he have?" Rick asked, looking at Peter and Lisa. He couldn't be sure, but they seemed to be pleased that he was implementing what they had been teaching.

Peter answered, "I don't think we have probed deep enough to know the answer to that question; we will have that opportunity during our times together as a Team."

Rick's heart began pounding with excitement—and fear. Soon it would be show time, not some distant dream. What if he failed? It was one thing to see the shortcomings of others. Was he ready to deal with his own?

KICK OFF!

Peter and Lisa had learned early in their efforts to disciple others how powerful informal fellowship was, and meals seemed to set that tone better than anything else. After talking over their options, the Team agreed that it would be easiest to meet Sunday afternoons directly after the worship service.

Peter and Lisa volunteered to host the first meeting. They had intentionally added several features to their home and yard to create an atmosphere conducive to building relationships: a grilling area on one end of an outdoor porch, commercial ice and beverage machines, and a playground with a splash pool for kids.

Frank and Sarah, an elderly couple with a passion for children, were also adopted into the Team because they agreed to have a study for the children while the adults were meeting.

It was a perfect late summer day. Garret was busy grilling, while several of the men stood around bantering over their expectations for the football season. Some of the women were visiting inside, enjoying the comforts of air conditioning. Others chatted as they set up tables. The teens were busy planning some boating on the river after the meal.

As Peter watched the Team members and their families interact, he whispered to Lisa, "The *Teen* phase has begun. We've been looking forward to this for years. I'm fairly confident about leading the Team through this phase; it's the *Adult* phase that concerns me."

"**One step at a time.**"

"But I have two legs," he replied with an impish grin.

SPIRITUAL DEVELOPMENT PROCESS

"All right, Team! The ideal test of a teacher is to see if he can keep his students awake after a meal."

"Especially after we have listened to him preach to us once already today," Vern joked.

Good-natured humor rippled through the Team as they moved inside for their first study time.

"What does the spiritual development process entail?'" Peter began, once everyone got settled.

When no one seemed to have an answer, he reframed his question. "If I labeled each phase of the physical development process as moving from *Infant* to *Child* to *Teen,* to *Adult,* would that make sense to all of you?"

As everyone agreed, he proceeded. "So what are the general characteristics and needs of each of these physical development phases? Let's start with *Infant.*"

"Characteristically, they coo or cry depending on how they perceive their little world," Misty said, remembering her own children.

Sam grinned, "They need their bellies filled and their bottoms cleaned."

His wife added, "They also need immunization shots."

"So, what would be the spiritual equivalent of the physical characteristics you've just mentioned?"

"My mothering skills would say, protection from spiritual hazards, biblical truth appropriate for the age level, and some messes cleaned up," Kim replied.

"How much work are babies in the *Infant* stage?"

"About as much as a husband!" Vickie teased, as Vern stuck his thumb in his mouth and slowly fell into his wife's lap.

Peter empathized before moving on. "We feel for you, Vickie! Okay, how about the *Child* phase?"

"Well, they're starting to do things independent of their primary care providers," Jan replied, "and they are beginning to learn some social skills."

"Character would be at the top of my list," Jared stated.

"They also need to be taught what is true and false, what is acceptable and unacceptable," Kim added. "Translated into spiritual characteristics, this would be the phase where a lot of teaching about biblical truth would occur, and commitment to the Body of Christ would become a consistent part of life."

Peter affirmed Kim's insights before asking, "What about the *Teen* phase?"

Several groans could be heard, along with expressions about being glad when that phase was over.

Lisa spoke up, "We don't have teenagers ourselves yet, but Peter and I have dealt with a lot of spiritual teenagers. I would have to say that I love the spiritual *Teen* years. They have finally got some maturity in their decision-making processes, they are seeing God begin to use them to make a difference in their sphere of influence, and, best of all, they believe that anything is possible with God on their side. If their slightly aggressive and maybe arrogant/obnoxious side is managed well, they go on to turn their world upside down. If it's mismanaged, they become problematic and self-destructive."

"That gives me some hope," Vickie sighed.

Peter moved on to the ultimate goal he had in mind for everyone on this Team. "Last of all, what description and needs fit the *Adult* phase?"

"A healthy *Adult* needs occasional encouragement, consistent accountability, and appropriate exhortation," Gary responded.

Maggie added, "They should have already discovered what contribution they have to offer society and should find fulfillment in making that contribution. I guess the spiritual equivalent of that would be knowing your God-given gifts and purpose, and then performing those with Spirit-controlled excellence and team alignment."

"Stop and **ask yourselves where you are in the spiritual development process.**"

As the Team slowly thought through the question, they agreed that no one was in the *Infant* phase. Most agreed that they fell into the *Child* or *Teen* phases. Rick stated that he felt like a *Child* in a number of ways, but desperately wanted to be a *Teen*. Gary and Kim hesitantly shared that they believed they were in the *Adult* phase. Many agreed and expressed appreciation for the mature example that they were for the Team.

As the meeting wrapped up, Peter had everyone pair off to pray for each other. He and Lisa sat there watching God at work. They had significant hopes for this Team; they had spent years preparing for this opportunity. Shivers of excitement ran up their backs, but they were also realistic enough to know there would be some rough sailing ahead.

ADVENTURE 1 —
WORLDVIEW PARADIGM

The following Sunday, the whole Team seemed to be turbo-charged.

The singles had agreed to put together a progressive dinner so that everyone could experience their housing accommodations and hosting abilities. Rick and Maggie had similar living situations, so they took the first stops—Rick providing the beverages, and Maggie, the appetizers.

Rick's situation was perfect for a single guy, but not much more. The plan was to have everyone come in, get a drink, and then head to Maggie's. Rick found himself getting irritated with Michelle when she held things up by letting one of her boys dump out his drink because he didn't like it. *Then why did you take it in the first place, you little twerp?* he thought.

Maggie's apartment was located just a block away from the school where she taught. It was brightly decorated and matched her disposition perfectly. She had everyone line up like a class of students and navigate an established path to pick up their appetizer before exiting for Penny's parents' home.

Penny's parents lived on West Canal Street in a modest but attractive home overlooking Columbia Park. They had agreed to host the Team for the main meal. Penny's mother proved to be an excellent cook, and her father an amiable host.

Garret provided the dessert and hosted the Bible study. His house and shop were located just west of the historic section of Kennewick. Before the study, several of the Team asked to see Garret's workshop and showroom. Looking at the detailed bronze pieces, Penny asked, "Where do you get your inspiration?"

"I love the West, which is probably obvious as you look at the overall theme of my displays. Some of my inspiration comes from being gifted with a vivid imagination. At other times, it comes from attending a rodeo or seeing a different art form. A couple of the busts were inspired by some old timers that I've known over the years."

Sam spoke with respect. "You're amazing!"

"I'm pleased with the art skills God has blessed me with, but lately I've been longing for my spiritual skills to grow up and surpass my artistic abilities.

At least you have abilities, Rick thought.

~ ~ ~

"What difference does it make whether or not God exists?" Peter's opening question made Rick feel like he was in a time warp. The discussion that followed was much like his first visit with Peter not so many weeks ago. He watched as his friend guided the Team through a series of Bible verses in order to develop biblical principles and make life applications for a worldview that was God-centered.

"So in conclusion, we see that **God exists in perfection, He wants us to know Him, and we are accountable to Him.**"

I wonder if Peter uses this same approach with everyone he disciples. Rick was lost in thought until Misty started to criticize her husband Kevin.

"If God exists and we are accountable to Him, then Kevin will have to answer for his lack of leadership in our home, won't he?"

Smoothly, Peter helped redirect Misty to each person's own responsibility outlined in Romans 14:12 before letting the Team know what the next week's session would involve.

On the way home, Rick vented to Penny, "What right did she have to jump on Kevin in public? I can't imagine being married to someone that critical."

Penny studied Rick with a quizzical look on her face.

ADVENTURE 2 – PURPOSE OF LIFE PARADIGM

When Rick got back to his apartment, he was in a foul mood but wasn't sure why. *Maybe I'm afraid that all the positives in my life right now will evaporate into nothingness. And then on the other hand, maybe I'm just a hopeless jerk.* He balled up his fist and hit the closest wall.

After his anger cooled a few degrees, he half-heartedly started looking over Adventure Two in his workbook. *What is the purpose of life? If I had the answer to that question, I'd have it made.*

The next probe question further aggravated him. *What does it mean to glorify God? How in tarnation am I supposed to know the answer to that?*

Just then the phone rang. "Rick, this is Vern. Any chance you could come o'va and help me with a small project this week? With the Team meeting at ou'a house next, I need to get a railing installed on ou'a back deck."

"Do you have the materials?"

"Ayuh, that much I do have. I just don't have the construction experience ta make it happen."

"Would tomorrow night be good?"

"Works for me. Why don't you come o'va right aft'a work, and we'll feed you befo'a we tackle things."

~ ~ ~

The thing Rick noticed from the street about the Roger's home, compared to the other houses in the neighborhood, was the large garage. Vern had a weakness for old cars.

After an incredible meal, Rick installed the railing in just a couple of hours. As he was putting his tools away and getting ready to leave, he asked Vern, "So what do you think of this week's adventure?

"It's a pow'aful remind'a fa' me."

"Do you know what it means to glorify God in *EVERYTHING* you do?"

"I think so. I struggle with applying it, but I believe I know what it means. It's worship."

"Worship?"

"Ayuh, worship! Today, we all worked a job. Tonight, Vickie cooked a wicked good meal and we ate it. You installed a railin' and we have spent time talkin'. If any a' those activities happened on just a horizontal level, then they were self-centa'ed acts of idolatry—substitute worship replacing the purpose God created us fa'. But, if we got out of bed this mau'nin' **thanking God for the opportunity to let otha's see Him in every activity we engaged in, that was true worship.**"

～ ～ ～

As Rick got in his pickup and headed home, he was mulling things over in his mind. *So maybe that's why I can do the same activity with two different outcomes; it's the motive behind what I do that makes the difference.*

ADVENTURE 3 – TEMPTATION PARADIGM

The following week Peter ramped up his discipleship efforts with Rick to prepare him to teach for the first time. The game plan was for Peter to review and discuss the previous week's lesson and applications on the purpose of life; Rick would then teach the concept of temptation.

The Larsons' house would tempt a few to envy affluence and the creature comforts that seemed almost limitless. Set on the river in Pasco, with Wade Park being the only thing that separated their front yard from the water, the house was spectacular. Though it was evident that the Larsons were well off, they had a unique quality of making everyone feel like equals. By the time the meal was over, most of the Team were more focused on what they were about to experience spiritually than they were their surroundings.

~ ~ ~

Rick's heart was beating a thousand miles an hour as he began his lesson on temptaion. To help diffuse his anxiety, he started with an engaging question. "What are your worst nightmares when you are on a road trip?"

"Construction," blurted out Jared.

"Fussy kids," Misty groaned.

"Safety issues—for me and my car," Maggie volunteered.

"Too much junk food," Vern confessed. "Just sitting tha'a I get bored, so my first pit stop is a well-stocked convenience sto'a to get my favorite snack foods."

Rick continued, "**I decided that the road trip concept would be a good way to help us visualize temptation. All of us prefer a smooth journey when we are on a trip. But the reality is that we often encounter challenges—some self-inflicted (like a lack of preparation or bad habits) and others imposed on us by circumstances beyond our control (like construction or breakdowns).**"

Everyone seemed to be connecting with the analogy Rick was using. He breathed a quiet sigh of relief and began to relax a little bit as he continued his lesson. "In Genesis chapter three and Matthew chapter four, we read of two different journeys with two different outcomes. In both stories, the main characters have a God-given destination. They also share the exact same satanic road hazards. But, in the Genesis 3 story, the road trip ends up in disaster, while the Matthew 4 story becomes a travel guide for all future travelers. Who would be willing to read Genesis 3:1-8?"

Kim just started reading. After she finished, Rick asked, "In this story, what was the destination objective?"

"It could be expressed in a number of ways," Maggie suggested. "Glorifying God, obeying God, not getting sidetracked or becoming self-centered."

"Good suggestions. So, what were the road hazards that Satan used to prevent Eve from reaching her intended destination?"

"Doubt would be one of the biggest road hazards," Gary ventured.

"What did Satan want them to doubt?"

"God's goodness and His wisdom."

"How so?" Rick probed.

"If people doubt that God knows what He's doing or that He has their best interests in mind, they will entertain other options."

Rick agreed and moved on. "So did Satan use a roadblock, or a scenic bypass, to introduce his options?"

"Definitely a scenic bypass," Burt affirmed.

"What does that tell you about Satan's temptation tactics?"

"He doesn't start with obvious departures from God's travel plans. He tries to deceive people into thinking that leaving God's plan will be an innocent detour with positive, pleasing benefits. Later, any questions about the consequences of taking a bypass are met with outright denial."

Several voices expressed agreement with Burt.

"As people contemplate Satan's bypass, what are the magnetic forces that influence them away from God's route?"

No one responded immediately, so Rick clarified, "Was Satan the only influence drawing Eve away from God's plans for her?"

Garret answered, "Not at all! In verse six, we see her bodily desire for food, her emotional desire for the value she felt it would add to her life, and the advantages she thought would be hers."

"I believe that is what First John 2:16 refers to as 'the lust of the flesh, the lust of the eyes, and the pride of life,'" Maggie added, providing the biblical reference point to Garret's answer.

Rick was pleased with the connections people were making. "So far, we have *Satan* and *Self* tempting us away from God's planned journey for our lives—one internal force and one external. Are there any other influences?"

"Another external influence would be peer pressure—what other people think, say, and value," added Kim.

"I agree, Kim. Let's record some of the principles we've covered so far," Rick continued. "The first involves the external and internal influences we just discussed. Each influence begins with an 'S.'"

- *Satan*
- *Society*
- *Self*

"For the next principle, we also need to record that *Satan* and *Society* (the peer pressure Kim mentioned) will be influencing *Self* in three areas:

1. Lust of the flesh (bodily appetites/addictions)
2. Lust of the eyes (value system issues)
3. Pride of life (self-absorption)

"And lastly, I have a list that begins with 'D's that describes Satan's temptation tactics from Genesis 3:

- Deception
- Doubt
- Denial
- Desire

Rick now addressed an aspect of temptation that he periodically found troubling. "I don't know if any of you ever struggle with why an all-powerful God allows temptation, but I do. First Corinthians 10:13 states that temptation comes to everyone and that God doesn't allow temptation to exceed our ability to resist it. This next story we are going to read helps me, as a visual person, to see how God illustrates those truths. Will someone please read Matthew 4:1-11?"

Betty volunteered. As she finished, Rick asked, "What similarities did you see between this story and the Genesis 3 story?"

"Satan tried to appeal to the lust of the flesh (with the bread), the lust of the eyes (with the treasures of the world), and the pride of life (asking Jesus to jump off the temple to show His power)," Burt outlined.

"And the pride of life could also be the same as *Society*, peer pressure," Gary added. "The Jews were looking for a king. Jumping off the temple and landing unhurt before a crowd would have been a powerful evidence that Jesus was their King."

"That's right," Rick agreed, as he began moving toward the conclusion. "Now, what are the reasons that this story turned out differently than Adam and Eve's?"

"Looking at the principles we have covered, I would say that the reasons would be the opposite of the four *D's*," Burt observed. "Jesus wasn't deceived by Satan's bypass attempts. He was firmly anchored in His Father's goodness and wisdom. Remember, it was the Spirit Who led Him into the wilderness to be tempted in the first place. He was so anchored that when Satan misapplied Scripture, Jesus was able to bring clarity to the consequences that would be incurred. And best of all, His only desire was to obey His Father's Word."

"Which reminds me," Rick added, "in Ephesians chapter six, there is a description of a soldier in battle gear. One of his offensive weapons is the 'Sword of the Spirit,' which is the Word of God."

"This is all fine and good," Ted interjected, "but, I'm not making the connection between temptation and paradigms. I thought this was supposed to help us develop a God-centered paradigm."

Rick was angry, assuming that Ted was questioning his competence. He had spent hours studying to get ready for this presentation, and he couldn't help but feel a personal sting behind the comment that he felt was slightly premature.

He began to performance choke. The pressure was mounting to say something intelligent, but he was coming up dry. The only thing coming to his mind was how much he would enjoy taking Ted out into the woods and teaching him a different kind of lesson. And then he felt ashamed for thinking such a thought.

Lisa looked at Peter. *Aren't you going to help him out?*

GROWING PAINS

Peter took a few moments to watch the Team's response patterns to this challenging situation. Rick had totally locked up. Vern started to tell a joke, but Vickie shook her head "*no.*" Jan tried to smooth over the growing silence by saying, "I'm sure Peter can explain the connection." Jared got up and headed toward the bathroom. *Interesting,* Peter thought. *It looks like we need to incorporate some mentoring in with today's teaching.* He slid forward in his chair.

"First, let me share that all of you at some point in this training process are going to get the experience of being under pressure to prepare and present biblical truth to the Team."

"Rick's done a great job at laying out the principles of temptation. Now, as to how that connects with developing a God-centered paradigm, let's hear what you think." Peter was not going to provide an answer before giving people the opportunity to process things for themselves.

Penny offered, "When Rick used the contrasting stories of Eve and Jesus, I could see that Eve's paradigm shifted to the Satan side. Her entire future was negatively affected by that paradigm shift. On the other hand, Jesus lived out a God-centered paradigm. The connection for me is that **temptation doesn't determine outcomes; it reveals the paradigm that already exists in a person's heart.**"

"What's the difference between *Past* problems and *Potential* problems when it comes to temptation?" Maggie asked. "They both seem to be evidences of a *Paradigm* failure."

"You're right. The difference lies in what the failure is connected with. For those dealing with temptations involving their *Past*, the connection is either with those in their childhood environment or with a traumatic experience. In both cases, temptation is connected to something outside of oneself. Even addictions that started in the past can be connected with the person that introduced the addictive behavior. Often in tragedy, the connection involves a question about why God would let such a horrible experience happen. When it comes to the *Past*, people tend to want to blame the actions of others rather than take ownership for their reactions. Unresolved issues from the *Past* get transferred to anyone or anything reminding people of their past. On the other hand, temptations involving someone's *Potential* are typically connected to the desires and values inside that person."

"Wouldn't that tend to make temptations involving the *Past* harder to deal with?" Misty asked. "There would have to be a separation between the external actions of others and your own reactions."

"That is true for most people." Peter agreed.

As things were heading towards application conclusions, Peter re-engaged Rick. "One thing that came up during today's study that I want to capitalize on is the observation that Jesus did the opposite of Eve. In essence, that is the *Replacement Principle* in action. Rick, would you please share that principle with us." Peter saw that his friend hadn't expected to have to teach any more, but, he wasn't going to let Rick off the hook that easily.

Taking a deep breath, Rick started. "Ephesians and Colossians describe the *Replacement Principle* with the words, 'put off' and 'put on.' The idea behind this concept is that, when something negative or sinful is removed from our lives, the resulting void needs to be filled with something spiritually positive."

"And didn't you bring some worksheets to help us identify negative and sinful issues in our lives?" Peter coached.

"Yes, but I want all of you to know that a lot of the issues listed on these worksheets came from discussions I've had with Peter about my own life. One worksheet addresses *Past* issues; the other worksheet probes for *Potential* problems. Hopefully this will help you identify where your greatest temptation struggles lie."

As the Team was leaving the Larsons' home, Peter praised Rick. "You did an awesome job teaching the lesson today!"

"But I choked. Ted made me see red for a few seconds, and then I didn't know how to regroup."

"Before you choked, you were doing as well at teaching as anyone I've ever met. Your road trip analogy and the comparison between Eve and Jesus was genius. And when I gave you the opportunity to re-engage, you recovered nicely and were able to continue. If you were in an educational setting, your grade would have been an 'A.' I'm really proud of you!"

Rick felt something warm burst inside himself. The words "genius" and "I'm really proud of you" kept repeating in his mind.

ADVENTURE 4 –
INTERNAL ENEMY
PARADIGM

After work the following Friday, Rick headed back to Enterprise with Penny and Miriam to spend that night and Saturday with Waylon and his folks. Suppertime was an interesting experience.

"So how is the *Reverend* doing?" Waylon asked with his customary wry sense of humor.

Rick was just getting ready to share about his teaching the previous week and Pete's positive feedback when Ray commented, "If you look at the tires on his pickup, you'd have a pretty good idea. They don't look like they've been rotated since he left. Probably thinks, now that he is involved with Bible studies, that someone less *spiritual* should do his work for him."

Son of a—! Why do I bother coming back here? Rick could feel hot bitter anger rising up inside himself. Jerking back his chair from the table, he got up and headed out to the garage where he violently performed the *suggested* tire rotation.

Penny told him later that, after he left the table, Ray had grinned and said, "That got him going, didn't it?"

"It's the same old story. No matter what I do, I can never please him. He doesn't give a rat's hind end about my life. He humiliates me any chance he gets."

"You've got a growing circle of people who do care about your life. Doesn't that help to offset the negatives of your family?"

"Don't I have the right to be respected by my own father?"

"Maybe the answer to that question could be found in our lesson for this week."

"What do you mean?"

"According the verses in our workbooks for this week's adventure, what is our internal enemy?"

"Our sin nature."

"Several of the verses also referred to it as 'Pride.' **I'm wondering if God is giving you an opportunity to give up your efforts to win your parents approval and the self-pity that comes when you fail.**"

Rick just stared at Penny in disbelief. *Had she just said that he was feeling sorry for himself?*

He turned abruptly saying, "I'm going to watch TV."

ADVENTURE 5 – SALVATION PARADIGM

Peter opened the next Bible study with a question that grabbed Rick's attention. "What images come to your mind when you hear the word 'condemnation'?"

Rick quickly thought, *Last weekend.*

"Nothin' positive," Vern answered.

"To help us picture the grace and our freedom from condemnation mentioned in Romans 8:1, I want to ask an even more probing question. Do you believe that salvation is conditional or unconditional?"

"I would like some clarification," Maggie stated. "Are you asking if we believe that someone can lose their salvation?"

"Yes, but for a practical purpose rather than for a theological position."

Burt replied, "From a legal perspective, I believe salvation is unconditional."

"What do you mean?" Maggie asked.

"Legally, everyone is convicted of sinful crimes against God's perfection. The verdict for such criminal acts is *Guilty,* resulting in condemnation and judgment. But God Himself, in the form of Jesus, visited earth and paid the sin debt in full when He died on the cross. Anyone who accepts that payment is legally declared *Pardoned*. No one can reopen the case against them."

"Doesn't that give people a license to sin?" Jared asked in a serious-sounding voice. "I've seen people who claimed that they were Christians and lived like the Devil himself."

"Misguided personal beliefs or lifestyles do not change truth," Lisa interjected. "At salvation, God's roles change; He moves from the role of *Judge* to the role of *Father*. As a judge, He must carry out His legal responsibilities of righteous justice. As our Father, He carries out His parental responsibilities of loving correction."

Ruth turned to her husband and softly spoke, "Which means, Sweetheart, that while God does not turn a blind eye to sin, neither can one of His kids be kicked out of His family just because they have sinned."

Peter agreed, adding, "As to the question of whether or not someone who is living in gross sin is a child of God, that is a determination that only God can make. We can only exercise external discernment based on the fruit we see, or don't see, in someone's life. God makes the internal judgment based on what He knows is in that person's heart."

"It seems you really want us to understand how someone's relationship with God affects his spiritual development. What application are you trying to show us?" Gary asked.

Rick's face remained expressionless, but inside he was smiling. He already knew the answer to that.

Peter explained, "We are going to be addressing some changes to personal areas of your lives that are necessary for spiritual *Teen* development. At times, this may stimulate guilt and shame, while at other times you may feel frustration over the lack of growth in your lives. If someone is secure in God's grace and in what God believes about him, he will be able to absorb these negative feelings and move forward. But if there is doubt about your *Paradigm* position, Satan will wreak havoc and prevent the growth God desires. So the bottom line is, **if you believe God views you as His child, there will be security in the development process,** even when it requires levels of correction. On the other hand, if you don't believe God views you permanently as His child, your focus will tend to be more on performance and the resulting feelings that go with that mindset."

"What about those who choose not to be part of a family anymore?" Michelle wanted to know.

Rick had an epiphany. "Maybe I can answer that. Even if I get ticked off to the point that I don't want to be a Thomson anymore, and I've been there more than once, that doesn't change the fact that my parents blood runs through my veins. I could change locations, change my name, and never speak to my parents again; but I'd still be their son."

"I've never thought of it that way," Betty responded, "but it makes perfect sense."

"I came from a church background that taught us that salvation was conditional, based on the choices that people make," Garret spoke. "So, are you saying that, since my faith is connected with God's offer of salvation, His spiritual blood unconditionally flows through me?"

"Great question, Garret. With this being a foundational issue to the spiritual development process, let me ask *you* a question. What do you think 'everlasting' means in John 3:16?"

"I've often wondered how *Eternal Life* could be conditional or temporary, and yet I've struggled with doubt about my salvation for years. I do the best I can to live out my faith, but I haven't viewed my relationship with God as a healthy father-son relationship. This may be a significant *Paradigm* shift for me."

"Understanding the grace of God and our resulting position in Christ is an important component to a God-centered *Paradigm* and the security needed for spiritual development."

Once again, Peter had the Team pair off for discussion and prayer. Rick's boss, Gary, ended up helping Rick process his recent trip home in light of what they had just learned. By the time they had finished praying together, Rick was back on track.

ADVENTURE 6 – SANCTIFICATION PARADIGM

The Williams' home was a little unusual. Even though the city had grown up around them, Jared prided himself that he still kept a few horses to let the neighbors know that he had been there first. Ruth explained that, when they were first married, Jared had competed in rodeos. To combine their mobile lifestyle with the need for a place to call home, he had built a pole barn to park their fifth-wheel trailer inside and to give them a few extra amenities like a laundry room and a full-sized kitchen. Over time, he had converted the pole barn into a house.

"I knew I finally had a place of my own when he pulled the trailer out, framed in the garage door, and laid carpet down for a living room where the trailer used to be." Ruth shared her story with the ladies while the men were in the den admiring pictures and trophies of Jared's rodeo adventures.

Penny noticed that, on one wall, there were family pictures of Jared, Ruth, and their girls, along with some older people. "Are these your parents or Jared's?"

"Those are mine," Ruth answered. "Jared doesn't really claim anyone for parents."

Penny thought that was an odd statement but chose not to pry further.

After the Williams' home had been politely explored and the meal had finished, Peter opened the Team's study by asking, "How would you describe the New Testament picture of baptism?"

Sam answered, "I think baptism is identifying with the message of Christianity."

"What does 'identifying with the message of Christianity' mean?"

The Team thought for several moments before Ted volunteered, "To me, it means that I have decided to publicly declare that I am a follower of Jesus."

"That is a common and good answer. The challenge is that in the Old Testament, God provided a multitude of icons—or pictures—to help His people learn how to follow Him; but in the New Testament, Jesus only provided two—the Lord's Supper and Baptism. I would like to suggest that, if authentic Christianity has only two visuals to picture its meaning, then it is vitally important to understand the significance of those visuals. So let's probe deeper. How are the words 'death,' 'faith,' 'love,' 'lordship,' 'surrender,' 'Holy Spirit filling,' and 'resurrection power' connected to baptism?"

Prolonged silence followed Peter's question.

Sam finally ventured, "I could share my thoughts about how to apply each of the words you listed on an individual level, but I'm not sure I could make their connection with baptism."

"Could you create a few more dots to help us understand what you are looking for?" Maggie asked.

"Certainly. When someone places faith in Jesus for salvation, that person experiences spiritual birth—they are a spiritual *Infant*. That is the starting point of a process by which the believer grows to be like Jesus.

"When Jesus died and was buried, the *penalty* of sin was paid; however the *power* of sin was still in effect because Jesus was dead. But because Jesus had obeyed His Father's will, the Holy Spirit empowered Him to come out of the grave so that He would also break the power of sin. Similarly, we are powerless to defeat sin on our own; we are totally dependent on the Spirit of God to unleash the resurrection power of Jesus in our lives."

"What about those who believe that baptism is *a* means of, or *the* means for, salvation?" Garret asked.

"Ephesians 2:8-9 answers that with the concepts of unmerited grace and faith. Also the book of Romans gives a good progression of condemnation, salvation, and sanctification. Chapters one through three show the need for salvation because of sin. Chapters four and five speak of justification through faith. Then, in chapters six through eight, *after* salvation has become a reality, God addresses the ongoing process of defeating the power of sin in believers' lives through the picture of baptism and the power of the Holy Spirit."

"Help me understand sanctification," Burt requested.

"First, I must know that my old self was put to death with Jesus on the cross and that it no longer has the power to control me. Next, I must appropriate that knowledge. By faith, I move from knowledge to actively surrendering to the will of Jesus. Surrender then unleashes the supernatural power of the Holy Spirit in my life that empowers me to live like Jesus."

"Saying 'no' to me and 'yes' to God," Gary simplified.

Peter responded, "Exactly. The choice to get baptized is symbolic of a believer's choice to leave his old sinful nature in the grave and have the resurrection power of Jesus flow through his life. It is moving from accepting Jesus as Savior to surrendering to His Lordship. In some cultures, those concepts are fused together and happen simultaneously, probably because of the severity of becoming a Christian. In North American culture, the two concepts are usually understood and acted upon separately."

"Is that why Western Christianity is often so weak and powerless?" Kim questioned.

"When a person chooses to replace total commitment and devotion with misguided busyness, comfort, convenience, or personal *rights*, how can the power of God flow through that kind of a life?" Peter asked with concern.

Rick's heart began beating a little faster and sweat started rising through his skin. He sensed the Holy Spirit asking him if there was *anything* he was unwilling to give up or deal with. *Why does it have to be so hard to live out New Testament Christianity?*

"It's unusually quiet in here. Are there any challenges coming to your mind right now?" Peter asked.

"I consider myself pretty hard core when it comes to accepting difficult tasks," Jared answered, "but I don't think I've ever been challenged to completely surrender to the Lordship of Jesus. That doesn't leave any middle ground."

"I think most of us would feel comfortable giving Jesus 75 percent of our lives, but 100 percent—that's quite challenging," Michelle interjected. "And, I've never made the connection of that decision with baptism."

I couldn't have said it better, Rick thought.

There was intensity in his voice as Peter pressed on. "Was it hard for you to make the decision to place your faith in Jesus as your Savior? When you made that decision, did you place 75 percent of your faith in Jesus or 100 percent?"

"Anything less than 100 percent faith in Jesus Christ is not salvation," Burt responded.

"The actual moment of placing my faith in Jesus wasn't hard, but it was challenging to get to the place where I was willing to make that decision," Sam agreed.

"And, that decision didn't magically make it easy for me to live like a follower of Jesus should," Jared re-engaged.

I can't remember anything easy about my journey with God. Rick was slipping into a funk.

"So, if you were discipling someone, what would you say was the key to living out authentic Christianity?" Peter probed.

"Reading the Bible," Jan called out.

"Going to church," Michelle responded.

"I would say prayer," Ruth offered.

"Those are all good answers, but is there a common denominator to the activities you just mentioned?"

Why don't you just tell us? Rick fumed.

"Obedience," Gary answered.

"You're on the right track, Gary; but let's go a little deeper. Can a follower of Jesus say 'yes' in two different ways?"

"Sure. One way is out of obligation; the other is out of desire."

"And how does desire form inside of someone?"

"Love," Ruth replied.

"The practical side to love is trust," Burt added.

"That's what I was looking for!" Peter continued with enthusiasm. "If a follower of Jesus is baptized out of a sense of duty, such as identifying with or obeying Jesus, rather than a sense of loving devotion, does he come out of the water with a true understanding of how to live out authentic Christianity?"

"Oh, I get it!" Maggie exclaimed. **"When a believer decides to get baptized because she understands that Jesus died so that her old identity does not have to control her anymore, and that choosing to love Jesus more than herself unleashes His**

resurrection power in her life, she establishes the pattern for all of the other decisions she will ever make."

The Team sat in awe of the clarity with which Maggie had just articulated the significance of baptism.

After a meaningful period of silence, Jared asked rhetorically, "So if we love Jesus completely, then wanting Him to have 100 percent control of our lives shouldn't even be an issue, should it? Baptism is a picture that should help us every moment of every day?"

Peter just smiled.

Rick sat there with the best poker face he had, but inside he was a boiling volcano of emotions. *Yeah, right. I got baptized years ago, and it hasn't helped me experience God's power in my life. And it hasn't cured me of my temper. And it hasn't stopped me from cussing. And it hasn't helped my father respect me any better. I'm not sure anything is going to change in the future, either. If I give Jesus 100 percent control, how do I know He'll treat me any differently than all the other authority figures I've known?* To make matters worse, Penny and several others prayed out loud to yield themselves completely to Jesus, but Rick just couldn't make that decision. Too many "*what ifs*" were ricocheting through his mind.

PARTIAL BREAKTHROUGH

Monday morning, Rick was still mulling over the previous day's discussions when his attention was arrested by his boss's voice. "Rick, can I talk with you for a minute?"

"Sure, Gary." Rick was panicking as he followed his boss to the pickup. *I wonder what he wants. Did I screw up? Am I in trouble?*

As they got into the cab, Gary handed him an envelope. "Rick, you're one of the best employees I've ever had. You're a fast learner, and you have a great balance between production and quality. This bonus should let you know that we greatly appreciate all you are doing for this company. I'd also like to know if you would be interested in training as a foreman. It would take some serious effort on your part to learn the ropes, but I believe you have what it takes. And there are considerable benefits, in addition to the pay increase, that should make it worthwhile for you."

Is this a detour or part of God's plan for my life?

"Thank you, Gary. I really enjoy working for you." After a brief pause, he queried, "When do you need an answer?"

"There's no hurry."

Rick breathed a sigh of relief; but as he left the jobsite, he was torn between the fulfillment of being recognized as a valuable employee and the clarity of what he thought God was calling him to do. *Yesterday Maggie said that what happened during baptism became the pattern for all future decisions. I wonder if that is true.*

Instead of going home, Rick found himself making his way over to the McCormick home, where he was immediately invited to join the family for supper.

"What did you think of yesterday's discussion?" Peter asked after the meal was over.

"Honestly, I'm really struggling. This whole baptism thing isn't making sense to me. It hasn't made the differences in my life, or in my family's lives, that you talked about yesterday. Now Gary is asking if I want to become a foreman, which really appeals to me. Yet, I feel like God is asking me to focus on ministry without fully understanding all that would entail. How can baptism help me with real life situations?"

"Do you remember the day you were baptized?"

"Sure. You were there; you're dad baptized our whole family."

"I know; that's partially why I asked the question. That was a great day! So, when my dad laid you back under the water, what would have happened if he didn't bring you back up?"

Rick raised his eyebrows and flatly stated, "I'd have died."

"And, in picture form, you did. Just as Jesus was laid in a tomb, your old sinful nature was put to death with Jesus. As you went under the water, you should have been making a public statement that you wanted the 'old you' put to death—*all* of you. So a basic application question for you to answer would be, 'Are you 100 percent committed to letting Jesus Christ control your life, or are you holding something back?'"

With a flash of clarity, Rick exclaimed, "Success—I want to be successful! I want my father to be proud of me. I don't think I could handle it if I had to go through life feeling like a second-rate citizen."

"Are you afraid that if you give Jesus total control of your life, He will keep you from experiencing what you want?"

With dawning realization, Rick quietly admitted, "That's it in a nut shell."

"Here's a question for you, Rick. When my dad lowered you into the water the day you got baptized, could you have lifted yourself out of the water, or did you need him to do it for you?"

"Lying flat on my back, I needed your dad's help."

"Would you have had my dad baptize you if you didn't believe he would lift you back out?"

"No way."

"On a human level, why did you let my dad baptize you?"

"I guess it was because I trusted him."

"Is it possible that all of your confusion about baptism and its relevance to your everyday life could be summarized as a trust issue between you and God?"

Rick sat in silence for quite a while before whispering hoarsley, "It kind of looks that way."

"Why?" Peter gently pressed.

"Maybe it's the combination of being hurt by others I trusted in the past and the fact that I feel too vulnerable when I'm not in control."

"So what are you going to do?"

"I'm not sure yet. It looks like I need to figure that out. At least now I know where I'm stuck and why."

ADVENTURE 7 – PROCESS OF CHANGE PARADIGM

Gary and Kim's house was located on the southwest side of the city and doubled as a model home for the fast-growing properties Gary developed. As the Team entered, there were expressions of admiration for Gary's abilities as a contractor and Kim's abilities to create an atmosphere of tasteful and comfortable warmth. The children really enjoyed the large play room where they were free to be kids, while the men found the pool table a major attraction. The ladies were quite animated as they discussed the unique design features of the Ingerson home.

As he listened to all the feedback the Team was giving his boss, Rick felt good about being associated with Gary and his construction business. The offer of being trained as a foreman was becoming more and more appealing.

After the meal, Rick began predicting how Peter would mentor the Team through this week's adventure. (He felt as if he were getting close to duplicating his friend's skills.) *He always starts off with something that grabs people's attention, usually a question.*

"Why are some people able to make positive and lasting changes, while others are not?"

I knew it! And, now he'll guide the Team's discussion without even looking like he is.

"According to the verses in our workbook, a significant reason is whether or not a person repents," Garret answered.

"Would that be simila' to being at rock-bottom?" Vern asked.

"That can be part of it, but it also involves moving in the opposite direction. In light of what you studied this week, what do think that movement looks like?"

"According to Romans 12:2, the answer would be changing our mindset,'" Vickie answered. "We need to stop worldly input and start finding out from God's Word what He thinks, so that our belief system reflects His character."

"The last group of verses in our workbook leads me to believe that the answer is accountability," Misty interjected. "We can know the right things, but God designed the Christian community to help each other make changes through the practice of transparency and accountability. I'm slowly learning that accountability is the key to my good intentions becoming reality."

Now he will affirm what's been said before putting the principles into words that everyone can easily remember.

"Good input! So if I took what Garret, Vickie, and Misty said, and used three 'R' words—'repentance,' 'renewal of the mind,' and 'replacement choices'—would those terms help you understand the process of change?"

He could have said that **change involves Repentance, Renewal of the Mind, and Replacement Choices;** *but making a statement wouldn't have been nearly as effective as asking a question.*

"*Repentance* and *Renewal of the Mind* make sense to me," Jared shared, "but I would like to know more about *Replacement Choices*, especially the transparency and accountability parts that Misty mentioned."

"Before we go to *Replacement Choices*, would you be willing to share what your take is on *Repentance* and *Renewal of the Mind* to give everyone another angle on those principles?"

"Sure. To me, those two parts are pretty straightforward. Either you are at a point that you want to change directions or you're not; you are either willing to get into God's Word to find out what He thinks about the area you are struggling with, or you're not. A lot of people's problems could be solved by realizing that they want to just pretend that they have repented, or that they are too lazy to find out what the Bible has to say."

"I would probably use different language than Jared, but I agree with his conclusions," Burt weighed in.

As Peter shifted the Team's focus to *Replacement Choices,* Rick was lost in random thoughts about his future. As a result, he didn't really hear the truths that the Team shared about how the level of transparency in a relationship equals the level of trust that is necessary for accountability to really work. And that, without accountability, change seldom occurs.

Rick mentally re-entered as he heard Peter ask, "So what are your take-aways for this week?"

He always includes take-aways. Now, he'll end with how we are supposed to put the take-aways into practice during the upcoming week.

And sure enough, that's exactly what Peter did. But then he did something that Rick wasn't expecting.

DISCIPLESHIP CHALLENGE

As the Team mingled after the session, Peter came over to Rick and posed some of the toughest challenges yet.

"We are just about one third of the way through this process, and you have done great with understanding the concepts and principles that have been presented. Now it's time to stretch you in the area of application. I would like you to go to an *Every Man's Battle Workshop* where they specialize in unpacking sexual addictions, and I want you to use your life next week as a case study that will give the Team a visual of the *Paradigm* truths we have been learning."

A million questions bombarded Rick's mind, but all that came out was, "Why?"

"Because I believe it will help with your discipleship development."

Ignoring the *Every Man's Battle* suggestion, Rick stated, "I'm not ready!"

"We seldom feel ready for the next step God has for us."

"Why not someone else? I'm still trying to figure out some of this stuff. Don't I have a choice in this, Pete?"

"Yes and no. Yes, you always have the freedom to choose. But in this situation, if your choice is 'no,' you are choosing to end your participation with the Team."

Peter knew that what he was doing with Rick right now was a necessary gamble. He had prayed a lot and then talked things over with Lisa to double check the wisdom of his strategy. She had agreed that Rick needed the extra pressure to help him learn that he couldn't sit on the fence forever. He needed to reach that place where he trusted God enough to fully surrender. Replacement choices would only become a reality if he learned to trust God and others.

"You see, Rick, we are not interested in helping you discover a head full of facts that never get fully implemented into your life. **Paradigm truth, by its very nature, should change the way you live.** I want you to articulate to the Team how you have changed. Will you?"

INTERVENTION

"A head full of facts that never get fully implemented into my life—what the heck does he think I'm doing here anyway? I left Enterprise to come to this place. I joined his Team just like he wanted me to. I complete every study and attend every session. What more does he want from me?" As Rick vented to Penny on their way to her house, she had a look on her face that he was slowly beginning to recognize as disagreement. What ticked him off even more was the fact that she wouldn't tell him what was on her mind. When she did speak, it was to tell him that she felt like he was yelling at her.

After dropping Penny off, he began to feel like a caged animal. He drove down to Clover Island and watched the sunset colors reflect off the river's water, but that just made him homesick. He began thinking about crossing the Blue Mountains and going back home; but how was that going to help him with work opportunities or with resolving his inner tension? Wandering around the ranch supply store didn't do anything except cause him to spend money on stuff he didn't need. Even his favorite barbeque joint did nothing to relieve his restlessness. Why was Peter being so hard on him? Quiet but colorful vocabulary rolled off his tongue as he struggled with his feelings.

Old feelings of abandonment and isolation began to surge through him as he headed back to his apartment. He tried praying, but the tension inside made him react like Dr. Jekyll and Mr. Hyde.

One part of him wanted so desperately to implement everything he had learned about *Paradigm* truths. The other part wanted to plunge into the oblivion of his past coping mechanisms. He could feel his hands trembling as they began unbuckling his belt and unzipping his pants. The adrenaline coursing through his body made his heart pound like it was going to beat out of his chest.

Just then the phone rang. Feeling like he was about to be publicly arrested, Rick almost didn't answer. *It's really late. Who'd be calling me at this hour? Maybe it's Penny!*

"Hey, Rick?" The voice wasn't Penny's.

"Yeah?"

"This is Garret. I know it's late; but for some reason, the Holy Spirit has been telling me to call you. I've been arguing with Him for the last half hour, but He won't leave me alone. So hopefully, I really did hear from Him, and you needed me to call."

Rick breathed a sigh of relief, and then slowly began to share what was going on. Garret listened and prayed before asking Rick to troubleshoot his problems using the *Paradigm* lessons they had studied so far.

"It doesn't seem to me that you are struggling with the existence of God in Adventure One or your salvation in Adventure Five. Where do you think you got stuck, Rick?"

"I'm not sure I know, but I have a feeling that Peter is pushing me to help me find out!"

Garret agreed. "This isn't his first time working with someone like you, or like any of the rest of us for that matter."

"That's for sure. By the way, you're doing a pretty good job yourself. Tonight would have been a disaster if you hadn't called. Thanks for your suggestion of using the *Paradigm Adventures* to troubleshoot what is going on inside of me."

PARADIGM
BREAKTHROUGH

After getting off the phone with Garret, Rick started reviewing the past sessions and evaluating his response to the truth he had been taught.

Adventure One: Garret is right. I am not struggling at all with God's existence; He's done too many things lately to reinforce His reality in my life.

Adventure Two: What is the purpose of my life? I wish I knew! I need to go over that session again.

Adventure Three: Satan is definitely my enemy, and he sure knows the tactics that work on me.

Adventure Four: I have no problem admitting my weaknesses. I know that my sinful nature is always pulling me toward sinful actions, especially the ones I have allowed to become coping and escape mechanisms.

Adventure Five: Thank God that I know I am one of His kids and a permanent part of His family. I know that I keep screwing up, but He never treats me the way my human father does.

Adventure Six: This one started causing me some heartburn. Why am I struggling to give God 100 percent, when it would allow me to experience the resurrection power of Jesus in my life? It's not like I have a better track record of running things than God does. Why can't I trust Him completely to do what I know I can't do anyway?

Adventure Seven: Repentance, Renewal of the Mind, and Replacement Choices. I think I'm stuck here, too.

Rick sensed that he was close to a breakthrough. He decided to keep pushing forward in his quest for answers, even though his construction job started in just a few hours.

As he opened his workbook, he saw a copy of the cross diagram Peter had drawn that very first weekend they had reconnected. Immediately the words "Identity Choices" were staring up at him from the cross on the page.

Adoption/Sonship Baptism/Resurrection Power Spirit-Filled Living	GOD Unlimited Glory Image
IDENTITY	**CHOICES**
Sin Idolatry Bondage	Satan Limited Rebellion

Identity Choices—could that be the answer?

Okay, so I know that every day I am faced with choices between doing things God's way or doing them Satan's way. I also know that my choices reflect who I worship and what I believe the purpose of life to be. **The motivation behind my choices is the solution to living out Paradigm truth.** *I can choose to live in performance mode based on my abilities with good intentions, which is probably the head full of facts Pete was talking about; or I can choose to live in an authentic relationship with God, based on faith. Would I be struggling to give God all of my life if I really knew and trusted Him? Maybe I'm trying to figure out what the rules are so that I can make God happy with my performance, just like I do with my parents. If I knew more about healthy relationships, this wouldn't be so hard.*

Rick began to go through a mental checklist of what he knew about God. When he finished, he was overwhelmed with the conviction that God had a personal interest in his well-being and a specific purpose for his life. God could be trusted—100 percent. He sealed his conviction by getting on his knees and verbalizing his complete trust and surrender to the Dad he was getting to know in a very real way. *God, You have ALL of me.*

After praying, he felt waves of freedom and peace wash over him, but he wasn't prepared for the full effects of his decision.

ON THE RIGHT TRACK

Rick couldn't believe how positive he felt after only a couple of hours of sleep. It was almost like he was standing on the top of a mountain summit that he had thought he would never reach. Now he was enjoying the awesome vistas all around him.

Everything seemed different, especially completing this week's discipleship study. Instead of the usual biblical principles format, Adventure Eight had case studies to solve, using the *Paradigm* sessions. As he worked through each case, Rick began to understand just how dedicated Peter was in helping the Team put into practice what they had been learning. At the end of the workbook lesson, there was a section where he was asked to use his personal life as a case study.

So Pete wasn't just singling me out, Rick mused, as he thought of his strong reaction just a few days before. *And even if he was, my reaction revealed* Paradigm *issues going on in my life that needed to be addressed. I guess what I fought so hard against actually turned out to be one of the biggest blessings in my life.*

Tuesday after work, Rick stopped by to see his friend.

"Pete, I need to talk with you about a couple of things that happened Sunday night."

Peter's face lit with pleasure. "That sounds good."

"I came so close to falling into one of my old sin habits."

Peter was mildly surprised and encouraged Rick to share. "Tell me about it, if you can."

"After you challenged me last weekend, I began to experience the same feelings of abandonment and isolation that I've always felt when I have interpersonal struggles. I tried praying, but the negative feelings only intensified. It seemed like things were hopeless; I couldn't think of any solutions."

"Prayer and even Bible reading are great tools," Peter interrupted. "But when those tools don't work, you need to reach for ones that do. (A screwdriver works great for putting in or taking out screws, but not so great for hammering nails.) Did you call any of the guys on the Team for accountability and encouragement?"

"I didn't even think of it. Even if I had, I still think I would have struggled with the idea of disturbing someone that late at night."

Peter's voice was a mixture of concern and compassion as he asked, "Did you fail then?"

"Thank God, no. Garret said the Holy Spirit prompted him for over a half an hour to call me. He finally did, for which I am extremely grateful. After he talked and prayed with me, the oppression and negative feelings subsided."

Relieved, Peter asked, "Can you see the power of external spiritual influences when internal ones aren't enough to make the changes you need to?"

"I think so."

"Periodically, even I have to call for help."

"Really?" Rick asked with surprise and curiosity. "Who do you call?"

"There are several people. They range from accountability partners to mentors. Dad is number one. But, I also have the O'Reillys, a couple of professors, and a collection of individuals that I believe excel in particular areas of life. Any time I see someone exhibiting a specific skill, I try to build enough relational rapport with them that I can ask them for help when I need to."

Rick nodded his head. "I think I can see that happening in my life this year. Garret and Vern have been very helpful to me. And," Rick continued, "it's pretty obvious that I need to attend the *Every Man's Battle Workshop* you mentioned."

Peter smiled and affirmed, "I doubt you will have any regrets." After a pause, he asked, "You mentioned that you had a *couple* of things you wanted to share about Sunday night. What else did you experience?"

"I'm finally free! Garret told me to troubleshoot my circumstances using the *Paradigm Adventures* we have studied, which was exactly what this week's lesson was all about. Even though I was struggling with the concepts of complete surrender from Adventure Six, I really was stuck on knowing Who God is. I came to see that the purpose of life in Adventure Two is wrapped up in the character of God and the relationship He designed me to have with Him. **I'll never surrender to someone I don't trust, and I'll never trust someone I don't really know. My ability to worship and make right choices is based on how well I really know and trust God.**"

"So, what did you discover about your trust in God?"

"As I reflected on all that He has done for me, especially this year, I realized that He really cares. I'm not sure what the specific purpose of my life is yet; but I discovered that I was more concerned about knowing His will than I was about knowing Him."

"Rick, I'm so proud of you! You've made a discovery that will help you throughout the rest of this discipleship process."

"Thanks! I'm actually looking forward to sharing my life as a case study with the Team this coming Sunday!"

ADVENTURE 8 – PARADIGM CASE STUDIES

Kevin and Misty rented a simple ranch house on 10th Avenue. Due to the limited parking space, they had asked everyone who could to carpool, which created some fun connections among the Team. The kids were excited because they got to use the travel trailer as space for their study time. Frank and Sarah were going to have their hands full directing all that youthful energy tonight!

Peter and Lisa had prayerfully prepared for tonight's session. They knew that it was going to be both encouraging and challenging in the upcoming weeks as they transitioned from *Paradigm* principles into helping the Team deal with their *Past*.

As the Team began to share their case study results, there was a little confusion about what the "right" answers were.

Peter smiled as he explained, "There are no right or wrong answers for trouble-shooting case studies. **Your trouble-shooting and problem-solving skills will be a combination of where you are in your spiritual growth and the wisdom the Holy Spirit gives you to discern where someone else is stuck.** Most of you had similar responses when you identified which *Paradigm* truths were needed to address the case study scenarios; that should encourage you. The areas of difference may be God's way of uniquely gifting you to read a situation, or it may be that you have some ongoing growth needs of your own. As you interact with others, trust God to guide you."

"It just doesn't seem possible that people could have different answers and still be right," Misty objected.

"That almost sounds like one of the case studies," Jared joked.

"So you think that's funny, do you, Jared?" Misty's face was as dark as a storm. She was almost yelling as she bit off her words. "What do you know about trying to please other people and never succeeding? I can't ever seem to get things right!"

Peter grabbed the opportunity to help the Team transition into dealing with their *Past*. "Rick, would you please share your personal case study."

"Misty, I can relate," he began with a look of understanding. "I have never felt like I could please my parents. Perfection was the expected standard and anything less than that was either punished or dealt with in a way that left me feeling worthless. The *Paradigm* truths we have studied have helped to set me free, though the journey has been a rough ride."

Misty still looked furious, and Jared definitely had something troubling him.

Rick began to share the details of the past couple of months. He was greatly encouraged as the Team affirmed the growth they were seeing in his life.

As the feedback slowed down, Misty responded coldly, "Well, I'm *still* not free, and I can't see how any of this is helping me."

This is perfect, Peter thought, before mentally preparing everyone for what was ahead. "As challenging as studying *Paradigm* truths has been, I would suggest that this next section on dealing with the *Past* may be the toughest material for most of you to deal with. Those of you who learn and apply the next several lessons will be emotionally and spiritually prepared to handle just about any discipleship situation." Looking around the room, Peter wondered, *Will everyone make it through dealing with their* Past? *Will Rick make it?*

ADVENTURE 9 –
POSITIVE NEGATIVES

Hebrews 12:5-11—*How does God use negative experiences in positive ways during your spiritual development process?*

The probe question from this week's study reverberated through Rick's brain as he ended what seemed like the millionth phone call. His mother had called at noon to let him know that Waylon was in the hospital fighting for his life after a logging accident. Rick was wanted at home, and the most challenging part of it all was that his family expected him to go back to work in the woods indefinitely to help out.

It felt like emotional and spiritual whiplash. For the past two mornings, he had awakened on such a spiritual high. After years of confusion and frustration, he finally felt like the *Paradigm* truths had set him free. Peter had suggested that studying truths about the *Past* could be the toughest challenge of all, but Rick really hadn't been convinced until now.

It's not fair, God! Haven't I had enough problems to deal with? Why is this happening? Why now—just when things are starting to turn around for me?

The voices in his head were driving him crazy.

Ray: *You know what you have to do; now do it!*

Mother: *How would you feel if you were in Waylon's place?*

Penny: *Rick, this is an opportunity to see how much you have developed spiritually. Will you make decisions based on the God-centered* Paradigm *you have been learning about, or in the self-centered, unhealthy ways you have made them in the* Past?

Peter: *Lisa and I are here for you.*

Gary: *I'll support whatever decisions you make.*

If I choose to go back and help, will I be doing it for the right reasons or because I lack the guts to stick to the truth I've been learning? If I choose to stay in Kennewick, will I constantly be living with a sense of guilt because I'm viewed as failing my family? Is God asking me to go back?

God smiled. **The brightest positives are always learned through the darkest negatives**.

ADVENTURE 10 – TRUST

The hosting had finally rolled around to Ted and Jan who had been quite hesitant to volunteer. They lived in a small but adequate house on Union Street, sandwiched between several commercial businesses. There was plenty of room to park in the front and enough of a yard in the back for the kids to enjoy, and the Team quickly settled into meaningful connection with each other.

Two opposing questions in this week's study quickly engaged everyone's interest. "Where is relational trust learned? Where is relational mistrust learned?"

Vern piped up, "I heard a story of a fatha' who wanted to educate his fou'a-yea'-old son about the practices of businessmen. After puttin' his son on the kitchen counta'top, he told him to jump and promised to catch him. Instead of catchin' him, the fatha' let his son fall to the floa' and then he bent o'va the cryin' boy and said, 'Lesson numba' one, Son—don't even trust you'a fatha'.'"

A vivid picture of his own father flashed through Rick's mind. As a five-year-old, he had climbed into the pickup and shut his hand in the door. His father simply told him to leave it there and drove down to the next-door neighbor's before helping him get his hand out of the door. The memory closed with the words, "That will teach you to pay attention."

All that taught me was not to expect help from my father when I screwed up, Rick thought.

"I remember having a stuffed animal," Maggie countered, "that I loved with all my heart. One night, my father, who was a very serious man, came into my room to kiss me; then he bent down to kiss my stuffed animal and told her to have a good night. That was when I knew it was safe to trust my father."

"That's so cool," Rick whispered.

"Rick, you look like something is bothering you tonight. What's going on?" Garret questioned.

"I didn't realize it was noticeable. I just spent the last three days in Enterprise watching my brother fight for his life. On top of that, my parents expect me to move back home to live with them until he is in the clear, and run Waylon's business until he is fully recovered. They didn't even want me to come back here today to be with all of you. My father told me that I couldn't leave, but I waited until he fell asleep and came anyway."

"In all the years I have been involved in spiritual development," Peter responded, "I am still amazed at how God creates real life opportunities for people to practice and apply the truths they are studying. As a Team, we can help Rick learn truths that authentic followers of Jesus are trustworthy. Our next study adventure teaches how to set healthy limits that will help Rick learn how to interact with his parents.

"Before we apply this week's truth specifically to Rick's life, let's do a couple of exercises that will help us as a Team to see the power of trust. First, I want you to *mentally* pick one or two people in this group that you might not trust; then process the question, 'Why do I struggle with trusting this person?'"

The silence that followed Peter's instruction was intense. After what felt like an hour, he moved on.

"Now I would like to have each of you share a Team member's name that you trust above ninety percent and tell us why you trust her or him that much."

Michelle spoke first, "I trust Gary and Kim because of how they treat each other as a married couple. I watched Gary a few weeks ago apologize to Kim after he spoke to her in a less-than-loving tone of voice. And then I watched Kim immediately forgive and kiss him. I struggle with forgiveness, and their interaction with each other deeply touched me."

"I trust Jared," Vern spoke, "because he is reliable and honest. I have asked him several times to help me with personal projects, and he often does it immediately; but he is honest with me when he can't. Not once have I felt like he was helping me out of obligation."

"As a mother," Kim joined in, "I trust Maggie because of the way she treats children. I have watched her help them get their food and drinks, mediate when some of them had problems with each other, and even sit them on her lap to listen to them as they tell her a story about their week."

After a healthy pause, Garret volunteered, "I trust Burt as a professional with integrity. One of my fellow artisans wanted some legal help to capitalize on a sketchy situation. He called me ranting and raving because one lawyer told him that what he wanted to do was unethical, and that he wouldn't be able to help him achieve his goal. When I asked who the lawyer was, he gave me Burt's name. I was so proud of Burt at that moment!"

"I know I'm talking a lot today," Michelle spoke again, "but I really trust Ruth. I have a lot of baggage in my life, and recently I shared something with her that has caused me a lot of shame. She really listened to me and then shared the unconditional way Jesus loves broken people. She has gone out of her way since then to affirm and encourage me. I didn't even have to ask her to keep my story confidential; I just knew she would."

Lisa thoughtfully added, "I trust my husband as a leader. I have seen him in some very challenging situations, and he consistently knows how to lead himself, our family, and the spiritual family God has called him to serve. He owns his mistakes and learns from them. And when he gets stuck, he is not too proud to reach out and ask for help from the network of mentors he has built into his life."

Rick watched with amazement at the way his friend was able to hear positive feedback and acknowledge it without losing focus. He also saw tears of gratitude as individuals heard how they had earned the trust of others on the Team.

Seemingly small actions make such a big difference in building relational trust. If that is true with positive experiences, it is also probably true with negative experiences, he thought. *That could be why trusting others is so challenging for me; I have a million little memories that warn me not to trust.*

Rick was brought back to the present by Peter's next question. "So, what can we do to help Rick through the challenges he is facing with his family?"

"I can assure him that his job is secure regardless of how much time he needs to take off," Gary replied.

"I can drive o'va ta Enta'prise on Friday nights and spend Sata'day with him to off'a support," Vern volunteered.

"Me, too," Garret added, "and we can make sure he comes back to Kennewick with us so that he can spend his Sundays here to stay connected with the Team and to keep working through this discipleship process."

"Betty and I can help him deal with any financial aspects," Burt joined in.

Rick was overwhelmed as he thought of how much this Team was willing to do for him after knowing him for such a short time. "Thank you," was all he could choke out.

ADVENTURE 11
– GROW UP!

Rick had very little problem readjusting to the rigors of logging. It was almost like his body and brain switched to auto-pilot. Work filled his days; hospital visits rounded out his nights. His parents seemed content that he was fulfilling their expectations.

Things were running just as he thought they would, with one significant exception. Several of the guys were checking up on him to make sure that he was staying connected to God and studying the discipleship material in preparation for the upcoming weekend. Both Vern and Garret reassured him that they would be over Friday night.

When his parents learned that he had friends coming for the weekend, they quickly offered to have everyone stay at their house. Mild concern flitted in and out of Rick's mind as he thought about how everyone would get along. His concern became supercharged when Penny and Miriam arrived and were also invited to stay at his folks' place. Burt and Betty came, but they had booked a room at the motel in the center of town next to the courthouse. They decided that their support for Rick could double as a weekend getaway.

Things went well Friday night, but cracks began to appear Saturday when Ray found out that Rick was planning to spend the rest of the weekend in Kennewick. "You're not leaving," Ray declared as he pulled Rick into the kitchen so that the others wouldn't hear.

Anger flared inside Rick as he felt the force of his father's domineering tactics. He was also infuriated with himself for feeling helpless in the face of Ray's demands. He knew from experience that reasoning with his father would be useless. Despite all the months of discipleship progress, Rick felt his bitterness and hatred start to return.

Why do I always seem to get stuck in my dealings with my father? I can't seem to stand up to him or get him to change. If I ignore him and simply leave, I'll have to face him when I get back. If I stay just to please him, then I'll hate myself for not having the guts to do what I believe in.

"Hey, Rick, where did you go?" Garret and Vern asked as they came into the kitchen. "What time do you want to head back to Kennewick?" Vern added.

"I—uh—don't think I'm going to be able to make it this weekend."

"Why not?" Garret asked with suspicion.

"It's nothing really. My father just doesn't want me to leave."

"Is there a reason why Rick is needed here for the next day and a half?" Garret asked, turning to face Ray.

"Rick knows the answer to that," Ray answered and turned to leave.

"Mr. Thomson, that's not going to work for us. As part of Rick's Discipleship Team, we have pulled together to help make it possible for Rick to be here and support his family during most of the week and then make it back to Kennewick each Sunday to continue his spiritual development with us."

Ray's body became rigid as Garret spoke, but he just walked away.

~ ~ ~

The next afternoon as the Team met at Jared and Ruth's, Vern brought up the incident with Ray and Rick. "So what's going to happen when you get back to you'a parents' house tonight?"

"My father will either give me the silent treatment to try to make me feel like I failed the family or he will threaten me."

"Are those responses biblical or healthy?" Garret probed.

"Probably not, but he doesn't care about that. He's going to do what he chooses to do regardless of what anyone else wants."

"Not if you stand up to him," Jared flatly stated.

"You don't know what he's—."

Burt cut Rick off. "I *do* know the way people try to control others; I frequently see that in the courtroom."

"If I went to court, maybe he would have to listen to me; in the real world, that doesn't happen."

Burt pressed on. "The legal system is part of the real world, Rick, and it was designed by God, along with other options not quite so drastic."

"So you think I should take him to court?" Rick chuckled at the thought.

"That would not be the appropriate starting place. First, **you need the strength of character to set limits on his negative behavior. Then, if necessary, levy progressive consequences when he crosses those limits.**"

"Can you give me some practical ways of doing that?"

"Sure. When you go home, tell your father that you want to be there to support your family during the week, but that you are also going to be coming back to Kennewick every weekend to engage in another important aspect of life that God wants you to be involved in."

Looking squarely at Burt, Rick replied, "He won't accept that."

"What if you added, 'If that's not acceptable, I won't be able to help out during the week.'"

"If he can't intimidate me like he usually does, he might get physical."

Jared quietly but stiffly moved into the kitchen to get himself a drink as Burt continued. "If you think that is likely, you probably shouldn't be living with your parents at their house in the first place. Why don't you take several guys with you as support when you talk with him, especially if they are men who know him. I doubt he would get physical with others present; and if he did, that would be the time to involve law enforcement."

Rick wailed, "It would be so much easier not to have to deal with him at all!"

Burt drove his point home. "Easy doesn't develop character. It's time to grow up Rick! If you don't deal with this now, you will react the same way every time you get into a situation with someone who reminds you of your father."

Rick looked around at Peter and the other Team members. They all nodded in agreement.

~ ~ ~

Rick wasn't sure what to do as he headed back to Enterprise. While he was talking things through with the Team, he was convinced that he could set limits with his father. But now, without the Team's presence, he felt powerless and subservient.

At the hospital, the doctors told Rick that Waylon was doing much better. The ongoing coma was medically induced to allow him more time to heal.

Maybe I won't have to worry about setting limits. Maybe Waylon will regain consciousness this week and come up with a plan that will enable me to go back to my life in Kennewick.

Monday, Tuesday, and Wednesday, the news remained the same. Waylon was continuing to progress, but the medical staff weren't sure when they were going to try bring him back to consciousness. Garret and Vern called to ask what Rick had done about setting limits with his father, and he just kept telling them that he was working on it.

On Thursday, he got the gut-sinking news that Waylon would remain in a coma through the weekend. That night, Garret pushed Rick to decide how he was going to handle his father.

"It looks like God really wants me to deal with this, doesn't it?"

Garret chuckled, "It sure does, my friend!"

"I'll tell him tomorrow night. Would you do me a favor and come over for support? I don't think I can do this by myself."

"Absolutely; but you are going to have to do the talking. I won't do that for you."

The next evening when Rick got home from work, he showered and packed his clothes and study materials. Garret had agreed to show up at seven. As Garret drove into the yard, Rick grabbed his duffle bag and managed to open the door before Ray asked, "Where do you think you're going?"

"Back to Kennewick. I'll be going every weekend."

"Like hell you will!" Ray slammed down the recliner and quickly moved to intercept Rick. "You're not going anywhere." He swung his clenched fist as he spoke.

Rick surprised himself by ducking the punch Ray threw and wrapping his father in a bear hug before they crashed through the front screen door. Their momentum carried them across the porch where they fell to the ground. As they were falling, Rick made up his mind to maintain the grip he had around his father's body and try to restrain him until he calmed down.

"Well, well, well, look what we have here," Jared commented as he reached down and pulled Rick up and away from Ray. Standing there beside Jared were Garret, Vern, and Burt.

As Ray stood to his feet and saw the group of guys standing beside his oldest son, he grumbled, "If you were in the hospital instead of Waylon, none of this would have happened." Then he turned, walked into the house, and threw Rick's duffle bag out into the yard before shutting the door.

ADVENTURE 12 – FORGIVENESS

Sam and Michelle were the last couple to host the Team by opening up their trailer home. They had procrastinated because they were uncomfortable with being viewed as trailer trash—that is, until they learned how many of the Team had lived in trailer homes earlier in their marriages. Vern and Vickie shared a story of one trailer home they called "The Zoo" because of all the creatures that wanted to make it their home, too.

As the Team transitioned from the meal and warm interaction into their study time, Vern's good-natured humor continued. "It looks like ou'a next Adventcha' was written just fa' you, Rick."

Forgiveness! Rick cringed. The events of the past couple of weeks had brought back a flood of bitter memories that seemed as new as when they happened. *How can I forgive my father when I can't even have a civil conversation with him? How can I forgive someone who never takes ownership for his actions?*

"Often people limit temptation to the realm of fulfilling inner cravings or engaging in *naughty* behavior," Peter began; "but temptation is often a pull toward losing emotional control. Bitterness is one of Satan's deadliest temptation tactics. In First Corinthians 10:13, we read that temptation is common to us all. Maybe it would be helpful, as we begin learning about the topic of forgiveness, to have those of you who are willing, share some of the deepest violations committed against you. Sometimes, until you hear stories of what others have gone through, it is easy to feel that no one has been violated as deeply as you have."

"I've only shared this story a couple of times," Lisa opened up. "In high school, I had a boyfriend and, during our junior and senior years, our relationship deepened to the point that I thought we would eventually get married. The night before graduation, we had planned a special date. When he didn't show up on time, I became concerned and started calling to find out where he was. The condensed version is that my best friend had been physically involved with him for a couple of months, and he decided that the best way to tell me was to stand me up."

Rick's mind flashed back to the conversation he had with Peter the first weekend they reconnected. Peter had shared his story of pain, but not Lisa's. Quiet admiration for this couple was growing inside him.

"My life didn't have the kind of betrayal that Lisa's did; I simply could never please my parents," Misty shared. "NOTHING was ever good enough for them—school grades, the way I dressed, my friends, the career I wanted to pursue, the husband I chose to marry. A few years ago, I found out that I was even cut out of any inheritance. My younger brother was the recipient of everything they owned."

"My mother was more of a monster than a mom," Sam's voice cracked as he spoke. "I never knew my father. As a kid, I didn't know that my mother made her living by *entertaining* men. I dreaded nights. Before a guy would come over, she would lock me in a dark closet and order me not to make any noise. If I did, she would lift my shirt and push a burning cigarette into my body."

Michelle began to sob. It took several minutes for her to say enough for the Team to get a picture of her broken and abused childhood.

Ted got up and walked out, waving his finger at Jan not to follow.

As Rick listened and watched, he began to understand the wisdom Peter possessed in helping others gain perspective of their own problems. And then, it seemed as if God rolled back the curtain between Earth and Heaven to allow him to see that moment in time when Father and Son made the decision to have Jesus leave the breathtaking perfection of Heaven to fulfill His cruel assignment of reconciliation on Earth. *He didn't do anything to deserve the treatment He got here, and yet He still offered forgiveness to everyone who violated His perfection.*

"Have I forgiven my father if I won't allow him to be around my children?" Michelle asked, after she had regained emotional control.

"Don't confuse forgiveness with the need to rebuild trust," Lisa responded. "Forgiveness can be immediate and complete. But, in harmful situations, the offender needs to understand and accept the need to go through a process of rebuilding credible trust. Putting healthy limitations in place does not mean that you haven't forgiven."

Lisa continued, "Jesus forgave everyone as He died on the cross, but that forgiveness isn't experienced until there is repentance on the part of offenders. And, though the love of God never fails, and though forgiveness is always available, He often asks people to prove their sincerity by the choices that they make."

*So **I can forgive my father and be free from the bitterness of the past, even if he never changes. And, if I have to set a healthy limit, that doesn't mean I haven't forgiven him.** I wonder how long it's going to take for these truths, instead of the* Past, *to control my life.*

ADVENTURE 13 – PAST CASE STUDIES

"Are you going back to Enterprise this week?" Garret asked.

"I have to."

"Why?"

"First of all, I don't know how things are going to turn out for Waylon. Secondly, I need to know that God can begin to heal my *Past*. How can I know that if I don't do my part and face the challenges He gives me? I need to figure out how to balance the tension between honoring my family and not allowing them to dominate the life God wants me to live."

Garret nodded and queried, "What's your plan?"

"I called one of my aunts and asked if I could stay at her place this week. She knows our family dynamics and was more than willing to help me out."

"Good job!"

"Tomorrow, I should know more about how things are going for Waylon. If he regains consciousness, I can talk things over with him later in the week and figure out what needs to be done during his recovery process."

"And your father?" Garret probed.

"I think he'll leave me alone. With me staying at my aunt's, he'll be worried enough about what people think that it should curb any physical encounters. It will still be awkward if he's there at the hospital when I am, but that's something I'll just have to work through."

"Do you have an accountability plan just in case your circumstances start dragging you down?" Garret pressed.

"I could check in every day and let you know how I'm doing. Would you be open to that much interaction?"

"You know I would!

Rick cracked a smile. "Yeah, but I had to ask."

"Choose a number from one to ten that represents your overall healthiness," Garret suggested.

"I will; and if it drops below seven, you have my permission to do whatever is needed to get me back on track."

"You got it," Garret responded as he slapped Rick on the back.

~ ~ ~

The week flew by. Waylon regained consciousness and became so impatient with his slow recovery that he was starting to be a pain in the butt to the medical staff. Their threats to send him to rehab much earlier than originally planned were music to his ears. It would be a full month before he was able to go back to work, so Rick, Waylon, and Gary drew up a phase-out and re-entry schedule that helped meet the needs of both businesses.

As Rick prepared for Sunday's Team session, he felt for the first time in a long time like there was hope that he could become a healthy follower of Jesus. He could see God actively at work. His *Paradigm* was changing. His *Past* was starting to lose its negative grip. Now if he could just discover his *Potential*.

ADVENTURE 14 – PRACTICES:REHABITUATION

"Well, Gang, this is the final stretch!" Peter's excitement was contagious as he introduced the *Potential* process of spiritual *Teen* development.

"Lisa and I are really proud of the progress our Team has been making with developing a biblical *Paradigm* and a healthy way of dealing with the *Past*. Now we are looking forward to each one of you discovering your unique God-given purpose."

Rick's heart began to pound in his chest. *This is what I've been waiting for.*

"Let's start off by outlining the five *Potential* building blocks:

- *Practices*
- *Partnership*
- *Personal Wiring*
- *Passions*
- *Perseverance*

"Concerning *Practices*—if you've ever looked at the table of contents in many discipleship materials, you'll see some fairly typical topics, often called spiritual disciplines. We'll be looking at some of these habitual components as part of the *Potential Practices* in the near future. Using Second Peter 1:5-7, and our acrostic H.E.R., (Habits/ Emotions/Relationships), we will also unpack the progressively challenging components of *Potential Practices*."

"What do you mean by 'progressively challenging components'?" Vickie asked hesitantly.

"Rick, why don't you answer Vickie's question."

He never seems to miss an opportunity to mentor me. Rick looked at his friend with admiration. "Well, Vickie, Pete explained it to me like this. As hard as it is to exercise discipline in stopping sinful habits and starting spiritual ones when you first start the discipleship process, the greater challenges are learning how to control ourselves emotionally and truly loving others. **We need the ground we gain by disciplining our habitual actions to control our emotional reactions so that we can show God's love in all our relationships."**

As an afterthought, Rick added, "I'm beginning to see how true that is after dealing with my family for the last several weeks."

It was just a look, but Rick felt affirmed as Peter transitioned into Adventure 14. "This week we are going to spend most of our time discussing with our accountability partners any remaining sinful habits that are crippling the *Potential* of our spiritual development. Those habits will haunt us and hinder forward progress if they are not dealt with before we start trying to live out spiritual habits.

"Next week, we will study one of my favorite spiritual habits." Silently he added, *and begin transitioning Rick into a more engaging aspect of discovering his Potential.*

Before Rick left, Peter reminded him that he needed to attend an *Every Man's Battle Workshop* and completely deal with the sexual addictions from his past. "There's a workshop scheduled in Portland next month. I'd like you to register and go."

Although Rick quietly nodded his head in agreement, he was experiencing some anxiety.

PRACTICES: BIBLE STUDY PRINCIPLES

Bible intake—the topic generated a lot of initial questions and thoughts.

Vern: "I try to read my Bible, but I don't get a lot out of it. I finally disciplined myself to read through the Bible this ye'a. I'm on track with my readin' plan, but I can't say that I unda'stand a lot of what I'm readin'."

Jared: "I catch some messages on Christian radio while I'm trucking. That's about the best I can do."

Garret: "If someone mentions memorization, I run for cover. I just can't seem to memorize anything."

Ruth: "I love the Psalms; they give me so much encouragement."

Maggie: "Which version of the Bible is the best?"

Burt: "Some parts of the Bible seem to contradict others. How can I know that it is accurate and trustworthy?"

Sam: "Sometimes the Bible doesn't seem very relevant to the 21st century. How do people riding donkeys and living in tents help me learn how to make a house payment or have a better relationship with my wife and children?"

"I mostly read the New Testament. God seems so harsh in the Old Testament." This from Michelle.

Peter sat there listening to familiar statements and questions while remembering his own journey towards a healthy view of the importance of meaningful Bible intake.

"What was your initial reaction when I explained spiritual *Teen* development as having three key components: *Paradigm, Past, and Potential?*" Peter asked.

"It sounded like I had a chance of making it through the process," Rick answered.

"I was amazed at the balance between complexity and simplicity," Gary replied. "You can study the God side of the *Paradigm* issues and never completely understand its complexity. But seeing that there are only two *Paradigm* choices makes it pretty simple."

Peter was thankful for the way God always directed the Team's feedback. "And that is also true of understanding and applying the Bible. Up front, it could look like a complicated task only attainable by those who go through a system of higher education; but in actual fact, it is very simple. I'm going to give you a few Bible tools that I believe will provide you with a sense of clarity.

1. *View Settings (telescope vs. microscope)*
2. *Structural Diagnostics (break it up/figure it out/put it into practice)*
3. *Reliability Index (John 7:17; Hebrews 11:6)*

"Let's start with the *View Settings*. The *telescope* view gives the *Big Picture* of the Bible as a whole, as well as the individual books that make up the whole. What would you say were the *Big Picture* themes of the Bible?"

"Sin," Ted replied.

"That's right. There is a black thread of sin that is woven throughout the entire Bible. What else?"

"Salvation," Garret responded.

"Right again. God weaves a red thread of salvation from beginning to end. With just those two *Big Picture* thoughts, what do we learn about the Bible as a whole?"

"God must love us very much," Vickie answered.

"Could we say then, that one of the *Big Picture* themes of the Bible is God saying, 'I love you, and I want you to love me'?"

"That's a beautiful way to express it," Vickie agreed.

"Using that *telescopic* discovery, we could then assume that God displays His love in sixty-six different ways, one for each book of the Bible."

Gary responded, "Like Michelle, I used to think that God was extremely harsh in the Old Testament. But the more I've studied, I have seen His extreme love. In almost every book that the prophets wrote, there is hope based on God's love for His people instead of what they really deserved."

"I don't know how to figure out what is going on in the Old Testament." Sam spoke of a long-term frustration he'd had.

Peter didn't want to wander too far from his main objective, but he did want to help Sam see that the Old Testament was a unique story of the Christian life. "Sam, the Old Testament story is told in just twelve books (Genesis, Exodus, Numbers, Joshua, Judges, First and Second Samuel, First and Second Kings, Daniel, Ezra, and Nehemiah). In Genesis, God gives the foundations necessary for faith. Exodus is the story of salvation. Numbers through Second Kings provide a vivid picture of spiritual growth. The end of Second Kings and Daniel tell what it is like to fall away from God; Ezra and Nehemiah are all about restoration. The remaining Old Testament books fall within that story line and are a complete picture of the spiritual development process."

"Wow! That certainly makes things easier to understand," Sam exclaimed.

"What kind of resources could you recommend for *Big Picture* study?" Maggie asked.

"I can show you some after our study. I've got one that takes you through the entire Bible in a short period of time. There are also excellent and thorough Bible surveys involving serious study with possible formal testing."

"So, I'm assuming that the *microscope* view involves paragraph thoughts and word meaning," Burt interjected.

"Yes, and that leads us to our next study tool—*Structural Diagnostics*. Once you have determined your *View Setting*, the next process is to *break up* the text you are studying into its divine divisions, *figure out* its meaning, and then plan how to *put it into practice.*

"God communicated specific thoughts He had. Finding those thought breaks makes study much easier; that's the *break it up* part of *Structural Diagnostics.*"

"How do you know that you have found the God-given thought breaks?" Rick asked.

"Let me answer with a question. Have you ever read a passage of Scripture and felt that God shared a specific thought with you; and then, at a future point in time, had Him share a different thought from the same passage?"

"Yeah."

"Then which thought was the correct one—the first or the second?"

"Are you saying that breaking up a passage is not a right or wrong exercise?" Rick asked with mild concern.

"I am suggesting that, if the Spirit of God wrote the Scriptures in the first place, He is more than capable of helping you break up a passage in such a way that you see the truth He has for you at the time."

"You are making it sound as if truth is circumstantial or relative," Burt responded.

"Truth is absolute; but, like a diamond, it has many facets that can shine, depending on how the light hits it."

When everyone seemed to understand the process of *breaking up* a passage, Peter took the Team through some practical exercises of breaking up small books of the Bible, individual verses, and even the shortest verse in the Bible—John 11:35, "Jesus wept." With that verse, he began to explain the need to *figure out* what God wanted to communicate to people in the 21st century.

Peter sat forward and studied the group intently. "'Jesus' is one thought; 'wept' is another thought. What is God saying to you personally with those two thoughts?"

After some lively group discussion about how God really can relate to modern-day needs that people have, Peter moved to the last aspect of the *Structural Diagnostics* tool—*putting truth into practice.*

Peter summarized this study tool by asking, "Based on what we learned about Jesus' compassion for His friends when Lazarus died, how does God want us to practice this truth throughout the coming week?"

"I can be pretty hard-hearted," Jared answered. "God wants me to be more understanding with people who are struggling emotionally, especially Ruth and the girls."

"I'm on the other end of the application spectrum," Michelle spoke. "As we studied the context of that verse, it dawned on me that Jesus had the power to prevent human suffering, but He knew that allowing it would have a greater impact for the Kingdom of God. I think I need to allow our children to experience some managed hardships so that they can see God at work in their circumstances. I'm sure that God also has things He wants to teach me as I help the kids through their hardships."

"I hope those managed hardships don't include me!" Sam looked at his wife with humorous concern.

"Are you sayin' you've got it easy?" Vern teased.

Sam feigned entrapment, but quickly switched to an amiable smile.

As others on the Team expressed specific ways they believed God wanted them to apply the truth they had learned, Peter was pleased to see each person fully engaged in the learning process.

"To reinforce today's truth, I want to hand out some verse references about the importance of the Bible and have you practice these study tools with each other. I'll pair you up and hand out the verses now so that you can make plans to get together sometime during the week."

"We'll give Joshua 1:8 and Psalm 1:1-3 to Kevin, Misty, Rick, and Penny.

"Garret, Maggie, Gary, and Kim, you've got Psalm 119:11, 105.

"Second Timothy 3:16-17 is a favorite for Lisa and me. Would you mind helping us with that passage?" Peter asked Ted and Jan. Peter had another motivation for this request. He wanted to talk with Ted and Jan about their insights into the discipleship process so far.

Ted nodded, "Yes."

"How about Jared, Ruth, Vern, and Vickie taking Second Peter 1:3-4?"

"You got it," Vern replied as he fist-bumped Jared.

"Hebrews 4:12 would be a good passage for a lawyer," Peter grinned as he assigned the passage to Burt and Betty.

"That sounds good as long as Sam and Michelle help to balance out Betty and me."

"Sure!" Sam and Michelle answered in unison.

"This *Structural Diagnostics* tool is a little challenging for me to wrap my mind around," Sam admitted.

Peter added some clarification. "It can be simplified from the *break it up, figure it out,* and *put it into practice* steps, down to two basic questions, Sam. First question—*'What is God saying to me?'* Second question—*'How can I put into practice what God has said to me?'*"

With his thumbs up, Sam grinned, "Thanks; that helps."

"What about the *Reliability Index* tool? Are we going to cover that today?" Rick asked.

"Not today," Peter answered. "When we get together next week, we'll see how many of you used it intuitively."

Peter ended the study time with a practical help. "Here are some suggestions for those of you who are struggling with letting God speak to you on a daily basis. Start with the books of Proverbs, James, or any of the basic Bible stories found in the Old Testament, the four Gospels, or the book of Acts. Read for five minutes, and then take five to ten minutes to go through the three-step process of *breaking it up, figuring it out,* and *putting it into practice;* or ask yourself the two basic questions, *'What is God saying to me?'* and *'How can I put into practice what God has said to me?'* Try that and see what God does in your life."

Even though many of the Team had expressed challenges about Bible study when they started that day, the conversation after they had closed in prayer was lively and filled with anticipation. They were eager to see what God would teach them in the week ahead as they studied His Word together.

Peter watched as Rick's discipleship passion and potential leadership skills went into motion. He gathered his partners around and worked out a game plan for the coming week.

Soon—very soon—Rick would take his discipleship development to a whole new level, mused Peter.

PRACTICES: BIBLE STUDY RESULTS

It was Jared and Ruth's turn to host again. During the meal, Jared expressed deep appreciation for Vern buying him a copy of the Bible on CD to play on his hauls. He was amazed by what he was learning, and Ruth praised how much more peaceful he had been. Garret shared what he had learned about memorization. Sam's excitement was infectious as he told about "rocking out" in the book of Proverbs. Most everyone agreed that it had been a transformational week.

After the meal, the usually quiet Kevin got the study time started. "I wasn't sure what to expect from our assignment. When Rick and Penny came over and we got to studying Joshua 1:8 and Psalm 1:1-3, God showed me that I'm spending too much time watching television. If I cut out just half of my weekly viewing, I could read through the Bible several times a year. We all felt that using our time more wisely was the part that we needed to put into practice. We also had to wonder why it was so challenging to spend time in the Bible when God promises so many benefits."

Jared jumped in at this point. "Speaking of promises, we had Second Peter 1:3-4 as our verses. Ruth has been living out these verses for years with her health issues and all. But I discovered that

I was a proud, self-sufficient man whose spiritual life was suffering as a result."

"He wasn't alone in that discovery," Vern chimed in. "I have seldom reached out fo'a God's promises." Looking at Jared and then glancing at their wives, Vern suggested, "I think the Holy Spirit was female the night we met. What do you think, Peta'—can the Spirit be feminine?"

"I'll ask Lisa," Peter chuckled.

Lisa rolled her eyes, smiled, and moved into the results from their study with the Maxwells. "If the ball is in our court, we might as well share what we got from Second Timothy 3:16-17. We discovered that the Bible is the source for stimulating right thinking and actions, as well as for exposing wrong thinking and lifestyles. Those who are engaged in living out the applications of Scriptural truths become completely equipped to live out their God-given purposes—their *Potential.*"

Gary added, "Psalm 119:105 echoes that and promises guidance. The Bible is equated with light. If we are spending adequate time in the Bible, we will have light to reveal where we are supposed to walk; if not, we will be doing a lot of stumbling and falling."

"And falling could mean into sin," Garret continued. "Psalm 119:11 was the verse assigned to us. It was very clear that memorizing the Bible is one sure defense mechanism against falling into sin. God knew that I needed to be challenged about memorization."

"Are you sure it was God? I thought Peter was the one who assigned you that verse," Kim quipped.

"He may have assigned the verse, but God convicted me so strongly that I did a lot of research to see how I could conquer my memorization difficulties."

Kim was intrigued. "What did you find?"

"The mechanics of memorization are simply *repetition* and *review*. Advertising uses those components all the time along with audio-visual associations. After critiquing several memorization systems, I customized one for myself."

"How does it work?" Kim probed.

"I just started, so I can only share what I've done so far. First, I pick a verse and commit all the words to memory using the *break it up* formula that we learned last week. After I know the entire verse, I say it twenty-five times the first day, twenty times the second day, fifteen times the third day, ten times the fourth day, and five times the fifth day. Then I'll say that same verse once a day for twenty-five days, and then once a week for five weeks. (I based everything on a five-day week.)"

"And memorizing Scripture is supposed to help you become victorious over sin?" Rick questioned.

"I know I'm just getting started, but I've seen it work already this week. A situation came up where I could have gotten myself into a business compromise. The Holy Spirit used the verse I'm memorizing to give me discernment to lay aside my personal preferences and make a principled decision."

"And that ties in with Hebrews 4:12," Burt joined in. "We learned that the Bible is the ultimate discernment instrument. Sometimes we can fool ourselves, but we can never fool God. His Word cuts through our excuses and false intentions to reveal what is really true. This week, I pictured myself on trial with God. I realized that sometimes I try to use my legal tactics to justify certain behaviors that I don't want to change. God did a great job at cutting away my excuses to reveal what He wants me to do."

"Me, too," Betty joined. "I can use the good that my career efforts accomplish as an excuse not to be more involved with the spiritual tasks that God gives me. The Holy Spirit was doing more cutting than I would have preferred."

Peter brought things full circle. "Which brings us to the *Reliability Index* tool that Rick asked about last week. **As you *broke things up, figured them out,* and made efforts to *put them into practice,* were any of you convinced that what you studied was more than human in origin? That it was, in fact, the supernatural Word of God?"**

"I know that what I experienced this week was more than any human could have manufactured," Jared asserted.

"If I wasn't convinced that what I studied was from God, I would never have felt compelled to put into practice what I studied," Garret affirmed.

Peter added, "In John 7:17, Jesus declares that the way to know if the Bible is true or not is simply to obey it. And in Hebrews 11:6, God promises that those with faith in His existence and His ability to reward will be the ones who please Him. Without taking things to a *health-and-wealth* extreme, God does indicate that His blessings are proof positive of His reality to those who place their faith in Him and in His Word."

"After all of the challenges I have been through in this discipleship process, I can honestly say that this week was one of the best week's I've ever had," Rick enthused. "As I studied, things just clicked together for me. I even started writing out potential sermons and Bible study lessons."

After the Team session was over, Peter approached Rick with a triumphant grin on his face.

"You're ready!"

"For what?"

"I have a ministry friend over in Pasco who is always looking for quality speakers to fill in for him when he needs to be away."

"Cool! When?"

"How about this coming weekend? Several older men have filled in for him in the past, but he was hoping for someone fresh and a little younger."

"This weekend! How will I be able to complete the next lesson for our Team study and get ready to speak for your friend in less than a week?"

Peter smiled as he answered, "I would like you to experiment with what you have learned this past week."

"What do you mean?" Rick panicked.

"Can you trust God to speak through you as you use the *Structural Diagnostics* tools with no other mental preparation?"

Rick's mouth dropped open. "NO PREPARATION?!"

"No scripted preparation. You definitely need to prepare your heart through prayer, which happens to be next week's Team study. And you need to believe that the Holy Spirit will guide you through the process instead of relying on your personal study preparation."

Rick demanded, "How will I know which passage to speak on?"

"I'm confident God will give you an innovative solution."

"You're the craziest spiritual leader I've ever met!"

"You ain't seen nothing yet—wait until you hear about the leadership ideas I have for the *Adult* phase."

Rick just stared at his friend in amazement.

"So, will you take a significant step this coming weekend and trust God to speak through you? This could very well be one of the ways God helps you discover the purpose you've been searching for."

Rick cautiously replied, "Yes."

GOD AT WORK

Never had six days seemed to fly by so quickly for Rick.

He was thankful to be studying the topic of prayer; it anchored his faith when doubt knocked on his soul's door. It was also after a time of prayer and fasting on Saturday that God showed Rick which passage he was supposed to speak on the next day. Each person would write down a favorite Scripture passage or one they had always wanted to hear a message about; then Rick would collect the papers in a box, pray for God's leading, and have someone from the congregation pull a passage from the box.

Sunday morning, as he anxiously drove to Pasco, a thought came to him with such powerful clarity that he couldn't help but be at peace. *I simply have to trust God to help me repeat what I've already been doing. He's helped me many times over the past two weeks to break Scripture passages up, figure out what the key principles are, and then give me creative ideas for putting those truths into practice. Why wouldn't He help me do that today so that others can begin to see how to have that same experience themselves?*

And that is just what God did! In fact, God did such an incredible job of helping him speak that several people asked him if he would be willing to mentor them in the use of the *Structural Diagnostics* tools.

As Rick crossed back over the river to meet with the Team that afternoon, his soul was filled to overflowing. Comments about how the Lord had used his message replayed in his mind. And now, he was headed to be with a group of people who were becoming his friends— real friends. Looking to the East, he saw the Cable Bridge and Clover Island. Geese were floating on the Columbia River, which was sparkling like diamonds in the autumn sunlight. And, like the river under him was carrying away debris and masses of tumbleweed, Rick felt God carrying away some of his pain, too. Maybe God did have a purpose for his life.

~ ~ ~

As Peter listened to Rick share his morning experiences with the Team, he saw an opportunity. Taking him quietly off to the side, he seeded and watered the idea. "Rick, let's see if you can trust God to lead you in teaching the Team how to apply the *Structural Diagnostics* tools for the topic of prayer."

Rick squawked, "You mean, like right now?"

With a hand on Rick's shoulder, Peter replied, "Yes. What parts of the process would be the same, and what changes would have to be made, to adapt from one passage of Scripture to many passages?"

Rick frowned thoughtfully. "*Putting truth into practice* should be the same. And, maybe the *figuring it out* would be similar. I'm not sure about the *breaking it up* part, though."

"You're on the right track. How would someone go about *breaking up* verses that were already separate from each other?"

"Maybe by finding their similarities and differences."

"You just cracked the code! That's all the adjustment you need to make. Now let's see what God can do through you this afternoon as you take the workbook content that you have already studied and lead others to discover and articulate how the habit of prayer can increase their *Potential*."

~ ~ ~

Most of the Team approved of Rick applying his newfound skills, using *Structural Diagnostics* to study prayer, and some were downright excited.

"What passages did you come up with for the topic of prayer?" Rick started.

"The Lord's Prayer," Michelle began.

"There are several verses about asking God for things and the promise that God will answer. I just don't remember where to find them," Sam spoke with uncertainty.

Rick wanted Peter to share the biblical research resources he had recently shown to Rick, but he knew Peter would want him to try it on his own.

"Depending on your preference between books or technology, you can use concordances or Bible word search programs that will surface all the places in the Bible where a topic is mentioned. Pete showed me several choices this past week."

Garret reached for his phone and, in just a few moments, was showing Sam his favorite App. Burt showed Sam the concordance he brought along with highlighted references he thought were especially meaningful on prayer. Rick was grateful for their help.

"Let's read the passages everyone has come up with, one at a time, and then ask, 'What principle could we learn about prayer from this passage?' Who wants to get the ball rolling?"

Vern started. "Matthew 21:22 indicates that pray'a doesn't work without faith."

Garret went next, reading John 15:7.

Rick asked, "Is John 15:7 saying the same thing as Matthew 21:22?"

Garret shook his head as he replied, "Not really. It is telling us that answered prayer flows out of our relationship with Jesus. I think this verse has a relational focus instead of a faith focus."

"That's a great observation. You just used the *break it up* tool. By seeing the differences between those two verses, you were able to see two separate principles. What's another verse?"

Kevin read Matthew 9:29 and Mark 11:22-24. After some thought, he stated, "These verses seem to be saying the same thing as Matthew 21:22."

"I can see that," Maggie and Vickie agreed simultaneously.

Over the next hour, Rick had the Team read verses and discuss their similarities and differences. The result was that the Team *figured out* several distinct principles about prayer:

- Prayer is a natural and relational exchange with God.
- Prayer is intensified by awe, desire, or need.
- Effective prayer is based on faith in God's abilities and character (best anchored in biblical promises).
- Perseverance and praise are evidences of faith; perseverance is needed until there is inner confidence that expresses itself in praise.
- Sin short-circuits prayer.

Rick asked, "What are the challenges of *putting* these principles *into practice?*"

"For the Team or for us personally?" Sam questioned.

"Always start with yourself."

"Why's that?"

"If you *break passages up, figure out* their meaning, AND *put them into practice* for yourself, you increase your credibility with people. **People want to see the truth in action more than they want to hear hard, cold facts.** I think my greatest effectiveness this morning wasn't *breaking up* a passage or *figuring it out;* it was in the stories God brought to my mind of times recently where I've had to *put truth into practice.*"

"For me, prayer has always been boring," Sam answered honestly, "probably because I viewed it as a mechanical exercise instead of as a relational exchange with God."

"It's weird talking to Someone I can't see," Misty joined in.

"I don't believe in asking for things more than once," Jared added.

"I believe God can answer my prayers, but I'm not always convinced He will. I give prayer wishes to Him more often than prayer requests," Michelle responded.

Rick resurfaced the application by agreeing. "Those are the same challenges I've experienced. Now, how do we put prayer into practice so that we can increase our God-given *Potential?*"

"By praying," Ruth answered; "praying alone, praying together."

"And then talking about what we're learning as we pray," Sam added.

With a grateful heart for an awesome day of seeing God at work in his own life, Rick closed his teaching. "So, let's pray."

ADVENTURE 15 – PRACTICES: EMOTIONS

Rick couldn't remember another time when he was so excited about God's activity in his life. It was as if he had stepped into a different world. Maybe that explained why the thought of going to Portland on the weekend for the *Every Man's Battle Workshop* didn't upset him like it had previously. He was still a little nervous, but he knew that his attendance would earn him credibility with Peter.

A young married man from the church family joined him at the last minute. Drew's wife Mandy had just discovered his sexual addiction, and they were now engaged in marital intervention with Peter and Lisa. Peter had called Rick mid-week to ask if Drew could ride with him, and Rick had gladly agreed.

The conversation on the way to Portland was a foreshadowing of their weekend experience. The rawness of Drew's situation reopened memories of Rick's past struggles. Standing in the hotel lobby as he waited to sign in, Rick looked around at the faces of nearly a hundred men. Shame was the word he chose to describe what they were all experiencing. As those not associated with the retreat walked by, he could sense varying degrees of judgment.

He was seriously doubting the sanity of Peter's parting comment. "Rick, I believe you are going to find emotional healing this weekend in ways you never thought possible. This could be one of the avenues God uses to unlock a significant facet of your *Potential*."

"Emotions are overrated," Rick had flippantly responded, but Peter just smiled.

Now, being here with other men who were suffering the consequences of their addiction, Rick began to wonder just how overrated emotions really were.

"Some of you here are wearing masks to cover up the real you," the speaker started out. "Those masks keep you from admitting who you really are and finding who God designed you to be. Part of your recovery will involve taking off those masks and dealing with the resulting emotions."

We'll see, Rick thought.

"Part of this retreat is designed to help you begin the process of getting in touch with reality. We will start by having each of you share your story with a small group of men in our next breakout session."

As Rick gathered with eight other guys of varying ages and listened to their stories, he moved from feelings of sadness to anger and from contempt to guilt to fear without realizing it. He saw glimpses of those same emotions in the men around him as he shared his own story, and they influenced the passion with which he communicated.

At the next general session, his anger reached an unexpected high. When he was asked to write down statements that he wished he had heard from his father while he was growing up, his anger simmered. *This is dumb. I doubt that I can think of anything I wish he had told me.*

But, as he began to write, statements flowed into his mind and out onto the workbook page designated for the assignment.

"I love you." "I'm glad you're my son." "I'm proud of you." "Great job!" "You can talk to me about anything." "You can never screw up so bad that together we can't find a solution." "I'd love to help you reach your goals."

Rick was surprised by the number of statements that he was writing down. He had pretended for years that it didn't matter what his father thought about him; but, truthfully, there was a huge hole in his heart.

"Now," the speaker continued, "I'd like you to take your list of statements and share them with your breakout group in the next session."

You dirty rat; you set me up! Rick felt betrayed. He wasn't aware that he would be expected to share what he had just written. His anger boiled as he left the general session and headed for the breakout room.

The breakout leader started, "I'd like you to hand your worksheet to someone in this room who you want to represent your father and have him speak the statements you wrote. This will be a surprisingly critical step of healing for many of you."

"It would have been nice to know up front that we'd be required to share our private thoughts in public."

"Rick, you seem upset. What are you feeling right now?"

"Like punching you in the nose!"

"That's an action that results from what you're feeling. Now, if you can, please give me a word that describes what you are feeling."

Trying to think when he was so angry was challenging, but he finally growled, "I'm ticked off. I hate being set up!"

"Thank you, Rick. I'm glad you were able to express what is going on inside of you. It might be helpful for you to know that feelings are like warning lights on a dashboard that signal when something is wrong. The feelings themselves aren't wrong, but they do indicate that something has to be dealt with."

"Why do you make such a big deal out of feelings?"

"Anger, discouragement, fear, guilt, pain, along with their varying shades of intensity, are indicators of need. **Identifying your need, managing the resulting feelings, and having your need met in legitimate ways are marks of emotional maturity**. What need do you think is driving your anger right now, Rick?"

Exasperated, Rick replied, "I don't know."

"Could you possibly be reacting to someone trying to control you?"

Rick answered thoughtfully, "Maybe. Why?"

"How could that of loss of control be handled in a healthy way?" the leader probed.

With some embarrassment, Rick replied, "I shouldn't have threatened you with force."

"Stopping negative expressions may be a starting point, but is it enough to cause the anger to subside?"

Rick shook his head, "Probably not."

"You're right. So the desire for control still needs to be dealt with. Do you have any ideas of how that need could be addressed without being defensive?"

"Right now, I'm under too much pressure to think straight."

"I understand. Let's ask the question a different way. Was there anything wrong with your statement about wanting to be informed that a private exercise would be used in a public way?"

"Are you suggesting that what I said was okay, but not the way I said it?" Rick puzzled.

"Yes, I am. Being honest about what you feel is always acceptable."

Rick's features hardened a little. "That never worked in my family."

"Many well-meaning, but wounded, parents have a hard time allowing their children to express their feelings. Did your parents have healthy childhood experiences?"

Remembering bits and pieces of comments from his parents' upbringing, Rick answered, "Not at all."

"Is it possible that your parents are struggling, too? It's hard to realize that adults can be emotionally immature, but many are, Rick. Only secure adults are able to allow others to express themselves honestly. If an adult tries to stop people, especially those who are under their authority, from expressing themselves, no matter how sincere or well-meaning they may be, they are emotionally immature people." As an afterthought, the leader looked Rick in the eye and asked, "You wouldn't happen to be the oldest child in your family, would you?"

Rick was surprised. "Yeah. Why?"

"It seems to be a common pattern for emotionally immature parents to have trouble dealing with their first-born child—father with son, mother with daughter."

With a shaky voice, Rick asked, "Is the way my father has treated me an indication of unresolved emotional pain in his own life?"

"What do you think, Rick?"

"That is probably true." Genuine sorrow flooded his heart.

"The pain caused by an unresolved need will result in emotional immaturity, which is the inability to express and manage feelings, and this is frequently the cause of addictions. Emotional health can best be gauged by the age people stopped growing emotionally. For example, if you got involved with sexual addiction at the age of 13, then for all practical purposes, your emotional maturity level would be equivalent to a 13-year- old. If your parents got stuck emotionally as children, then that is the level of their emotional maturity."

"Then how in the world can I ever find resolution if both of us are emotionally immature?" Rick questioned.

"You can't. You need to find emotionally healthy people in order to have your needs met in legitimate ways. That is part of the purpose of this retreat—to stimulate you to build a network of people that will safely help you to meet your needs God's way. Rick, do you have people in your life that you believe are emotionally and spiritually mature?"

Rick's face relaxed a little as he answered, "Not until recently. But in the last several months, God has gifted me with several people who are and others that I believe could help me in the ways you are describing."

"How do you feel about God providing those people for you?"

*"Better than I can describe." Rick paused to reflect on all that God had done in recent months before asking, "Are you saying that if I deal with getting my emotional needs met in the right way, that I won't have to deal with sexual temptation?"

"Emotional health is the primary battle front. Getting your needs met legitimately is where the battle of addictions is primarily won or lost. If you learn how to identify your need and then meet it in an emotionally mature way, you will have decreasing problems in battling temptation and the resulting cycle of addiction. Addiction temptation is the secondary battle front where people often lose if they have already failed emotionally."

"So when I focus on winning the battle over sexual temptation without being aware of my emotional needs and the warning lights I have already blown through, I'm pretty much set up for failure."

"I think you've got it, Rick!"

～ ～ ～

On the ride home, Drew asked if Rick would be willing to be a primary accountability partner, to which he gladly agreed. It felt great to be giving back to someone after all that he had been receiving. He was also able to connect with the guys on the Team during the week to hear how their study on emotions went and to share his take-aways from *Every Man's Battle.* Most of them agreed to partner with him to give daily accountability for his emotional and spiritual health.

As Rick reflected on all the positive changes in his life and the powerful resources that God was providing for him, his heart overflowed with optimistic joy. He was realizing that the *Replacement Principle* was also a vital part of breaking negative emotional responses. As he focused on negative emotions he wanted to remove, he also needed to focus on a positive emotional replacement. He remembered that, in Galatians, Paul talks about the *Fruit of the Spirit*—love, joy, peace, patience, kindness, goodness, faithfulness, gentleness, and self-control. Those *Fruits,* which are anchored in the character of God, are the exact opposite of human nature.

God, You are a greater reality than I have ever known. I believe that You are going to use my life in a significant way. I must be getting close to discovering what my purpose in life is.

DARK FORCES AT WORK

The strong smell of sulfur permeated the air as Sector 648 met to discuss Rick's growth and his potential harm to the *Cause of Evil*.

Goth Hard-A started the meeting. "The kid's got *Potential*, and he's beginning to see it for the first time. If we don't stop him now, we will be cursing ourselves in the not so distant future; not to mention that we'll be doubly cursed by Lucifer."

"But how?" Screw-up asked. "He's starting to conquer all of the normal problems that trip Christians up."

Goth grinned slyly, "Betrayal."

"By whom?" Cynicia questioned.

"Who do you think, you nitwit?" Goth paused for effect and then hissed, "His very own father." Ghoulish approval wafted through the darkness.

"How?" Screw-up pressed.

"We'll have Ray pin the consequences of his secret activities on Rick in such a way that Rick will have to pay for his father's behavior."

The room rang in blasphemous agreement, and after a few minor details were ironed out, the demons exited their lair and rapidly moved into attack mode.

~ ~ ~

"You're not going to believe this, Penny! My father just invited me to come home so that I could preach at the church he attends. The pastor had a family emergency and, when my father mentioned that I was involved in a spiritual development process with the goal of being in ministry, the pastor suggested that I come and preach!"

Penny's alarm surprised him. "Rick, I don't think you should go."

"Well, I do. This is the first time my father has ever shown approval for something I've done—ever!"

"But, Rick—"

"Don't you care?" Rick cut her off. "You've always been supported by your parents, and you've never had to grow up in a dysfunctional home where everything looked good on the surface but was a churning pit of abusive oppression underneath."

"That's why I am concerned, Rick. How do you know that what is on the surface this time is genuine?"

"Why would my father suggest to his pastor that I was capable of speaking if he didn't mean it? Don't *you* think I'm capable?" Rick steamed.

"We're talking about your father, not me. Have you talked with Peter or anyone else on the Team?"

"Why would I do that? Can't you see that God is giving me this opportunity to prove to my father what I can do? The Team already knows what I am capable of."

"This isn't about capability; it's about making a wise choice based on where you are in your spiritual development. It's only been a few weeks since you set limits with your family, and you are right at the start of learning how to manage your emotions. Wouldn't it be safer to get the Team's input before making a final decision?"

"Safer...does everything have to be safe? Doesn't learning to trust involve some risk? But I suppose accountants don't take risks, do they?" Rick's voice dripped with sarcasm.

Quietly, Penny responded, "I was just sharing my thoughts."

With a hard edge to his voice, Rick retorted, "Well, I don't really care what you think. I've never had a chance like this before, and I don't want to blow it by worrying about safety."

After a long pause, Penny replied, "Then maybe, if you don't value my opinions, I need to rethink how much you really care about me. I want to be with someone who isn't threatened by my input and isn't an affirmation junkie. If you go without asking advice from the Team, I'm going to have to step back and decide whether or not we should stay together."

ADVENTURE 16 – PRACTICES: "ONE ANOTHER" RELATIONSHIPS

"Pete, I blew it again! It seems like every time I gain a step, I end up going three steps backwards. I'm a jackass of astronomical proportion!"

Peter couldn't help smiling. "What happened?"

"Penny and I had a major disagreement that may lead to the end of our relationship. With all that I have learned about emotions lately, you'd think that I would have applied at least some of it to our argument. But no, I reverted to my old hard-core way of handling things."

"Why do you suppose that happened?"

"Just a week ago, I wouldn't have had a clue. But now I know exactly why I did what I did. She made me feel like a little kid who didn't have the capability or right to make decisions on my own."

Peter probed, "Do you think that was really her intention?"

Rick shook his head. "Not at all; she even tried to get me to ask the Team for help with working things through. But that ticked me off, and I said some hurtful things to her."

"The quality of your relationships with other believers is an important aspect of your *Potential*, Rick."

"I know," Rick hung his head down.

"What was the disagreement about?"

"My father invited me to come home so that I could preach at the church he attends. I thought it was God giving me an opportunity to prove a lot of things." Rick sighed.

"Doesn't it seem a little odd that he would invite you back home when just a couple of months ago he was trying to physically control you? When that failed, he essentially threw you out."

"I guess I'm so used to the dysfunction that it didn't seem unusual. I've seen him go from one extreme to another in a matter of hours. I just wish that I could have a normal relationship with my folks."

"You can develop relationships with others that can provide what God intended you to have with your parents, can't you?"

"I guess so. No, I know so." Rick began to speak with passion. "The last several months have proven that to me. I just have to accept the fact that I may never have the kind of relationship with my parents that I've always wanted and then learn to be grateful for the wonderful friends God has provided."

"This is the place, Rick, where *Practices* flow into *Partnership*. You are moving from *Habits* and *Emotions* into the *Relationship* dynamics of spiritual development. **In the New Testament, there are many verses that show how followers of Jesus are to treat *One Another*.** These *One Another* verses are seldom practiced to the extent that Jesus intended because of cultural preferences and people's pasts. It is our desire to see this Team live out these passages as Jesus originally intended. In reality, Penny was probably trying to practice *exhort one another*, but you couldn't or wouldn't hear her."

"You're right, Pete. So what should I do now? I know that I will never reach my full *Potential* if I keep screwing up my relationship with others."

"Maybe our next lesson on listening and questioning skills will help you navigate through those challenges."

ADVENTURE 17 – PARTNERSHIP: LISTENING & QUESTIONING

"Can you give me an overview of listening and questioning skills, Pete?"

Peter was puzzled. "Why?"

"I need to talk with Penny, and I don't want to make things worse than they already are!"

"Is your primary concern to convince her not to end the relationship between you?" Peter prodded.

"Honestly, that's a large part of it. But, I also know that you typically lead me to a higher level than I initially see. So, I'm assuming that, if I can see things differently in the way I communicate with others, it will help me in all my relationships, not just with Penny."

Peter wrapped his arms around Rick in a huge bear hug and then slapped him on the back. "You know, that is one of the most mature answers I've experienced from you in this spiritual development process!"

Rick grinned. "Well, I must protect my status of immaturity by saying, 'Let's get on with it!'"

Transitioning into teacher mode, Peter spoke one word, "Noise."

"Noise? What are you talking about?"

"Noise is the greatest barrier that hinders people being able to listen to each other and communicate effectively."

"What kind of noise are you talking about?" Rick asked.

"When you are listening to a radio, what do you do when there is too much background noise or static?"

Thoughtfully, Rick offered. "If it's background noise, I turn up the volume. If it's static, I change the station or shut it off."

"What would background noise represents in a conversation?"

"I want to say other people talking, but I think you are pressing for something deeper than that."

"You're right!" Peter grinned before giving Rick the clarification he needed. "Was there any background noise in your conversation with Penny?"

Rick paused before asking, "You mean, like baggage from my *Past*?"

"Would that affect your ability to listen to Penny?"

"You bet it would! In fact, it did. I cut her off more than once because my father's offer represented something that I have always wanted and never felt I had."

"Now what do you think static represents in a conversation?"

"Something that distorts clarity."

"What distortions happened when you argued with Penny?"

"I got mad. From there, it all went downhill."

"Does the static of being self-centered improve or reduce the clarity God wants in communication?"

Rick just rolled his eyes.

"Dumb question, huh? But you get the point. **The background noise of *Past* baggage and the static noise of self-centered sin are two huge barriers to effective communication.**"

"So how do I learn to communicate effectively?"

"That's a great question!"

With some exasperation Rick asked, "And, your answer is—what?"

"Why don't you tell me what you think it is?"

"Obviously I have to eliminate *Past* baggage and self-centeredness, or I'm doomed from the start. But I'm not seeing what the positive side should look like."

"Has this conversation helped you?"

"Sure it has."

"How much have I told you?" Peter continued.

"It feels like a lot," Rick answered.

"Have I been telling you how to communicate or asking you questions that have led you to answers that you could own?"

"Now that I think of it, you have been asking questions!"

Peter now pressed for meaningful applications. "What are the downsides to making statements, especially negative ones?

Rick considered before he answered. "A statement tends to put people on the defensive. It also shifts the burden of proof to the one making the statements, which can produce a heated debate or a battle of wills. If a more passive person disagrees with the person making the statements, he will just dismiss the conversation as irrelevant to his life."

"Good answers. So, what is the power of a question?"

"Good question!" Rick grinned at his own play on words. "A question makes me think before I give an answer."

"Have you ever noticed how many times in biblical conversations, God uses questions?"

"Can't say that I have."

"How did God communicate with Adam after he had sinned?"

"He asked him where he was."

"Had God lost Adam?"

Rick laughed. "No! He knew exactly where he was."

"So, why did God ask the question?"

"Probably to give Adam a chance to come clean on his own."

"Was the question open-ended or closed-ended?"

"I'm not sure," Rick answered with a puzzled look on his face.

"Open-ended questions provide complete freedom for someone to answer any way they want. Closed-ended questions are basically a list of options to choose from."

"Then it was an open-ended question."

"That's correct. How about the next question He asked Adam?"

"That would be a closed-ended question because all Adam had to do was answer Yes or No to eating the forbidden fruit."

Peter moved toward his conclusion. "Did Adam take ownership for his behavior with the questions God asked him?"

"Nope. He tried every trick in the book to keep from taking ownership."

Peter leaned forward. "That's when God began using statements."

"So if I apply this to my conversation with Penny, I need to go back to her and take ownership for letting the baggage of my *Past* and my self-centered emotions get in the way of our conversation. Then I need to ask good open-ended questions and really listen to what her answers are."

Peter smiled. "Why don't you try that and let me know how it goes."

"What if it doesn't go well?" Rick worried.

"If you don't have self-centered motivations, how could that possibly happen?" Peter questioned to connect Rick with truth.

"I think I'm beginning to see what you mean!"

Peter warmly affirmed, "I knew you eventually would."

ADVENTURE 18 – PARTNERSHIP: ENCOURAGEMENT & EXHORTATION

"Your conversation with Rick must have helped," Lisa commented as she and Peter were getting out of their car at Gary and Kim's.

"Why do you say that?" Peter asked.

"Here comes his pickup, and it looks like Penny is with him."

"It was a little hard for me to tell; she's sitting so close to him that they looked like one person until you said something."

Peter and Lisa grinned at each other as they waited for Rick and Penny. When the two couples began walking toward the house, Penny looked at Peter and quietly mouthed, "Thank you."

Peter simply smiled and nodded. He was pretty sure that Penny had been used by God to interrupt evil. If he could have seen the spirit world he would have seen Goth, Cynicia, and Srew-up headed to a fiery meeting with Lucifer.

Deep in thought, Peter was thankful to see something positive come out of it all. *Rick's on his way to the most meaningful experiences of his life if he keeps his head and heart in the right place. I just wish I knew whether or not he has what it's going to take to be the leader to replace me.*

After the meal, Peter began the Team's study time by stating, "Today we are going to start with two complementary and opposing *One Another* directives—*Encouragement* and *Exhortation*. How many of you feel that you experience biblical encouragement on a regular basis?"

A few Team members acknowledged that encouragement was a normal part of their spiritual experience. The others expressed varying emotions over the lack of encouragement in their lives.

"What makes someone a good encourager?"

"Knowing others," Ruth responded. "Sometimes we think we are being encouraging to someone, when in reality we are just doing what we want done to us. Not everyone receives encouragement in the same way; so in order to really encourage someone, we have to know her or him as an individual."

"I also think it involves being an *others*-focused person," Michelle added. "Most of us are self-centered and don't take the time to notice what is going on in someone else's life."

Peter thought he saw Rick flinch a little at Michelle's answer. He paused before asking, "Now for the harder question. How many of you regularly give and receive biblical exhortation?"

"What is biblical exhortation?" Rick asked. "Hopefully it isn't like some of the 'exhortation' I experienced growing up."

For the next several minutes, Peter asked members of the Team to read Galatians 6:1; Hebrews 3:13 and 10:24-25; Proverbs 27:17, 28:23, and 29:1; and James 5:19-20. Then he asked, "What do these Scriptures show us about biblical exhortation?"

Garret volunteered, "It certainly doesn't skirt difficult issues, but neither does it beat people up."

"It seems like God is saying that, without biblical exhortation, we won't be adequately prepared to stand before Jesus on the *Judgment Day*," Maggie interjected.

"And that it is one of the safety cables that God has provided to prevent us from slipping into a lifestyle of sinful destruction," Gary added.

Peter knew the next application would stretch many of the Team. "In the next few weeks, we are going to practice, at a higher level, the biblical and practical need of vulnerable transparency and accountability with each other. To help continue building trust, we are going to do a Team exercise that practices encouragement and exhortation."

"What if we don't feel comfortable with this exercise?" Ted asked.

"Maybe the best way I can answer that question is by using parenting as a reference point. How many of you parents ask your children to do things for their own good that they would prefer not to do, or initially think they can't do?"

Heads were nodding all around the group.

"At times, we are going to reach critical development barriers that you will either choose to push through or choose to ignore and remain where you are. Remaining where you are does not make you a *bad* person, but it will be a point of exit from the Team. For the sake of where we are going and the Team expectations that we've laid out, we must have everyone moving in the same direction, regardless of how challenging that becomes. We will encourage and provide help to everyone seeking to move forward, but we will not allow someone to disengage from the development process."

A couple of Team members looked like they were experiencing spiritual development indigestion. Jan's voice trembled, "I don't think you know what you are asking some of us to do."

Very calmly, and with as much empathy as he could display, Peter affirmed, "As hard as it may be for you to believe, I really do know what I'm asking you to do."

Rick was all eyes and ears as he watched Peter's leadership skills in action.

Without allowing tension to build from a lengthy silence, Peter began to explain the Team exercise. "The Apostle Paul used a very strategic formula in the New Testament when he wanted to exhort those to whom he was writing: *positive—negative—positive.* He started by sharing *positive* words of encouragement; then he moved into the constructive *negatives* that he exhorted them to change; and finally, he closed with *positive* words of encouragement. During the next couple of weeks, we are going to practice that formula with each other. I want you to come prepared next week to share the positives you see in each other's lives and any constructive criticism that you believe will help stimulate spiritual development."

Lisa added, "What we are trying to do is help you, as future leaders, to increase your relational strength and to reduce negative consequences. The time frame between you making a negative action or decision and another believer speaking truth into your life should be very short. And **every disciple and leader is better when there are encouragement and exhortation feedback loops.**"

The atmosphere had changed from warm to tenuous. Fortunately Peter and Lisa had been through this before. They were convinced that this would be only a temporary setback. Once the Team saw the benefits of this exercise next week, things would relax again.

ENCOURAGEMENT & EXHORTATION PRACTICE

The following week, Ted and Jan had an "unexpected" obligation come up at the last minute. They called Saturday night to let Peter and Lisa know that they wouldn't be coming. Peter gave Lisa a knowing smile, both over the timing of the cancellation and the fact that the Team would still be dealing with the same exercise next week. This was the part of the process where things could get interesting.

"Let's get going." Jared was eager to volunteer for the Team's input so that he and Ruth could rest easy for the remainder of the exercise.

Encouraging comments about their commitment, sincerity, and transparency followed. Jared was complimented on his efforts to increase his biblical intake. Everyone expressed warm appreciation for Ruth's life of faith in dealing with her health issues.

"Jared, you have already identified the one area I could recommend for improvement. A few weeks ago, you mentioned that you could be hard-hearted. I agree that it is an area that needs the touch of God." Gary was speaking with conviction; but he went on to say, "I do want you to know, though, that I have seen improvements already this month; so please be encouraged."

Everyone agreed that it was challenging to find something to exhort Ruth about. They finally settled on her need to learn to be more vocal about things that bothered her instead of stuffing her emotions inside.

Gary and Kim Ingerson were next. Input for Gary was quite similar to Jared's. In addition to all of his positive qualities, the pressure of his business sometimes stimulated him to make cryptic and terse remarks. Kim nodded her head in agreement.

Kim received positive compliments for her mothering and marriage skills. The only constructive feedback for her was that she could be more transparent. The Team felt that because of her proficiencies, she could at times portray herself as someone who had no short-comings.

"But, I want you both to know that I would very happy if I could measu'a up to even half of what you model as followa's of Jesus." Vern's closing comment completed Gary and Kim's feedback on a positive note.

"Another couple that I think has their act really put together is Burt and Betty," Misty interjected. "You seem to use your professional lives as platforms to live out your faith, and you take your jobs very seriously."

"I would agree," Garret joined in and then went on to add, "I have wondered at times, though, if you take your professions so seriously that it might have a straining impact on your marriage. I know how consumed I can get with my business, and I'm not married."

The Larsons both agreed, Betty more so than Burt.

"This exa'cise hasn't been as bad as I thought it would be," Vern jumped in. "We might as well be next." Then he made motions like he was buckling himself up for a high-impact crash test.

"Well, let's start with your sense of humor, Mr. Rogers." Sam loved joking with Vern, so he was only too glad to provide some positive feedback. "I can be having a p-poor day; but whether it is here with the Team or during a weekend church connection, you always lift my spirits."

"I love Vickie's spiritual intensity," Misty added. "You have faithfully served our church family with passion ever since I have known you."

Penny broadened Misty's insight. "I also know that you both have used your occupations to bless people within our church with vehicles and dental care. You are some of the most giving people I've ever known."

"So what's the bad news?" Vern jokingly grimaced.

"Like me, you get into comfort zones that are sometimes hard to break out of," Jared answered. "You seldom fail to move towards positive challenges, but it can take you a considerable amount of time to become motivated to act."

"Are you saying my Yankee stubbornness is not a virtue?"

"He may not be, but I am," Vickie teased.

"Well, just don't fa'get, my lovely wife, you'a turn to be exho'ted is coming up quickly!"

"I already know what I need to work on."

"What's that?" Michelle saw an opportunity to become part of the process without having to share something negative.

"My mouth. I should hold the world record for clean feet; mine are frequently in my mouth. I know I hurt people's feelings many times because I speak before I think."

Vern was sitting there with a smile on his face that let everyone know he agreed with his wife's self-assessment. But he was also careful not to let his humor get out of control and hurt her.

Peter stepped in, preparing the Team for prayer by asking, "What do you think of this exercise so far?" As he asked, he was watching Rick's body language. *He's got his poker face on today; I wonder what's going on in that mind of his.*

"I can see why you wanted us to practice this as a Team," Maggie answered. "It is biblical. And, if we can't do this in a safe environment, how would we ever learn to implement it outside of this Team."

"I'm amazed at how much we really do know about each other. We tend to believe that our lives are camouflaged by anonymity," Kim shared.

"Thanks for stretching us." Garret vocalized a thought that represented the majority of the Team's feelings.

~ ~ ~

With the exception of the Maxwells, there was definitely a more relaxed atmosphere the following week as the Team gathered at Peter and Lisa's house to finish up the *Encouragement and Exhortation* exercise.

After the meal and time of catching up, Peter decided to start the study with Matthew 22:37-39. "I'm going to ask you a question that someone once asked Jesus. 'What is the greatest commandment?'"

"To love God completely," Misty answered.

"And the second greatest command?" Peter continued.

"To love others completely," Misty answered again.

Making eye contact with each member of the Team, Peter gave some parameters before he continued. "Pause a little before answering this next question. Does God want us to love others less than we love Him?"

Burt volunteered, "At first, your question sounds like a no-win proposition. Jesus made it clear that we are not to love others, regardless of their relative association with us, more than we love Him. But, I believe His final instruction before He was crucified was that love would be the new 'rule' for those who follow Him. Our love for each other reflects our love for Him."

"That's exactly right, Burt. **Our love for each other is a direct reflection of our love for Jesus.** What does an unwillingness to exhort each other appropriately reveal about our love?"

Maggie joined in. "Sometimes we pretend to love by saying that we love someone too much to hurt them. In reality, we love ourselves or others' opinion of us too much to get involved, deeper than surface level, in lives that God clearly instructed us to be involved in."

"You hit the nail on the head. So, let's not just complete an exercise today; let's start a lifestyle that God designed to be an integral part of the Christian community. Every believer will be held accountable for practicing *Encouragement* and *Exhortation.*"

For the next hour, the Team wonderfully encouraged and exhorted Sam and Michelle, Kevin and Misty, and Peter and Lisa.

Rick sat there with a mixture of anticipation and dread over what he was going to hear about himself. When he saw where things were going the week before, he decided to take the exercise seriously. During the week he asked Waylon, Gary (from an employer perspective), and Drew for their positive and negative feedback. Waylon wouldn't take the exercise seriously, but Gary did an excellent job at both *Encouragement* and *Exhortation.* Drew did nothing but encourage, which felt good; but Rick knew that it wasn't an accurate assessment simply because everyone has areas where they need correction and exhortation.

Now, as he listened to the Team's feedback, it was very similar to what he had already heard from Gary. First, there was overwhelming affirmation of his passion and commitment to learning, along with his ability to help people understand biblical content. The real challenge for him was summarized by Jared's comment about his lack of interpersonal skills. Several others elaborated on his social discomfort and rigid interaction. There was plenty of affirmation, which took some of the sting out of the *Exhortation* part. But he also knew that he was going to have to be careful in processing the collective negatives; he couldn't afford to let them get the best of him emotionally. Fortunately, he had the recent success with Penny as a benchmark.

Ted and Jan were the last couple to go through the exercise. People provided *Encouragement* and *Exhortation,* but it seemed very superficial. Rick wondered if that was because others felt as uncomfortable with them as he did, or if their lives were really that shallow.

Peter concluded by increasing the Team's accountability interaction. The Maxwells either didn't hear, or ignored, the parameter of accountability partners not being spouses.

Peter also gave the Team a week off from meeting together as a group; instead, they were going to be held accountable for connecting with another couple or two to help strengthen relationships on a smaller scale.

During the next two weeks, Peter and Lisa received many telephone calls from individuals on the Team expressing what a blessing it was to connect with others at a level deeper than they imagined possible. As a couple, they were grateful to God for seeing His principles at work in the lives of those in whom they were investing.

FUN TIME

Fun time! Peter decided that with all the intensity surrounding the *Encouragement and Exhortation* exercise, a fun outing would provide a healthy release. The concept of having fun stimulated feelings of anxiety or disinterest in some, while others couldn't seem to get enough.

All week long, Peter and Lisa had been praying for God to give the Team an experience that would continue to strengthen relationships. They could organize the fun, but God was the One Who would make the spiritual impact.

The afternoon started off with a special meal. As the meal was winding down, Lisa handed out some instructions for a timed scavenger hunt between the guys and the gals. Five action items were listed with a scaled point system for each item. The last item was to be back at Peter and Lisa's one hour after the starting signal. Points would be deducted for each minute that either side was late.

During the usual adult study time, the kids typically were involved in a study of their own. This week, however, they were included in the fun. As the instructions were being read, the guys started to strategize. When Peter gave the signal, it looked like a cross between a football team and a mob running towards the parked vehicles. Vickie's car was abandoned when she figured out that Vern had snitched the keys from her pocketbook. A few tires squealed as cars and trucks headed off to get as much of the list completed as possible.

Over the next hour, it was amazing to watch the transformations that occurred. Each person's unique abilities started to go to work. The organizers were strategizing. Those wired aggressively were motivating others into action and passionately working at executing plans. The more compassionate were giving children things that they could do and still be safe. Some were the watchdogs, looking for signs of the other team and trying to determine how far ahead or behind they were. A few had managed to figure out how to booby trap the other team by bribing a cashier to stall a checkout process.

Time was running out. As both teams headed back toward Peter and Lisa's, the guys saw the gals just ahead of them. That was when the fairly easy-going Garret became a junk yard dog and yelled, "Hang on! We'll take them at the intersection. They had to stop for a red light."

He did a super job of anticipating when the light would turn green, and he couldn't resist stepping on the accelerator as he passed the gals. Vern was following right on Garret's bumper. What neither of them expected was the police cruiser in an oncoming lane about three cars behind an SUV. In a matter of seconds, the guys lead came to a roadside halt as flashing lights and a slightly ruffled police officer wrote out a couple of speeding tickets. One of Sam and Michelle's boys was crying, wondering if they were all going to jail.

The ladies just waved as they drove past.

Back at the house, some were laughing. Others were mock arguing over the techniques used by the other side. Garret was passing a hat to raise money to pay for the fines. Jared asked Burt if he could use his legal experience to get them out of the fines. And most of the gals were in a group huddle, jubilant about their win.

Michelle was in the bathroom, cleaning up an accident in her son's pants.

After things calmed down a little, Maggie vocalized what many were feeling, "I wasn't too sure about the value of a *non-spiritual* activity when fun was first introduced as part of our discipleship process, but I get it now. **Relationships need real-life interaction, not just intellectual stimulation."**

"Especially in light of the intensity of our recent studies," Vickie added.

Smiles and nods went around the room. Rick couldn't have agreed more. Never had he felt more connected to a group of people, and a lot of it was because of the fun factor.

Sam was standing next to Vern and, hearing his "ayuh" response, he saw an opportunity to try to uncork Vern's accent.

"Vern, you eva' had this much fun back ta Maine?" he mimicked.

Rick saw the setup and watched as Vern hesitated, playing Sam like a fish on a line. "Daow," he responded.

Sam looked a little crest-fallen before Vern continued, "But ole' Walta' Duffy come close."

"Walta'?" Sam was back in the game.

"Ayuh. You see, Walta' wa-n't a very religious man, but his wife Muert'l come to ou'a church pretty reg'la. One night, Walta' got inta the kick-a-poo joy juice with a coupla' his buddies dow'n ta tha ba'. On his way home, he hit one a' those frost heaves that rocketed him inta space. When his ca' come back dow'n, it landed on a patch of black i'ce. Well sa', he begun to spin 'round and 'round a thousan' miles ta hou'a—hit all fou'a co'nna's of that ole' Impala he wuz drivin' befo'a endin' up in the pucka'brush. Fautunately Earl McGinnus was followin' him and managed to get him down ta the hospital—roum three fau'teen, I think it wuz."

"Three fau'teen? You shu'a?" Sam fed the fire.

With a straight face, Vern just kept going. "Well, Muert'l, she saw her chance ta have the pasta' talk sum religion inta Walta'. The pasta' walked inta Walta's room (I'm pretty shu'a it wuz roum three fau'teen), and he didn't waste much time gettin' ta the point. 'Walta, the Lau'd wuz shu'a watchin' out fo'a ya.'

"Poo'a Walta' laid the'a lookin' like a co'nna'd bobcat with his brain tryin' ta figu'ya a way out. Finally, he looked up and said, 'Well, I wish't He'd been a drivin.'"

When Vern finished, Burt jokingly asked Vickie, "Where did you find him anyway?"

"Ba' Ha'ba', Maine."

Everyone laughed.

"By the way, Burt, maybe everyone else knows, but where's Betty?" Vickie asked.

"She had to prepare for the Capital Campaign Recognition Dinner tonight," Burt replied.

The Discipleship Team was having a ton of fun with each other on a very real level; but Betty was headed toward spending time with someone at a very low level; at least, that's what it would look like on the surface.

PARTNERSHIP OOPS

Betty had been a leader in a recent Capital Campaign to raise several million dollars needed for public improvement projects for the Tri-city area. After a year and a half of very hard work, they had reached their goal. Betty was being recognized as the integral catalyst for that success.

She listened to the words of praise being spoken about her and couldn't help but sit there with flashbacks of similar experiences from her childhood and early adult years. No matter what the accomplishment, the one person she wanted recognition from—her dad—was never there. And now, she was being recognized for one of the most significant achievements of her career without Burt.

He had fully intended to be there but had stopped by the office to take care of a few pressing case details for the next day. His short stop turned into several hours and, before he knew it, it was ten o'clock. He went home and dropped into bed exhausted, expecting Betty not to be too far behind him.

Usually, Betty could shake off the negative feelings that pressed in on her soul at times like this. Her typical method of coping was to focus on the next goal with hopes that it would become the time she'd be valued by the one from whom she most wanted praise. But on a couple of previous occasions, she had found that alcohol was a powerful escape from the pain of reality.

As she sat there, she began to look at the rich color in the refilled wine glass. Brief thoughts of what she had been learning about her *Paradigm* and *Past* flitted through her mind. Slowly, though, she reached out and let her fingers caress the glass's smooth contour before raising it to her lips; the wonderful taste and internal warmth it provided was a comforting sensation. She didn't remember asking for more, but she must have… several times.

Later, old but familiar feelings of nausea began to come over her. Somehow she had the presence of mind to excuse herself and head for the ladies' room. From that point in time, she had faint memories of someone helping her through a blurred series of events until she found herself slowly waking up in unfamiliar surroundings, in an unfamiliar bed.

Burt woke up to discover that Betty hadn't come home the night before. He tried calling her cell phone, but only her annoying voice mail message greeted him.

Hearing the phone ring and seeing Burt's number, Betty was torn between her desire to get home as fast as she could and fear of what Burt was going to think of her. Fidelity was one of their strongest values as a couple. Now she wasn't even sure where she was in relation to that value. Thinking about it added to her nausea, physically and emotionally.

At home, Burt was talking out loud to diffuse his anxiety. "Get a grip, Burt! Panic will not help you at a time like this."

Before calling the police, Burt decided to call Peter and let him know what was going on, and to ask him to have Rick and Garret come over for support.

The next hour passed in slow motion for Burt. Before he could call the police, Betty pulled into the driveway. All she could do when she got inside was cry. Moments later, Peter, Rick, Penny, Garret, and Maggie arrived. Betty was sitting on the sofa in tear-stained anxiety. Maggie and Penny quickly surrounded her, which seemed to give her comfort.

Garret volunteered to pray and afterward calmly asked, "What happened, Betty?"

Bursting into tears she sobbed, "I'm not…exactly…sure."

As pieces of the puzzle came together, Burt sat there trying to digest what he was hearing. Waves of regret crashed down on him as he listened to Betty express the voids of affirmation she felt at important times of her life. He was also wishing he knew how to express his feelings of inferiority as he constantly tried to measure up to Betty's successes, not to justify himself, but to let her know that he understood how she felt. He empathized with her lapse in judgment over having too much to drink. But when he heard about someone helping her to one of the hotel rooms, he came unglued.

"You slept with someone last night?!"

Betty buried her face in her hands and, in a voice that could barely be heard, said, "I don't know, Burt."

"You don't know? How could you end up in one of the hotel rooms without knowing whether or not you slept with someone?"

"What *do* you know, Betty?" Peter quietly asked.

"I was still partially dressed when I woke up. My blouse was on a clothes hanger, but other than that, it looked like I slept in my clothes."

Just then, Betty's phone rang. Someone from the hotel's service desk was calling to tell her that Mr. Osborne had left her an envelope marked "Personal."

"Who's Mr. Osborne?" Burt asked.

"Joseph Osborne. He's one of the managers from the firm we hired to help us with our Capital Campaign."

"Was he the one who helped take care of you last night?"

"Maybe. Honestly, Burt, I was as drunk as I've ever been. I don't remember much."

"Well, it looks like we'll find out soon enough. Let's go back to the hotel and pick up that envelope."

"You go. I'm not up to it."

"I can't go and pick up an envelope marked 'Personal' in your name."

"I'll call the hotel and let them know I'm sending you."

Betty called to make the arrangement and, moments later, Peter and the guys headed to the hotel with Burt. On the way, Peter asked, "Burt, are you prepared for what you may find out?"

"How can I be?"

Gently Peter tried to help Burt remember and apply the truths he had been learning. "For starters, would you say that the events of last night were generated from Betty's *Past*, *Paradigm*, or *Potential* issues?"

Somewhat mechanically, Burt responded, "Her *Past*."

"Are you prepared to forgive and support her as she deals with those issues?"

"I want to; but what if this is more than a *Past* issue? "What if she's been having an affair?"

Keeping his voice low, Peter asked, "What truth do you have to support such an idea?"

"None. It's just that you hear about things like this, but you never really think that it could happen to you. Then—just like that—the possibility is staring you in the face."

Peter sat quietly praying, refusing to give trite answers to Burt's grief. He knew that everyone dealt with situations like this differently and was just thankful to be present with other members of the Team to help both Burt and Betty process the truth of their circumstances, balanced with the grace of Jesus. *"We have seen Jesus' glory…full of grace and truth,"* Peter quoted to himself.

After picking up the envelope, they headed back to the Larsons' home where Betty read the letter out loud.

"Betty, this was the most discrete way I could think of to save you from an embarrassing situation. You have been nothing but motivated and professional throughout this entire campaign, so I'll not presume to guess the reason for your over-indulgence. You do need to know, though, that you ended up going into the men's room to relieve the effects of the alcohol you consumed. I just happened to be there to intervene. Weighing the options, I felt that your physical well-being and reputation would be best protected if you slept things off in one of the hotel's rooms. I took you to my room to expedite your safety, and then got myself another room. As far as I'm concerned, this is in the past. However, please know that, in the process of helping you, I've never been so scared in my life. If there's ever a next time, you're on your own. Respectfully, Joseph Osborne."

Initial relief was visibly evident in both Burt's and Betty's faces. Burt gently pulled Betty to her feet and gave her a long, warm hug while whispering in her ear, "I love you."

Looking at Peter, Burt asked, "Where do we go from here?"

"As hard as this is, it could be the turning point that takes your marriage, and your relationship with the Lord, to a level higher than you could possibly have imagined. I would suggest that the two of you take whatever time you need to process the causes behind the choices you have made as a couple. Address changes that you feel are needed. If you get stuck at any point, we are more than willing to help however we can."

"Thanks," Burt replied.

"What about the Discipleship Team as a whole?" Betty asked. "They are going to need to know what happened, aren't they?"

Exhaling slightly, Peter asked, "Do the two of you trust your Team well enough to use this experience as an opportunity to address perhaps the most difficult and sensitive issues of the spiritual *Teen* development process?"

"I do," Betty answered. "If someone can risk their reputation trying to protect mine, it's time I took ownership for my actions so that I can move forward."

"How about you, Burt?" Peter gently pressed.

"I'm a little torn. To be honest, I don't want to be viewed as an uncaring husband. Neither do I want Betty's reputation and career jeopardized. I'm thankful for the support of those of you who came, but that seems like it should be enough. Do we have to do this in front of the whole Team?"

Quietly, Peter asked, "What kind of answer do you think God would provide for that question?"

"You've alluded to the fact that **holistic spiritual growth cannot be achieved independent of the Christian community.**"

"In this case, Burt, you are not going to be forced to do something you are unwilling to do. But, are you willing to test whether or not that allusion is true?" Peter respectfully challenged.

"What if someone breaks confidence? What if the information we share privately with the Team becomes public knowledge?"

Rick joined in. "Are your 'what if' questions motivated out of a God-centered *Paradigm* or a self-centered *Paradigm?*"

Out of long habit, Burt responded from his legal background. "The number one expectation for this Team is credibility. How can I know that the entire Team is trustworthy?"

Garret ventured, "Is God trustworthy? Is He big enough to walk you through a possible breach of confidentiality within the Christian community?"

"Yes, He is. But I still struggle with human nature."

"So do I," Rick agreed; "but the starting point of obedience is to determine what God wants us to do. Then, it's a matter of trusting Him to walk us through the process regardless of the choices other people make. **Walking by faith is not always a smooth journey; in fact, it can be downright messy at times. But we have a reliable Guide.**"

Peter gave Burt time to process what he was hearing before adding, "Burt, you are free to choose what you want to do with this. I'm sharing how I think you can experience optimum growth. Not everyone is ready for that. I will respect your decision either way. I did want to give you all the positive reasons to incorporate your Team members into your spiritual development process, but I will truly understand if you choose not to."

After several moments, Burt agreed to move forward with disclosure and Team discussions. Peter was confident he would not regret that decision; but he did underestimate one couple's reaction.

ADVENTURE 19 – PARTNERSHIP: CONFLICT RESOLUTION

Having obtained Burt and Betty's approval, Peter and Lisa decided to meet with as many of the Team members as possible before their next regular study. They wanted to stop the rumor mill and lay a foundation for positive and productive communication before the Team got together with Burt and Betty. Surprisingly, everyone was able to make it Wednesday evening.

After stressing the importance of confidentiality, Peter briefly outlined the events that had transpired in Burt's and Betty's lives over the last few days. When he finished, he asked if there were any questions or points to clarify.

Ted was first to respond. "Should they even be on the Team anymore?"

"I can't believe you would think such a thing!" Misty exclaimed. Several others nodded in agreement.

"Well, if Betty's going to get drunk every time she doesn't get the support she wants, that's a huge breach of credibility, not to mention the likelihood of infidelity," Ted responded defensively.

An awkward silence followed Ted's comment, but Peter didn't let things hang for very long. "What do the rest of you think?"

Garret interjected, "If I remember correctly, Peter was pretty clear that failure was not the focal point of credibility." Looking at Peter, he continued, "Didn't you say that failure with ownership was acceptable?"

"Yes; blame-shifting and making excuses for failure is what disintegrates credibility."

"That's exactly what I mean!" Ted responded hotly. "Everyone who gets drunk has some reason they hide behind to excuse their behavior."

Penny, who was generally quiet, looked at Ted and asked, "Is your response towards Betty's behavior motivated out of a concern for her *Potential* or out of challenges from your own *Past?*"

Ted's eyes narrowed to icy slits. "What would you know about drunks and cheats?"

Rick's blood pressure was rising fast. Just as he was about to put Ted in his place, Penny gently placed her hand on his leg. Looking at Ted, she calmly responded, "Ted, I do empathize with all that you went through with your first wife, but I don't think that—"

"Don't think?!" Ted exploded. "You have no idea what you're talking about!"

Jan tried to calm her husband and run interference. "Maybe it would be helpful if we just moved on. Ted always gets excited when it comes to the topic of alcohol."

By this time, several Team members were very uncomfortable, and Michelle looked like she was going to burst into tears.

Peter knew that he needed to move on and talk with Ted one-on-one. He tried to bring some stability and clarity to the Team. "First of all, I want you to know that you're doing well at expressing your feelings, as long as it doesn't turn into personal attacks. Right now, we have two topics on the table; so let's separate them. At some point we need to talk about the principles of conflict resolution. We also need to finish talking about the principles of spiritual discipline without it being solely about Burt and Betty."

"Could you give us a crash course in conflict resolution?" Rick asked. Murmurs of agreement skittered around the room.

"Sure. It's not too hard to explain; the challenge is putting the principles into practice. You can study more about what I'm going to share with you by going to the website of PeaceMaker Ministries (www.peacemaker.net). I attended one of their training seminars years ago, and it was the best conflict resolution material I've ever been exposed to."

As Peter was gearing up to teach, Rick reached for paper and pen. He was learning that Peter's insights were valuable information and that life lessons could come at any time and in some very unusual settings.

"To start with, there are two basic responses to conflict: biblical and natural. Natural responses also fall into two patterns: aggressive and passive."

Wheels were spinning as everyone processed this information in light of the evening's conversation.

"In keeping with the *Two* pattern we've got going, there are two types of conflict: principle-based and pride-based. Principle-based conflict will always resolve itself with biblical responses. Pride-based conflict will result in aggressive or negative response patterns."

Rick looked up and noticed Ted's body language. He was not enjoying the information he was hearing.

"I learned from Peacemaker Ministries that pride-based conflict is caused by a four-step idolatry process: *Desire, Demand, Judgment, and Punishment.* Conflict starts with a *Desire,* which may or may not be principled. The way you determine whether or not it's principled is to see if the desire turns into a *Demand*— 'I have to have my *Desire* in order to be happy.' Once someone is in *Demand* mode, he very easily transitions into *Judging* those who don't give him what he wants. He ends the cycle by *Punishing* those standing in the way of his *Desire.*"

Peter continued, "Biblical confrontation and negotiation, as well as confession and forgiveness, are the tools needed to resolve pride-based conflict."

The teacher in Maggie was asking for clarification. "Disagreement doesn't necessarily mean that we're involved in pride-based conflict, does it?"

"Not at all. In fact, passionately stating your beliefs often becomes the window people can look through to discover truth. The problem comes when a person *Demands* that others see things his or her way instead of letting the Holy Spirit lead people to the truth."

Ted was sulking now. Jan put her arm around him for support.

Gary voiced what many were thinking. "So what are the principles we need to discuss to be able to resolve the situation with Burt and Betty? What did you mean by 'spiritual discipline principles'?"

Peter was glad to move forward. "Some of the questions about failure that need to be answered by us as a Team are

(1) *Why* does God discipline His children? (2) *How* does God discipline His children? and (3) *When* does God discipline His children? "Let's start with the *Why* question first."

Kevin cautiously asked, "Isn't this question a lot like the 'What does God think about us?' question you asked when we covered *Paradigm* growth?"

Peter was excited about this observation. "Good connection, Kevin! God is always looking at the redemptive potential in each of us. He has a special interest in His children. God does not randomly discipline His children. He is always motivated out of a desire to help them live up to their highest redemptive *Potential.*"

"How does God discipline His children?" Michelle asked tentatively.

"Think about biblical stories like Adam and Eve's disobedience, Sarah's unbelief, Lot's love for this world, Joseph's brothers' mistreatment of him, the Israelites' frequent complaining and unbelief, King Saul's partial obedience, Peter's denial of Jesus, and Ananias and Sapphira's lying to Peter. What are some conclusions we can draw?" Peter queried to stimulate their thinking.

"From a case worker's perspective, I would have to say that God doesn't initially employ a heavy hand," volunteered Misty. "He gave Adam and Eve ample opportunity to repent before he used discipline. His discipline of Sarah is actually humorous; His name for her son was a constant reminder that God is greater than her unbelief. With Peter, God asked soul-piercing questions that subtly got to the heart of his issues. Even with Sapphira, He didn't immediately strike her dead with her husband; He gave her a chance to be truthful, independent of her husband."

"But He does hold people accountable for their actions," Gary pressed.

Peter responded, "That's where I was hoping someone would go. We need to add the balancing principle. My personal philosophy of ministry is to **grant grace until it has a crippling effect on others or until there is indication of a hardened heart**. One of the ways to determine whether or not someone has a hardened heart is by creating a diagnostic evaluation and feedback plan."

Peter worked to set the stage for their next Team meeting. "Between now and next Sunday afternoon, take some time to answer the following question in your own mind and heart: How should we balance grace and truth in relation to failure and discipline? We are going to talk about *Diagnostic Evaluations and Feedback*, which will help us answer tonight's final question, *When* does God discipline His children?"

Peter had Garret close in prayer. Several stayed behind to ask questions and encourage each other, but Ted and Jan didn't waste much time preparing to leave.

"Should I talk with Ted?" Rick quietly questioned Peter.

"How do you think he will respond?"

"Not very well."

"Are you ready to skillfully walk him through the truth he needs for inner resolution?"

"Probably not, but he needs help!"

"How do you think God wants you to help him?"

"I'll pray for him first, and then see if someone with more skill than I currently possess would talk with him."

Peter smiled and gratefully watched Rick walk over and talk to Garret instead.

ADVENTURE 20 – PARTNERSHIP: GRACE OR DISCIPLINE?

Sunday afternoon brought a mixture of warmth and nervousness as the Team gathered for lunch. Several people went over and gave Burt and Betty hugs.

Rick couldn't help but notice that Ted hung back and kept to himself. Jan seemed okay, carrying on conversations with several of the ladies. Rick couldn't be sure, but it seemed to him that she was avoiding Betty.

Peter had talked to Rick earlier in the week about leading this week's lesson. Rick had strongly objected because of the sensitive nature of the Team's current challenges. Peter reminded him that, if he was heading for pastoral ministry, he would have to learn how to deal with delicate situations calmly and with confidence. Reluctantly, Rick agreed; but internally, he was wondering if Gary's offer to train him as a foreman was a better fit for him.

During his preparation, Rick could imagine Ted's reaction to what he would share. No matter how hard he tried, he couldn't seem to get Ted out of his mind. The closer Sunday came, the sicker to his stomach Rick began to feel. Finally, just before the worship service, Rick told Peter what was going on.

"That's completely normal!" Peter reassured his friend. "Never let one person rob your message. God made your nerves to help you communicate; you just need to learn how to manage them instead of allowing them to control you."

Now, with the Team all around him, Rick breathed a quick prayer. "Okay, Dad; we both know that I need Your help right now. Please speak through me."

"All right, everyone, we're going to get started with our study."

Ted looked up at Rick, and then took a seat where a recliner blocked his line of vision. Rick was silently grateful to God for the intervention, and his confidence rose a little.

"Last Wednesday night, Pete challenged us with the question, 'How should we balance grace and truth as it relates to spiritual failure and discipline?' He was asking, in essence, 'When do you move from grace to discipline?' I've asked Penny to pass around a handout that I put together to help us process this concept. On the front side of the handout, I would like you to evaluate where you would place yourself, on a scale of one to ten, with one being total grace and ten being total discipline. Those of you who are willing to share the results of where you fit on the continuum will be encouraged to do so."

Michelle was first to volunteer her results. "I've struggled all week with the concept of discipline. Most of you know what a soft-hearted person I am. I would place myself at a one or two at most."

Jared spoke next with a chuckle. "I'd be clean to the other end. I struggle with what I call *Sloppy Grace* where people are free to do whatever they want without consequences."

The rest of the team were more moderate than Michelle or Jared, but they were pretty evenly divided between grace and discipline. Ted managed to avoid scaling himself.

Rick continued, "From the biblical study I did this week, God seems very interested in the performance of His children. Every place God gave responsibility, He also incorporated accountability. He also seems to exercise grace in the way that He gives responsibility to people."

"What passages did you study?" Lisa asked.

"Jesus told several parables about a master giving responsibility to his servants and then demanding an accounting when he returned. The grace factor in those parables was that the master didn't demand more from people than he knew they were capable of delivering. He varied their responsibility and then held them accountable only for that level of responsibility. I also studied the final judgment for followers of Jesus at the *Judgment Seat of Christ.*"

"Those are good observations, Rick," Lisa affirmed.

Encouraged, Rick moved forward toward an application he felt God had given to him. "It seems to make sense that, **if God is holding us accountable for living out His plan for our lives, it would be beneficial to evaluate our performance before we stand in front of Him with no further opportunity for adjustments.**"

"Did you learn that from the Bible, or from being part of my company?" Gary teased him.

"I really did learn it from the Bible. But, now that you mention it, I can see that you are actually practicing this principle with those that work for you. We know exactly what you expect from us. You let us know when we are doing well, and you tell us the areas where you want to see improvement."

Gary continued, "What do you think would happen if you ignored my suggestions for improvement?"

Rick was excited as he watched God providing practical illustrations that he could never have dreamed up. "That would take us to our original scaling question of where you place yourself on that line between grace and discipline, wouldn't it?"

Gary grinned. "Yes, it would."

"If I remember correctly, you were around a seven on the discipline side. If I'm making the correct assumption, that would mean you would give me a thirty percent margin to get my act together before you started implementing consequences."

Gary agreed, and everyone seemed to make the connection.

Rick presented four questions for Team discussion. "These questions will summarize all that we have been learning this past week. First, Where does God want us to scale ourselves as a Team on that line between grace and discipline? Second, How willing are we to identify our God-given responsibilities? Third, Are we willing to evaluate our performance in each of those areas and give honest feedback to each other? And last of all, How will we communicate when we are moving from grace to truthful discipline when we fail?"

Lively feedback followed. The general conclusion to the first question was that it is a wisdom issue, depending on personal growth variables and the visible attitude of the individual.

The second question was turned into homework. During the upcoming week, everyone had to identify their God-given responsibilities.

For the third question, Rick requested that everyone scale out and share their answers. Most everyone was willing to have their own performance evaluated; however, they expressed insecurity about giving honest feedback to others for poor performance.

Rick closed his lesson. "Peter would like to lead us through a direct application to answer the final question, How will we communicate when we are moving from grace to truthful discipline in those areas where we fail?"

PARTNERSHIP: RESTORATION

As Peter took over the teaching, he acknowledged Rick's work. "What did everyone think about Rick's teaching abilities today?"

Almost instantaneous clapping and whistling erupted. Rick didn't know whether to smile or turn red. He ended up doing a little of both.

"And now, for the delicate part of this application. I've talked with Burt and Betty ahead of time, so they are prepared. They both have courageously agreed to be the first to apply this process to their recent circumstances." Peter continued passionately, "But I want to make it abundantly clear that, from time to time, any one of us can end up where they were last weekend. And, to help illustrate that point, as well as to diffuse Burt and Betty's discomfort, let me ask you how many of you have your act completely together right now?"

Vern and Vickie looked at each other in tacit agreement before Vern spoke. "Truth be told, Vickie and I have ou'a own issues. I can put on a good front, but behind the scenes it is not uncommon fa' me to use alcohol as a stress relieva', and that has caused problems several times in our marriage."

Peter caught Ted rolling his eyes as Vern spoke.

Kevin and Misty joined in. "Our finances are a mess. We made poor choices early in our marriage, and they have haunted us ever since. At least once a month, we get into a knock down-drag out fight over our financial situation."

Sam choked up as he shared. "This whole experience has resurfaced a variety of challenges Michelle and I have faced. A few years into our marriage, I was sexually involved with a co-worker. We've been to counseling and worked through a lot of stuff; but when something touches those scars just right, we find that we still have struggles. This week, I actually saw the same pain in Michelle's body language that stimulated some of those gut-wrenching, debilitating feelings of shame I had during the months we worked through our reconciliation. Sometimes, I just want to run and hide from the shame of my failure. I'm still not sure if Michelle completely trusts me."

It took obvious effort for Michelle to control her emotions. "I'm finding that forgiveness does not equal a pain-free life. Sam's infidelity caused me such acute pain! It was like being in a serious accident. At first, I didn't even know if I was going to live. Then, slowly, I began to heal. But at the slightest bump, those wounds would start to bleed again. In time, things healed; but I needed rehabilitation to learn how to do life a different way. And even now, after all the therapy is over and I've discovered a new normal, all it takes is an unexpected hit for the pain to return. At those times, I have to repeat the healing process."

Peter and Lisa were encouraged as they watched the Team's response to these members' courageous admissions. Instead of awkward silence, there was an outpouring of genuine empathy and support.

Jared placed a can of chew on the coffee table. "It probably doesn't seem like much compared to what some of you have shared, but I've been a slave to smokeless tobacco for twenty years. The longest I've ever been free from it was a month. Ruth doesn't say much, but I know she would appreciate it if I quit. And the Holy Spirit always lets me know what He thinks about my addiction."

Ruth slipped up behind her husband and wrapped her arms around his neck.

To lighten things up a bit, Maggie quipped, "I kick my cat. My psychologist thinks it's because I was not allowed to express myself between the ages of two and three."

Garret reached out and pretended to choke her, then deadpanned, "I have no issues."

Good-natured responses let Garret and Maggie know that they succeeded in diffusing the emotional overload.

"I think you're beginning to see what I mean." Peter focused the Team on the application. **"The two greatest negative factors to discipline are (1) an *I'm-better-than-you* attitude and (2) the lack of a restoration plan."**

"Why is that?" Ruth puzzled.

"My experience with the first factor is that, the harder it is for someone to identify with failure, the greater their pride. With the second factor, many people dislike confrontation so much that, when they finally get up the nerve to address a failure in someone else, they are just relieved to get the confrontation behind them and ignore the other person's need for a restoration plan."

"How do you create a restoration plan?" Garret asked.

"It's helpful to find out if the failure is conditional or constant. If the failure is conditional, then a *Preventative* restoration plan can be developed. If the failure is constant, a *Corrective* restoration plan needs to be developed."

Misty spoke up. "Based on that information, it sounds like what Burt and Betty need is a *Preventative* restoration plan."

Everyone breathed a sigh of relief, as Burt initiated a portion of the process. "Maybe a *Preventative* restoration plan is what Betty needs, but I need a *Corrective* restoration plan. My entire life has revolved around proving myself to those that matter the most to me. I'm a workaholic driven by unhealthy motives."

Peter could now move forward productively. "What I'd like to do next is collectively develop those restoration plans and then, as a Team, commit ourselves to implementing them."

"How?" Michelle asked.

"By identifying the specific areas that need evaluation and feedback and then developing a plan for how that evaluation and feedback will continue until it is no longer needed."

"That makes a lot of sense to me," Garret piped up. "Let's get started."

Soon the room was buzzing with helpful questions for Burt and Betty. With the exception of Ted and Jan, there was a stronger sense of Team camaraderie than ever before.

Betty identified that, before a significant event, she needed to communicate to Burt what her expectations were for him. She agreed with Lisa's recommendation that she read at least one book to help with her God-centered *Paradigm* identity. Betty also felt that it was necessary to have someone she could call to diffuse negative emotions if she felt like Burt had failed her. Kim asked if Betty would like to partner with her for two-way diagnostic evaluations and feedback, and Betty gladly agreed. Kim had her own list of things she wanted Betty to hold her accountable for.

Burt determined that what he needed was a realistic weekly schedule, with a fudge factor of no more than three to five hours. He also wanted to be held accountable for taking Betty out on a date at least twice a month. And he agreed to attend every significant event where Betty felt she needed support.

Vern interjected, "I don't see why we all a'un't doing this. I would think that all of us have issues that need a *Preventative* plan befoa' resta'ration or ca'rection becomes necessary."

In the next ten minutes, nearly everyone on the Team identified a couple of things that they wanted diagnostic evaluation and feedback on and shared those results with their accountability partners to help the process succeed.

Peter closed the lesson by having everyone pray a one-sentence prayer of blessing for the person to their left. As the team began to pray for each other, the Holy Spirit ministered in ways not previously experienced, with one exception.

PARTNERSHIP DEPARTURE

As the rest of the team began praying for each other, Ted and Jan quietly worked their way to the door.

Hearing the door open, Peter and Lisa followed Ted and Jan outside.

"Are you two all right?" Lisa asked.

"Yeah, we just have to get home," Ted answered vaguely.

Peter pressed the issue. "Are you sure, Ted? It didn't appear that you agreed with the processes we laid out tonight." He knew where the Team was heading, and so far Ted and Jan hadn't displayed, by actions or attitudes, that they were heading in the same direction. "Are you still in support of our five Team expectations?"

Ted's response wasn't too much of a surprise. "If you prefer alcoholics, perverts, and addicts to people who take real biblical standards seriously, we don't want to be part of this supposed 'Team'."

"I believe you need this Team for your own spiritual development and growth. Don't you think it would be a mistake to leave before you see things through to the end?"

Ted exploded, "*Staying* would be the mistake. And that includes attending this church, which you seem bent on turning into some wishy-washy group therapy clinic. You've just helped me decide that we need to find a church home with expectations that focus more on biblical standards than sloppy 'touchy-feely' stuff. *Trust— Teamwork—Two-way Talking....* What a joke!"

Peter and Lisa were experiencing that strange but familiar mixture of gut-wrenching turmoil and wonderful release. They hurt because this couple's growth would be stunted; but they were also relieved that the rest of the Team would be protected from Ted and Jan's unresolved issues.

As the Maxwells got into their car and drove away, Lisa put her arm around Peter and stated, "From time to time, I *almost* want to change what I believe about Christians not being able to be demon-possessed."

Peter answered, "It's obvious that some serious spiritual warfare has been taking place this week. Let's pray before we go back inside to break the news of the Maxwells' decision to the rest of the Team."

Prayers from the Team inside the house, and now prayers from Peter and Lisa outside, were already being acted upon. Heavenly task forces were barring demon access to and influence on the Team; enemy plans were effectively foiled. God's kingdom would advance through this Team; faith would prevail.

"Hey, where did you two slip off to?" Maggie jokingly asked, as Peter and Lisa re-entered the house.

"Ted and Jan have decided that they would rather be part of a different type of Christian community than the one we are creating here."

Garret spoke what the others seemed to be thinking. "That really doesn't surprise me."

"Is this because of us?" Betty asked.

"I don't think so," Penny replied. "Ted never really answered my question last week about the struggles from his *Past*."

"Is this a living illustration of how powerful a person's unresolved *Past* can be?" Sam asked, looking at Peter.

"That is a very real possibility; however, I will add some balance to my answer. Sometimes when truth intersects a person's life, he or she is not in a position to respond effectively.

"You mean he could still be in the *Childhood* phase?" Vickie questioned.

"That's also a possibility; but, that doesn't mean that our time spent with Ted and Jan over the last several months won't yield fruit at a later time. **Some people respond to truth immediately; others experience a progressive journey where the response is gradual and genuine. The saddest cases are those where the heart is so hard that penetration requires spiritual shock treatment or ends in a fatal heart attack.**"

As the Team sat there processing this recent turn of events in light of all they had been through this past week, there was a spirit of unity that created determination to live out the truth they were learning.

No one was in a hurry to leave.

HE, WHAT?

Rick found that, every other weekend, he had a roommate. Waylon found his way to Kennewick to be with Miriam one weekend, and then she would travel to Enterprise the following weekend.

One weekend, Waylon shared some disturbing news with Rick. "I saw The Old Man parked in front of the school in Wallowa on my way over here."

Rick raised eyebrows. "And?"

"It was strange. I stopped to see what was up and, when I tapped on the window, he didn't roll it down; so I just opened the door. There was a kid in the front seat with him and neither one of them seemed very happy to see me. It was like I interrupted something. When I asked what he was doing, he told me it was none of my business. I gave him a long, hard look and, about that time, the kid said, 'I'll come back later.' When the kid got out, The Old Man just fired up his truck and drove off, but not toward home."

Rick's forehead wrinkled. "What do you suppose he was up to?"

"Beats me; but, just as I opened the door, I thought I saw something in the kid's hand. Whatever it was disappeared so quickly that I don't really know what I saw."

"Maybe it was one of the kids from church."

"I already thought of that, but I don't remember seeing this kid before."

"You ain't exactly been a regular attender lately."

Waylon gave one of his rare, goofy smiles, but it quickly turned into a frown. Rick could tell that something was eating at him.

"Hey, Pete's helped walk me through some pretty tough issues. Why don't you talk to him about it?"

Waylon looked up hopefully. "Maybe I will."

That night when the brothers got back to the apartment, Rick asked, "You talk with Pete?"

"Yeah. I'm still trying to connect some of the discipleship stuff he mentioned with The Old Man, but he really helped Miriam and me with a couple of little hiccups we've been having."

"Speaking of Miriam, how are things going for you two?"

Waylon smiled. "I think she's the one!"

Rick had to admit that he, too, was slowly but surely becoming convinced that he would feel privileged if Penny would agree to marry him. He said as much to Waylon. And that was all the two of them needed to begin to conspire what the ultimate proposal would look like. After getting permission from Penny and Miriam's parents, the brothers executed their New Year's Eve proposal plans.

WEDDING PLANS & WHIPLASH

Leaving early on New Year's Eve morning, Waylon and Miriam headed down the interstate toward Portland to "do some shopping."

In the Gorge, Waylon pulled into the Multnomah Falls parking lot and, arm-in-arm, they walked up the trail towards the Falls. As they neared the bridge, Waylon asked a stranger if he would be willing to take a picture of him and Miriam. Positioning Miriam against the rail slightly off-center of the Falls, he reached into his vest pocket and removed a ring while getting down on one knee. Looking into her eyes, he asked if she would be willing to become Mrs. Waylon Thomson. Just as she said a resounding 'Yes!' the stranger immortalized the moment on camera.

As they finished their drive into Portland, they discussed possible wedding dates and surprised each other by deciding to catch a flight to Vegas and bring the New Year in as husband and wife.

Back in Kennewick, Rick had planned a special evening, starting at Penny's favorite restaurant. After a delightful entrée and pleasant conversation, the waiter asked for their dessert orders. Upon his return, he placed a dessert at each place, along with a third plate slightly in front of Penny with a small velvet box on it. Reaching for Penny's hand, Rick looked into the eyes of the woman he had grown to love like no other and asked her if she would accept his offer to become his wife. With a blush creeping up her neck and into her face, she quietly whispered, "Yes."

For the next hour, Rick was floating on clouds; he couldn't tell for sure where he was. But one question quickly changed that. "Penny, when do think we could get married?"

After what seemed like an eternity, she replied, "A year from this coming summer."

Instantly, Rick crashed back down to earth, fighting anger and confusion. "Why wait so long?" he asked tersely.

She smiled sweetly. "It's not really that far away, Rick. I've always wanted an outdoor summer wedding, but there are too many details that need to be figured out for me to feel comfortable getting married this summer. I don't want to go into this feeling pressured. I want to be able to enjoy every minute."

Rick was storming inside. *How many details could there possibly be? Pressured?! Are you sure ten years wouldn't be better? I thought you said you loved me! Is this some kind of stall technique?* Later, he was grateful that he hadn't known about Waylon and Miriam's decision to get married that night. It might have pushed his temper over the edge.

The rest of the evening was just plain weird for Rick. Penny had a glow on her face that showed she couldn't have been happier. He, on the other hand, didn't know how to express that she had just given him an unjust jail sentence. Her parting hug tried its best to win over the raging confusion in his head. As he drifted off to sleep, his last thought was, *Maybe Pete can help me again. I can't seem to make sense of what's going on.*

ADVENTURE 21 –
PERSONAL WIRING

The next morning Rick called Peter as early as he dared and asked if he could come over.

"Lisa and the kids are sleeping in, so why don't I take you out to breakfast?"

As Rick was walking out the door, Waylon called to tell him about his proposal and wedding. A half hour later, Rick found himself pouring out his guts. "I don't get it, Pete. Waylon asks Miriam to marry him, and they get married the same day; Penny wants to wait a year and a half. What's with that? Does she love me or not?"

Peter just reached for a napkin and began to draw a box. "Rick, how much do you know about personal wiring, also referred to as temperament types or personalities?"

"Not much; but what does that have to do with waiting to get married?"

"Everything. **When God creates people, he wires them in unique and specific ways. If you understand the basic wiring differences in people, it will help you to interact with them more productively.**"

"I hope so, because this isn't making any sense to me at all."

"First, let me start by explaining the basic wiring differences, and then see if we can apply that information to what you are experiencing right now."

Rick had received enough help already to know that he could trust his friend. "Okay. Let's do it."

A-1 Powerful	R E L A T I O N A L	A-2 Playful
ACTION / REACTION DIFFERENCE		
B-1 Perfectionist	D I F F E R E N C E	B-2 Pleasant

Inside the box that Pete had drawn, he added a horizontal bar through the middle. "This line represents the action/reaction differences between people. I'll label the top side as A-type people, typically characterized by high energy and action. Their action indicators include being assertive, competitive, demanding, extroverted, and optimistic. Their primary reaction is typically anger.

"On the bottom side are the B-type people, typically characterized by low-key actions. They are reserved, cooperative, negotiating, introverted, and realistic/pessimistic people. Their primary reactions would be fear/worry.

Next Pete drew a vertical bar through the middle of the box. "This line represents the relational differences between people. Those on the left side, I will label as 1's. These people are Contributors who measure their value by what they accomplish or create. They are emotionally guarded, reserved, rational, and task-oriented people. Their greatest expression of love is what they can do for someone.

"Those on the right side, I will label as 2's. These people are Relaters. They are emotionally expressive, affectionate, friendly, feeling-oriented, and relational. Their greatest expression of love is the time they can spend with people.

"There are a number of assessment tools that go into a lot more detail than what I am sharing with you. Every assessment has its own descriptors for each category ranging from adjectives and character qualities to animal names and colors. But for now, let me give you the basic descriptors that I use for the four basic wiring categories.

Peter took the napkin and added descriptor words for each of the four sections. In the A1 box, he wrote the word *Powerful*; in the A2 box, he wrote *Playful*; for the B2 box, he wrote the word *Pleasant*; and in the B1 box, he wrote *Perfectionist*.

"Now, let's see if you can identify yourself from these basic descriptors. Do you think you are more the A-type or the B-type?"

Rick looked at the napkin. "What if you feel like you are both types?"

"That is possible. There are actually sixteen different personal wiring combinations with a wide range of intensity levels, making no two people exactly alike. If you are thinking you could be both A-type and B-type, which one represents more than fifty percent of your personal wiring?"

"I would have to say that I am more A than B."

"If you could put a percentage ratio that represents your A/B combination, what would you write?"

"60 A/40 B."

""How about the 1/2 descriptors—which of those represents you?"

Pointing decisively at the left side of the chart, Rick declared, "Number 1 all the way."

"That gives you an A1/B1 personal wiring combination, which means that you are an aggressive person who likes to get things done but keeps an eye on realistic details."

Rick's eyes lit up in agreement.

"Let's make this real to you. From what you know about your brother and Miriam, what do you think their personal wiring combinations would be?"

"Waylon is definitely an A1 all the way. Miriam, on the other hand, might be an A2/B2. She loves to have fun, but there is also a peaceful side to her."

"I'd say your attention to detail is definitely at work. With what I've seen of Waylon and Miriam, I agree with your observations. How do you think God wired Penny?"

Rick's forehead wrinkled as he studied the napkin chart in front of him. "My guess would be that she is a B1/B2 combination." He looked up to see what his friend would say next.

"Rick, assuming that your observations about everyone's personal wiring are true, how would you interpret yesterday's events for Waylon and Miriam?"

Rick again pored over the napkin chart. "Well, it looks like Waylon can make a fast decision to get something done. If it's exciting to Miriam and doesn't cause any negative feelings for those involved, she's going to be good with whatever he decides."

Peter smiled. "Now, how about you and Penny?"

Rick winced. "Similar to Waylon, I want things to happen quickly. If all the details are figured out, I don't see a reason to delay. Penny, on the other hand, isn't going to want to be rushed. She is going to want a peaceful and relaxed approach, with every detail figured, out before she moves forward."

Pete grinned from ear to ear and Rick knew he had done a pretty good job of applying what he had just learned.

"So where do I go from here, Pete? Does this mean that I can never make a decision without giving Penny all the time in the world to get on board?"

"I don't think you two are going to have an easy time figuring things out, but life from God's perspective requires balance. If you yoke a race horse with a plow horse, they will either adjust or end up killing each other. You are going to have to learn to slow down, and Penny will have to learn how to speed up a little."

"How do I talk with Penny about this? I don't want her to feel pressured, but I don't think that it's necessary to wait a stink'n year and a half before we begin life together, either."

"You've done really well today figuring out wiring combinations. Let's see if you can take this crash course to a practical level. Look at Penny's descriptors. How do you think you need to communicate and interact with her about your difference of opinion?"

"I don't know. I'm feeling stuck again."

"Do you think Penny even realizes that you are upset over her time frame?"

"Absolutely not! She seemed totally oblivious to what I was thinking and feeling."

"Look at the descriptors again. How do you think she will react when you tell her that you would like to get married earlier than she suggested?"

Rick focused on the charts in front of him. "I guess she will want to know all the reasons why I want to get married earlier. She'll probably also want to be reasonably sure that she won't feel pressured getting ready for the wedding."

"Armed with that information, do you think you can have a productive conversation with Penny?"

With a sigh, Rick replied, "I'll have a much better chance, now that I am beginning to understand her personal wiring, than if I had tried to talk with her last night."

Just then the waitress brought out their breakfast order and Rick's world became temporarily a little brighter. Peter, on the other hand, realized that his discussion about personal wiring stimulated growing fears—one related to Rick and another related to a long-desired dream.

VISION FEARS

Throughout the spiritual *Teen* development process, Peter and Lisa had been observing each person on the Team to learn their unique leadership contributions. Knowing the overall goals they had for this Team, Peter and Lisa began to test many factors, hoping to discover smaller ministry team alignment. Several possibilities were solidifying, but Peter was struggling with fear that his total expectations wouldn't become a reality; and, worst of all, he was beginning to agree that Rick might not have the gift mix and personal wiring needed to become the pastor who would replace him. The dream he believed in and desired to execute was at stake. After all these years of waiting and preparing, would this be the time that everything came together, or was he facing another dead-end? The only *Potential* building blocks left to cover for spiritual *Teen* development were *Passions* and *Perseverance*. Time was running out.

Lisa could see that Peter was growing frustrated, even bordering on depression. Though his times of discouragement were few, she had become adept at reading the man she loved. She made up her mind to sit down with him and find out what was going on. Over the years, she had learned to be his sounding board and to breathe encouragement into him. Tonight, she would do that again, with flair.

After the kids were in bed, Lisa quietly went to the kitchen and brewed a cup of Peter's favorite coffee. Then, coffee in hand, she guided him to the loveseat where much of their meaningful interaction occurred.

In a low, disturbed voice, Peter asked Lisa, "Is it going to work this time? We've been in two churches where we made a difference, but we've always run into roadblocks that keep us from living out everything we believe in. As a church, we're philosophically aligned, and there is more potential here than we've ever had. But, I'm beginning to doubt that we're going to realize the whole dream."

Lisa just sat there listening.

"And, worst of all, have I built Rick's hopes too high? He's expressed doubt about his ability to become a lead pastor, and I've just kept encouraging him. After all he's been through, I can't bear the thought of adding more pain to his life. He's definitely got the gift of teaching; but even with all his growth, he is still very uncomfortable in social settings. I've taken him on hospital visits, and he can't wait to get back outside. He loves helping anyone who wants to grow spiritually, but he doesn't have that special touch that people long for in a pastor. Garret has more of that than Rick does."

Quietly, Lisa spoke, "Honey, that doesn't mean that Rick can't be repositioned as a vital part of one of the teams. Besides, you have been trying for years to **challenge and change the status quo** of American ministry expectations. Rick may be part of God's answer to help us change those expectations."

Peter sat there trying to digest what his lovely wife was saying. Rationally, he agreed with her; emotionally he was having a hard time believing that everything would work out. One thing he was sure of—he wasn't going to have peace until he at least talked things over with Rick. He turned to look at Lisa. "I'd like to call him tonight, but it's way too late. He's probably sound asleep."

Slowly, with a teasing look, Lisa started unbuttoning her blouse. "Maybe we should think about going to bed, too."

Peter looked around and began to notice that Lisa had prepared for this moment—the coffee…the loveseat…her quiet listening and support. Without a word, he reached over and shut the light off.

RICK'S WIRING APPLICATIONS

The next morning, Peter woke to the pleasant sight of his beautiful bride gently sleeping beside him. He was thankful for the quiet moments God gave him to reflect on the love he had with this wonderful woman.

Slowly, his thoughts turned to his friend, and how he should address the concerns he had shared with Lisa. Deciding to call, he was a little concerned when Rick didn't answer the phone. His concern grew as morning turned into afternoon and his messages still weren't answered. Finally, toward evening, his cell rang and a quick glance told him it was Rick.

Before Peter could speak, an excited Rick began to talk a million miles an hour. "Pete, you know that wiring diagram you showed me in the restaurant? That is the coolest thing ever; it really works!"

Peter wondered why Rick was so excited. "What do you mean?"

Rick was exuberant. "I wanted to test it out before I talked with Penny, so I asked if some of the guys could meet with me yesterday afternoon to help with an experiment. Garret, Sam, and Drew showed up, and I walked them through the diagram just like you did with me. Then we all tried to guess what each other's wiring combinations were."

"And?"

"That's the cool part; it really works! We came pretty close to pinpointing the personal wiring combination for each of us. Garret got so hooked that he researched some online assessments and had us take a few free ones that he found. They confirmed what we had already discovered. Isn't that cool?"

"It sure—"

"And guess what?"

"What?" Peter settled back with an amused chuckle. He could tell that it was going to be a few minutes before he could fit a word in edge-wise.

"Drew went home and had his wife take an assessment, and they had an incredible conversation that unlocked some of the problems that have simmered between them for most of their married life."

"That's—"

"Isn't that awesome? I mean you helped me yesterday morning, and already I've been able to help others!"

"That's—"

"And that's not all! I haven't told you the best part yet!"

"Go—"

"It's about Penny and me! When we got to talk this morning, she was able to take the wiring thing and help me understand more about her than I have ever since I've known her! After hearing about why and how I learned about personal wiring, she was even willing to move our wedding to this coming summer."

"Rick! That's great!" Peter finally slipped in.

"Yeah; but here's what's even greater to me—I decided not to."

"Wha—?"

"Surprised you, huh?" Rick sounded confident and peaceful as he explained, "I can see how my impatience has had a very negative impact on my relationships with others. I began to realize that I could show more love to Penny if I began to honor the way God wired her. And I quite possibly would have a better marriage if I practiced before we got married."

Peter responded warmly, "That's real progress, Rick!"

"I was hoping you'd think so."

Holding his breath for a moment, Peter moved the conversation towards his concern. "Are you open to talking about some other applications of how God put you together?"

There was dead silence on the other end of the line. "Rick, are you there?"

"Uh-huh. Just struggling with whether I've done something wrong."

"Why would you wonder that?"

"D—I mean—blasted baggage from the *Past* still haunts me." Rick paused before continuing, "I trust you, Pete; I really do. So, what other applications did you want to help me with?"

"When we started this discipleship development process, do you remember me sharing that I thought you possibly could replace me as the lead pastor?"

"Yeah."

"Do you remember your response?"

"At the time, I didn't see how I possibly could."

"What do you think now?"

"Strange you should ask! In addition to what happened with the guys this morning, I also got a call from our home church in Enterprise; they're looking for a pastor. They asked if I would send them a resume, which, by the way, I will need help with."

Peter's mind started spinning at warp speed. "How did that happen? What do you think about that?"

"As you know, the church has a history of not being able to keep a pastor since your dad left. This last guy was from the inner city of New York. In their own way, they told him to go back where he came from. It seems that somehow Waylon gave them my name and said I might be interested."

"Are you?"

"I'm not sure. I know that I've grown a ton through this discipleship process, which has created a personal stability that I absolutely love. But, I'm getting more and more confused as to what God's plan for my life is. Gary sees my passion and abilities for building and wants to develop me as a foreman. I can see that I'm making a difference in Drew's life, so I wonder if God wants me to focus on mentoring others. You have mentioned that I am gifted to teach; and when I teach, I see God at work. And then, the church in Enterprise might be a place where I could make a difference in a culture I'm familiar with."

"Could you have a sense of fulfillment if any of those options became reality?"

"I think so. I can see *Potential* in each and every one of them, which only adds to my confusion."

Peter blew a quiet breath of relief. "Good." After a pause he added, **"Living out your God-given *Potential* does not necessarily mean finding one specific activity you believe to be God's exclusive will for your life**. I think the next several Team sessions will be invaluable in helping you discover what God has chosen you to do." Peter was relieved that Rick was open to more than just one option. The next couple of months would be interesting.

ADVENTURE 22 – PASSIONS (SPIRITUAL GIFTS)

"What is a spiritual gift?" Peter posed the question to get things started.

"It's what you're good at," Jared answered.

"Does that mean if I'm good at robbin' a bank that I've discova'ed my spiritual gift?" Vern asked, looking at Jared with a quirky expression on his face. Jared just grinned at the extreme illustration.

"Let me ask a clarifying question," Peter interjected. "Is there a difference between abilities and spiritual gifts?"

"I'd say yes," Betty answered.

"In what ways?"

With the confidence of a lawyer Burt asserted, "Natural ability is the result of inherited genetics; acquired ability is the result of personal development; spiritual gifts are supernatural capabilities given by God alone for specific purposes."

"Well put, Burt. So my next question is this: What is the purpose of spiritual gifts?"

"According to the New Testament passages we studied this past week, aren't spiritual gifts presented in the context of the Body of Christ?" Rick asked.

"That's right," Peter agreed. "So what would that context indicate about the purpose of spiritual gifts?"

Rick answered, "They are not meant to build any one person up; they are meant to be an interdependent asset to help believers carry out God's purpose for the Church."

"Yes," Peter affirmed.

"Can a believer have more than one spiritual gift?" Penny asked.

"Some definitely possess more than one gift, based on God's purposes. However, no one receives every gift, or they would become self-sufficient. Every believer does, however, receive at least one gift to benefit the Body of Christ. Romans 12:3-8; First Corinthians 12:1-14:40; Ephesians 4:7-8, 11-16; and First Peter 4:8-11 are the major Bible passages that describe spiritual gifts."

"How many spiritual gifts are there?" Ruth asked.

"I'm not sure," Peter replied. "The Apostle Paul's writings give lists that contain similarities and differences. That leads me to believe that **anything that a believer does where he consistently makes a supernatural difference could be considered a spiritual gift.** I've also done enough studying on this topic to know that authors do not totally agree with each other. That cautions me not to be overly dogmatic on details surrounding spiritual gifts."

Sam spoke decisively, "Well, one thing I do know is that I'm not supernaturally gifted in the area of giving money."

"Does that exempt you from giving at all?" Peter asked.

"No, I know I'm still responsible to give. I'm just saying that I know my capability to give isn't greater than my responsibility."

"That's a great way to express it, Sam."

"How do we discover our spiritual gifts? Is there some kind of test that we can take?" Maggie inquired.

"There are several spiritual gifting tests that you could take. In my opinion, though, those tests only reveal personal preferences and wiring characteristics. How can you adequately test for supernatural results if you haven't experimented with each gift and watched for God's activity in the experiment?"

"So is that how a Christian should discover his or her spiritual gift(s)?" Rick asked.

"After becoming familiar with the gifts mentioned in the Bible, experiment first with those gifts you have the strongest desire toward. During the experimentation, look for internal joy and external impact—you should experience joy in exercising your gift(s), and others should express *sincere* appreciation for your supernatural capabilities. Ask mature believers who know you what they think your spiritual gifts could be. Take every opportunity that God sends your way; picky believers will be hindered in the discovery process. Those would be some of my discovery suggestions."

"This process could also require some honest self-diagnosis and group feedback," Burt interjected.

Peter was grateful that Burt had brought up the subject. "In what ways?"

"It would be easy for me to say that I didn't have specific gifts because I was too afraid to try them. If I were serious about discovering the gift(s) that God has given me, I would need to evaluate how much effort I really put into the area of a specific gift. It would be invaluable to have others who know me speak frankly after a specific experience."

"Self-diagnosis and group feedback are some of the hallmarks of a mature believer, not only in the area of spiritual gift discovery, but in every area of spiritual development. Outline the starting point and end result of each gift you try on a scale from 1-10 to help those of you who are visual."

Rick had a pretty good idea where Peter was headed. "I'm feeling some practice exercises in our near future."

Lisa looked at Peter with a grin as he responded, "You are feeling correctly!"

Rick began to list all the activities they had already experienced as a Team, "Let's see. So far, we've had opportunities to teach, encourage, exhort, and provide hospitality. What is next on the agenda?"

"Evangelism."

As Rick looked around the room, he was pretty sure that he detected the same kind of emotions from most of the Team that he was feeling about the upcoming exercise—trepidation.

GIFTING PRACTICE: EVANGELISM

Vern and Vickie asked Peter if they could teach about evangelism the following week, believing that God had given them the gift of reaching lost people. Sam overheard the request and asked to join them.

After a great meal and lively interaction at the Rogers' home, Vern started off with the goal of the lesson. "This session is to prepa'e you to sha'e you'a faith in a meaningful way with someone in you'a ev'ra-day life."

"With someone we know or someone we don't know?" Misty wondered.

"We are leaving that up to you," Sam answered. "One of the things we spent a lot of time talking about as we prepared was how frequently only one method of sharing our faith is taught. We believe that Jesus wants every believer to share the Gospel; but we do not believe He has only one particular method for doing that. Child evangelism, door-to-door, inviting people to evangelistic outreaches, street preaching, relational evangelism, radio and television programs—they all have their place in leading people to Jesus. **It is important to stimulate and equip believers to share their faith without a one-size-fits-all approach.**"

"We've been stimulated before, but I can't say that we have really been equipped," Ruth offered. "How are you going to equip us?"

"We are going to look at (1) why we should share our faith, (2) why we don't share our faith, and (3) how we can share our faith."

"I know why I don't," Betty spoke transparently. "I'm not confident that I'll know what to say. I don't want to flounder and turn someone away from Jesus."

"I'm just plain scared," Penny confessed.

Sam responded, "Fear and failure were the two reasons we came up with for *why we don't* share our faith. We discovered that fear is defeated through faith in our God (Second Timothy 1:7-8; First John 4:18). We also decided that developing a personal plan for sharing the Gospel is the best way to overcome your fear of failure (First Peter 3:15).

Rick had his notebook and pen out, ready to write, before asking, "What does a personalized plan look like?"

Vern and Vickie tag-teamed this question. "You should think through how to make a *Point of Contact* to get a conversation started. Eventually, you will face the *Point of Confrontation* where the bad news about sin must be faced before you can move toward the *Point of Confession* where the good news is believed and accepted. As you close, there should be a *Plan for Continuation* where you help new believers begin their discipleship development process."

After Vern and Vickie shared thoughts on each of the *Points*, Sam brought the lesson to a close by sharing the biblical motivation for evangelism. "Jesus commissioned us to share the Gospel. Sharing our faith is not a suggestion; it is a direct command. And, if that seems too cold, God's amazing love for the lost should warm our hearts. He does not want anyone to experience the torments of condemnation and eternal separation from His presence. Those are powerful motivators to help me get outside myself to share Jesus with those who don't know Him."

The lesson closed with some application exercises. "For the next half hour, we want you to gather in groups of two to four and identify the person you plan to share your faith with next week so that we can be praying for the Holy Spirit to prepare both us and those we will talk to."

GIFTING PRACTICE: EVANGELISM RESULTS

As the Team planned and prayed about how to share their faith, demonic forces were gathering. Peter and Lisa knew that **few topics other than interpersonal conflict, stimulated spiritual opposition more than prayer and evangelism.** As a couple, they had been fervently praying for the Team.

Monday night, Rick called Sam to brainstorm about some ideas of how he could share his faith. "I know that evangelism is not my spiritual gift, but I would like to get better at sharing my faith."

"What have you tried?"

"Door-to-door; but, I'm just not a salesman. I get stuck at the *Point of Contact*; I need relational credibility before I can have an effective conversation with someone about their soul's needs."

"Who do you have relational credibility with that needs to hear the Gospel?"

"I've got an uncle that I really respect, but he has been turned off by my father."

"Do you think he would listen to you?"

"Maybe. I know that he respects me because he has told me so a couple of times."

"Would writing, calling, or face-to-face be the best way to communicate with him?"

"Definitely face-to-face!"

"Cool!" Almost as an afterthought, Sam continued, "Hey, do you think you could use your teaching gift to present the Gospel to a group of people who were trying to find out more about God if someone else got them together?"

"Yeah, if someone else would create the *Point of Contact,* I could teach the *Point of Confrontation* without much difficulty."

"That would be a venue to explore. I could even be the guy to get a group together for you."

"That sounds great!"

~ ~ ~

Mid-week during a lunch break, Rick shared with Gary and Kevin that he was experiencing some inner oppression over the evangelism exercise. They both admitted that they were having similar feelings.

"Why don't we call the Team and see if we can get together Friday night for some serious prayer," Gary suggested.

"That would help us in a number of ways," Rick and Kevin agreed.

The three of them decided which Team members each would call. On Friday night, the entire Team met at the church's Equipping Center.

Rick started off by asking, "How many of you have experienced spiritual opposition or oppression this week?"

"I thought I was just struggling with depression at first," Michelle agreed. "The only relief I've had was when Misty called to let me know about our prayer time tonight."

"And Michelle's downer resurfaced a lot of relational issues between us that haven't been a problem for a long time," Sam added. "It was like she became Dr. Jekyll, and I became Mr. Hyde."

"Nice play on words, Sam! You weren't the only couple going through macabre metamorphosis," Betty joined in. "Burt and I have been at each other's throats since the beginning of the week. And, as usual, we just started working extra hours so that we didn't have to deal with each other. Gary's call helped us re-focus."

"We're usually a pretty upbeat couple," Vickie said. "But this week, there has just been an unexplainable heaviness that has surrounded us. We didn't give it a lot of thought until Rick called. We were so encouraged, knowing that we weren't the only ones feeling this way."

As the Team began to pray, the oppression intensified. Prayers became passionately bold as they began to plead with God for supernatural help. Praise for God's character could be heard as the basis for their bold requests. As the Team became unified in prayer, their hearts united and the forces of darkness were driven back; freedom became reality.

When prayer came to a close, the Team was certain that God was going to do something special as they shared their faith this weekend. They decided not to meet together for their usual meal on Sunday, but to take that time to try to connect with those they had chosen to share their faith with. They would meet at six in the evening to share how things went. Rick decided to drive to Enterprise on Saturday to talk with his uncle.

~ ~ ~

Sunday evening, Vern opened by asking, "What did God do this afta'noon as you sha'ed you'a faith?"

"Kevin stayed home with the kids so I could take one of my co-workers out for lunch," Misty started. "We have one of those relationships where there is mutual respect, even though we are miles apart philosophically. I would have to say that God really helped me to articulate my faith to her better than I ever have before. She listened and asked questions, and I learned more about the reasons for her belief structure, which helped me. I feel like our relationship was strengthened, and I believe God will continue to give me opportunities to share my faith with her."

Sam was bursting at the seams to share his afternoon's experience. "I've got an old friend named Jay who I used to run with in my wild party days. He owns a bar over in Richland, so I went over there to have lunch with him. Michelle and the kids ate a fast food lunch on the way over and prayed in the car for me the entire time I was with him. God really revved things up; it was like I couldn't say anything wrong. Jay's at that spot where his lifestyle is catching up with him, and he's searching for something. After I shared my journey of becoming a follower of Jesus, he agreed to come to our church next week! It was epic! I'm so amped!"

Everyone enjoyed Sam's enthusiasm and praised the powerful part Michelle had in partnering with him.

"Garret asked me to go to the mall with him," Maggie shared. "Before we went inside, we prayed that God would lead us to someone who needed to hear His Good News. We went to the food court, placed our orders, and sat down at different tables. An older sister of one of my students came around the corner. I could tell she'd been crying, so I asked her to sit down. When I asked her what was wrong, she opened up about troubles she was having with her boyfriend. God gave me such a wonderful opportunity to share some of my dating challenges and then to point her to Jesus, the most reliable relationship I've ever had. She thanked me and, when I asked if I could have her phone number so that we could stay in touch, she seemed glad that I had asked."

Garret jumped in, "And I got a unique opportunity to share Jesus with an older guy whose wife was off buying some lingerie for their fiftieth wedding anniversary."

"Very interesting," Vern chuckled. "How did ya' run with that?"

"I was able to ask him questions about his marriage, and that led into the marriage dynamics of Jesus and His Bride. He listened reasonably well, but I got the feeling he thought I was part of some cult. Our conversation ended when his wife came back."

"Well, we did a first," Vickie stated. "Vern and I picked up a hitchhiker and took him out to eat at a nice restaurant. It was actually fun for us to get to know a total stranger. His spiritual views were as broad as his travels, but he really listened as we shared our faith with him. Vern was able to give him one of the small New Testaments that he carries for such occasions. We came away feeling like we had planted a seed in good ground."

"I think I watered a seed," Rick chimed in. "The conversation I had with my uncle yesterday was very open, but I know he's still processing the facts of Christianity and looking around at Christians he knows. Sadly, some of them aren't very helpful."

"If he listened to you, that's a step in the right direction!" Sam encouraged.

One-by-one, the Team shared their afternoon experiences; some were great, some simple, but almost all of them had been meaningful. Fears had been absolved, risks had been rewarded, and they were all amazed at the intense reality of spiritual warfare and how unified prayer had made such a difference.

This encouraged them to embrace the upcoming experiments.

PASSION (SPIRITUAL GIFT) PROBES

Over the course of several weeks, the Team allowed themselves to be stretched and evaluated as they tried a variety of experiences.

Maggie's school had a budget to purchase playground equipment but not enough funds to hire out the installation; after presenting the opportunity to the Team, she also managed the installation through to completion.

Peter incorporated several Team members to help him organize a four-day multi-missions trip in Portland. Vern and Vickie led a team to serve in a homeless shelter, while Gary and Kevin led a crew to help with a church's building project. The rest of the Team helped with a seminar for a church that was serious about revamping their entire approach to discipleship.

Rick was invited to speak a couple of times at the church in Enterprise. He found that, by bringing Drew and Mandy along, he and Penny had some mentoring opportunities.

Peter knew that all of these experiences would be catalytic in discovering spiritual gifting and personal passions. He also lived with the deep hope that some patterns would emerge that would make it possible to create the ministry teams which would enable him to live out the passions and dreams of his own heart.

As Peter directed the Team toward discovering their passions, he shared several verses that tied personal passions with God's purpose for their lives (Jeremiah 1:5; Luke 4:43; John 4:43, 12:27, 17:4; Romans 8:28, 11:29; Ephesians 1:11, 2:10). Some of the Team were skeptical about whether or not God had an individualized purpose for everyone. He was pleased when people were willing to challenge the premises he presented to them. **Skepticism is a useful catalyst that drives people to search for answers.**

To aid the Team in the process of discovering what they were passionate about and their spiritual gifts, Peter gave them a list of questions.

Passion Probes

> ➤ *If you could do anything you wanted to and be guaranteed that you would succeed, what would you do? Why?*
> ➤ *What one change or influence would you make on the world if you could? Why?*
> ➤ *What are some things that you can't stand experiencing, or hate to see happening to others?*
> ➤ *If you knew that you had only five healthy years left to live, how would you spend them?*
> ➤ *When you die, what do you want others to remember the most about you?*
> ➤ *Who do you enjoy helping the most?*
> ➤ *When others express appreciation about you, what do they typically mention?*
> ➤ *If you had unlimited financial resources, how would you spend them?*
> ➤ *When you have discretionary time, what are your favorite things to do?*

➢ *As you look back over your past, do you see God's hand leading you in any particular direction?*

➢ *Do you have a dream or vision that hasn't become a reality yet? Is God calling you to adjust your vision or to persevere? Are those closest to you supportive of your dream or vision?*

➢ *What are your favorite Bible passages?*

➢ *If you could summarize your life's passions in just one word, what would that word be?*

PERSONAL PLANS

"Those were some soul-searching questions you had us answer this week." Betty started the discussion energetically, with Burt in obvious agreement.

"They were supposed to be," Peter responded. "What did the two of you discover as you answered them?"

"We realized that we each have two sets of passions. Our career passions have been dominating us so that we are ineffective at living out our spiritual passions."

"What direction do you see God leading you?"

Betty started. "I'm making a significant adjustment in my career goal. Many of you know that I've had my heart set on becoming mayor for years. With all that's transpired during this spiritual development process, I'm confident that becoming mayor is not what the Holy Spirit wants me to do with my life."

Burt added, "We're feeling that we need to take this next year and work on our marriage, reduce our career loads, and quietly wait for God to let us know how He wants us to serve Him. If we don't, we'll just end up swapping a crazy career schedule for a crazy ministry schedule. Through this discipleship process, we have learned that God is more concerned about the quality of our relationship with Him and with each other than with what we think we can do for Him."

Lisa's face glowed with approval. "You will not regret following through with that joint plan."

"Who else discovered God's voice as they answered the questions this week?" Peter continued.

Vern announced with obvious excitement, "Vickie and I discova'ed that ou'a combined answa's indicate that we love evangelism! We have resolved to become mo'a intentional at sharin' the Gospel."

"My passion is giving," Gary joined in. "Years ago, I committed to give ten percent of my gross income to God. During our last building fund campaign, I committed to give an additional five percent. This week, God laid a percentage figure on my heart for the upcoming year that has challenged my faith. I'm nervous, but also excited about how God is going to help me make that happen."

Kim piped up, "And that is where I come in. I believe my answer to Peter's last *Passion Probe* is *Encourager*. I can see God using me to encourage Gary as he lives out his passions. I also have a number of ladies that I believe God wants me to encourage through this next year."

Jared looked a little uncomfortable. "Ruth and I feel like we need more time before we can accurately answer the questions you gave us."

Misty looked relieved as she glanced at the Williams. "I can relate to Jared and Ruth needing more time. I have so many passions that it is hard for me to figure out how to move in a specific direction, and that has had a somewhat negative impact on our marriage."

Sam wrapped his arm around his wife as he shared, "Michelle and I aren't sure exactly how to go about it, but we do know that we can't stand seeing other couples experience the kind of marital pain we have been through. We believe God is calling us to help turn around marriages that are in distress."

"I had a hard time seeing any pattern to my answers at first," Garret began. "When I finally got to the question that asked me to summarize my life in one word, I went back over all the answers I had written down. The one word that summarized all of those answers was *Pastor.*"

The Team murmured agreement with Garret's conclusion. It wouldn't have been too many weeks ago that such a conclusion would have produced jealousy in Rick. Today, he was just thrilled that Garret had made the discovery, and he wholeheartedly agreed.

Peter saw the peaceful smile on Rick's face and ventured, "How about you, Rick? What was the one word you felt summarized your life's passions?"

"I can't tell you in one word. *Teacher*, *Mentor*, and *Builder* all accurately describe things that I love to do. For years, I pursued pastoral ministry as a symbol of success and the answer to my broken longing for affirmation from my father. Through the *Teen* phase of this discipleship development process, the Holy Spirit has helped me to see that, **if I'm in a correct relationship with God, nothing else matters.**"

Penny gently squeezed his hand before adding, "And I see my abilities and God-given gifts as being a complement to Rick's. I believe that God has blessed me with administrative abilities and the gift of wisdom. I'm sure that, when we're married, I'll find out whether I'm right." Penny's comment garnered smiles from the ladies and good-natured jokes from the men.

"When are you getting married?" Karen asked.

"A year from this summer," Rick smiled, remembering the growing process that produced such a distant time frame.

After the excitement about Rick and Penny's news died down, Lisa asked Maggie, "What did you discover about your passions from the questions?"

"Even though I'm a teacher, the one word that kept coming to me was *Supporter.*"

Lisa smiled, and said, "Me, too. Peter has been a pastor ever since I've known him; but each ministry setting is different and requires different things from me. No matter what the ministry setting is, I seem to flourish just by supporting Peter and those we are serving. Lately, I've seen Peter serving in the capacity of *Equipper;* and yet the shift has brought no challenge for me because I still get to support him. I've also felt so blessed to be able to support many of you through this spiritual development process."

As Lisa continued to speak, something clicked in Rick's mind. Peter had been a pastor for years, but now his ministry was changing from *Pastor* to *Equipper.* God could use people in different capacities at different points in their lives. The important thing was to **let life be defined vertically instead of horizontally.** Though he wasn't sure of his specific God-given purpose, Rick had more peace than he could ever remember possessing. He felt confident that his *Paradigm* was biblical, his *Past* was being healed, and his *Potential* was being discovered.

ADVENTURE 23 – PERSEVERANCE: TIME MANAGEMENT

The following week, Rick was scheduled to preach in Enterprise. His plan was to work four 10-hour shifts for Gary and then to spend a long weekend in Enterprise, interacting with the church leadership and preparing for his Sunday presentations. Before leaving, he asked Garret to make sure to take good notes on the Team's time management discussions for him.

The Team met at Burt and Betty's, and Garret meticulously recorded the conclusions that came from everyone's research and interaction:

- **A de-cluttering tool can produce clarity and reduce stress. At times, life can seem messier than it really is; so when things become overwhelming, it helps to write down all the responsibilities, demands, and desires you are dealing with and group those that are similar.**
- **It helps to know your big-picture priorities. When time is managed from what seems urgent at the time, then what is really important can get lost. Knowing where you want to end up (at the end of a day, a week, a**

month, a year, a life) helps to prioritize decisions. At the Judgment Seat of Christ, there are no do-overs, so get rid of time wasters.

- **Intentional accountability protects against drifting. The best internal time management plans will only work when there are external checks and balances.**

Garret looked forward to sharing what he had just learned with his friend. Little did he know that Rick's life was about to get cluttered with someone else's decision that had the potential to blow him off course. Both God and the Devil were at work. Time would show who would win.

RAY'S FINAL DECISION

The Team was wrapping up their time management session when Peter felt his phone vibrate. A quick look let him know that Rick was calling. He walked outside onto the Larsons' patio to accept the call.

"Pete, my father has committed suicide." Peter recoiled in pain for his friend. Flashbacks of losing his mother ran through his mind. He knew from experience that, at times like this, **actions were more important than words.**

"If it's all right with you, I'll tell the Team, and then Lisa and I will be on our way."

With a husky voice, Rick answered, "That would be great."

"What's the matter, Honey?" Lisa asked as Peter stepped back inside, shock and sadness written all over his face.

Peter just took her by the hand and spoke to get everyone's attention. "Hey, Gang, Rick just called to let me know that his father took his own life."

Michelle began to tear up. "Why?"

"I don't know any of the details, but Lisa and I are headed to Enterprise right now."

"Can I come, too?" Garret asked.

"I'm sure Rick could use all the support we can give him."

A peculiar look came over Jared's face, and he and Ruth quickly left for home.

Several felt they could offer the best support after they learned more details. Others made arrangements so that they could drive over with Peter and Lisa. Rick determined that it would be best for his mother if he and Penny met everyone at the motel where people would be staying instead of the home place.

It was nearly midnight when Rick and Penny, along with Waylon and Miriam, met the Team to share the circumstances surrounding Ray's death.

In a flat, expressionless voice, Rick related the story. "Late this afternoon, I got a call from Waylon. The sheriff had come to his house asking him questions about drug involvement. His pickup had been seen in Elgin on Friday, and several school kids were busted for drug possession that same afternoon. The school's surveillance cameras caught one of the students getting out of Waylon's truck with a package in his hands."

Waylon interjected, "I was furious. Father had told me that his pickup was at the garage being worked on, so he needed to borrow a truck. He said he knew Rick was in town and that he wanted to borrow his, but I told him that it wasn't fair to take Rick's only vehicle when I had several.

"Then, last night, Miriam was driving home and saw our father's pickup parked out behind an old shed as she drove past the home place. She thought that was a little strange but forgot about it until the sheriff showed up this afternoon to accuse me of drug dealing.

"At that point, I told the sheriff to follow me to our father's house so that we could get to the bottom of things. I think the Old Man sensed that consequences were about to come crashing down on him because we found him out in the workshop shot up with a concoction that guaranteed he wouldn't have to answer any questions—ever."

Peter looked over at his friend and could only imagine the tension in his soul. How was Rick going to handle this unexpected challenge? Would what he had learned during the discipleship process be enough to guide him to a healthy resolution?

Rick caught Peter looking at him and remembered a promise he had made. "Do you think your dad might be willing to come back and do the funeral? Mom wanted us to ask you."

Knowing the family the way Peter did, he warmly answered, "I'll be glad to find out."

BURIAL OF MORE THAN A MAN

A phone call from Waylon jump-started Rick's day early the next morning. "You up?"

Rubbing his eyes and trying to get his bearings, Rick answered, "I think so."

"Can you come over t' my house—alone? I got somethin' you should see."

With anxiety building inside of him, Rick assured, "Be right there."

It took only a couple of minutes to drive to Waylon's, but it was enough time for Rick to start feeling sick to his stomach. *How can things possibly get any worse?*

Waylon was leaning against the side of his pickup as Rick pulled into the driveway. He rolled down his window and looked into Waylon's face, hoping he could get some kind of indication of what was coming. Waylon simply handed him a large envelope before warning, "You ain't goin' t' like this—I didn't."

Rick opened the envelope and, after a quick glance, shot a look of disbelief at Waylon. "What the…?" He paused before muttering, "Is this for real?"

"Afraid so. The sheriff found it behind the seat when he searched my rig. There wasn't much of a chance to show you with all the people that were around yesterday. It looks like the Old Man was involved with more than just drugs."

Rick's hands shook as he quickly scanned the contents, and his anger boiled. "That dirty, rotten, stinkin' hypocrite!"

~ ~ ~

A few days later, a collection of family and friends, along with the entire Discipleship Team, gathered for Ray Thomson's funeral. Once again, Rick found himself dealing with the gap between the natural beauties that he could see from the hilltop where the cemetery was located and the ugly reality of his father's death.

Pastor John McCormick had gladly accepted the invitation to come back and perform the service. He did a wonderful job at delicately balancing truth with respect, reminding everyone of the need to be prepared for eternity. He gently touched on the fact that even followers of Jesus can make poor decisions, but then he moved on to highlight the positive characteristics of Ray Thomson's life.

As Pastor John was speaking, Rick's mind raced and his emotions ricocheted. He was struggling with the huge inconsistencies between the standards his father had imposed on Rick and others, and his inability to live out those standards himself. Rick was reeling with anger and shame for the association between his family and authentic Christianity.

As the service moved forward, he appreciated Pastor John's reminder to think of the positive things his father had done. Gradually, he recalled some of the benefits of his upbringing. He was also thankful that this hadn't happened before Peter's discipleship influence on his life. As hard as Rick was struggling, he could still feel an invisible arm around his shoulders; he still had a Dad—One that would never fail him.

As the casket was lowered into the vault, Rick was sobered by the realization that **the way a person ends his life is a huge statement about the life he has lived.** It made Rick more determined than ever to have the last chapter of his life story be an epitaph of a life lived for the glory of God. Satan would never get his soul; and, by the grace of God, neither would Satan get his reputation or minimize the eternal purpose God wanted to live out through his life, whatever that was.

ADVENTURE 24 – REFLECTION & REPLENISHMENT

As the Team met at Gary and Kim's the following week, there was a sober, but healthy, discussion about the *Potential* building block of *Perseverance* and **the part that *Reflection* and *Replenishment* play in staying in the game over the long haul**.

"Did you realize," Peter asked, "that, of all the characters in the Bible where there is enough information recorded to tell, only about a third of them finished well?"

Burt was shocked. "That's not a very encouraging ratio,"

"I agree. So what can we learn from those who do and those who don't finish well? How can they teach us about what it takes to stay true to our God-given *Potential?*"

"I think it requires us to step outside of ourselves, through whatever means necessary, to gain a big-picture perspective," Garret answered.

"Can you give an example of that?" Peter asked.

"Sure," Garret continued. "Have you ever sat in a Bible study where people were dissecting a Bible character's life like they were an authority on how to do everything right?"

Vickie chimed in, "When you are not in the story, it's always easy to see what should have been done, because it is void of the personal defaults, fears, and emotional desires of real life."

"Taking those thoughts," Peter continued, "could we say that it is necessary at times to *Reflect* on our own lives without emotional interference?"

"Yes," Garret answered. "I would also take that one step further. When we find it challenging to do so ourselves, we must search out the rational *Reflection* of other authentic Christians."

"Which is the last thing most of us want to do," Betty added.

Rick was processing what he was hearing in light of his father's life. "For years, I could see the direction my father was headed, though I never could have predicted the end would be so dramatic and devastating. Through this discipleship process, I have learned that rational *Reflection* connects me to reality; but, if that reality is less than what God desires for me, I have to do something to change it."

"That's where *Replenishment* comes into play," Peter smoothly transitioned into the next concept. "How many of you know how to keep yourselves filled up emotionally, physically, and spiritually to protect against the draining effects of life?"

"I don't do it well yet," Rick responded, "but I'm learning."

"So that you don't end up like your father?" Jared jabbed.

The question caught Rick a little of guard, but he quietly said, "Yeah."

A moment of discomfort passed through the room, but Peter quickly moved on. "What are some things that successful people do to keep themselves *Replenished?*"

Betty processed her thoughts aloud. "In the Bible, David wrote his feelings out and turned some of them into songs which he played on musical instruments. I know that, for me, worship is a powerful source of *Replenishment.*"

"I like to go down to the Park and just sit by the water," Penny shared. "The quietness somehow fills me up."

"Kinda' like the ocean in Maine whe'a I grew up," Vern added. "Sometimes I just have to drive to the Coast for a weekend to recha'ge."

A sparkle of humor twinkled in Garret's eyes. "My grandfather enjoyed playing poker every Friday night with a bunch of his friends."

"Do you think it was the cards or the camaraderie that helped him the most?" Vickie pointed out.

"Probably the friends! He was a horrible card player."

"Does one size fit all when it comes to *Replenishment?*" Peter began to wrap things up.

"Not at all," Burt replied. "I think that, like other areas you have walked us through, self-awareness is vital in knowing what works. After the discovery process, it's simply a matter of practicing what you know so that you don't allow yourself to get drained dry."

"Well put!" Peter nodded in agreement.

Rick looked around the room at the group of people he considered to be his closest friends. He felt certain that several of them had learned how to *Reflect* and *Replenish* themselves. Some, like himself, were still in the process of learning. And a few were just starting to struggle with the concepts.

Seeing the hard look on Jared's face, Rick began to wonder, *Is something eating Jared? He doesn't seem to be himself tonight. I wonder if I did something wrong, or if he's just having a bad day?*

CELEBRATION & TESTING PREPARATION

Peter started off the Team session with a teaser. "I've got some good news and some bad news."

Vickie's bubbly voice was the first to respond. "I want the good news first."

With fun written all over his face, Peter announced, "We're going to have a party!"

Sam was ecstatic. "Sweet hallelujah!"

"When?" Gary asked.

"In two weeks. We are going to have an afternoon of games followed by a celebration feast where we will share memories of the discoveries we have made over the past year as we have grown together, as well as the future direction God is leading us."

"Why?" Misty questioned.

"In the Old Testament, the Lord would often ask His people to celebrate victories to strengthen their faith and prepare them for upcoming challenges. In the New Testament, God is pictured as an intense Master; but **when His servants performed well, He would throw a party to celebrate.**"

Burt spoke soberly, "You mentioned upcoming challenges. That would be the bad news, I'm guessing."

"Your legal mind doesn't miss much, does it, Burt?"

"Like I said, it was just a guess."

"Part of the celebration will be recognizing those of you who pass the Discipleship and Leadership Testing Interview."

Rick gave a quizzical look. "What's that?"

Peter was both nervous and excited. "For those of you who believe that God is calling you to serve Him in a leadership capacity, there will be an all-day interview and testing process to qualify you for the *Adult* phase of training."

Vern made a motion like cracking a whip. "I think he's moved from *Equippa'* to *Tortura'*."

Peter just smiled. "To help take some of the dread out of it for you, I've prepared a list of questions we're using so that you will know in advance what the process will be. You are free to use ANY resource you deem helpful as you prepare for this interview. The goal is to help you solidify the *Teen* discipleship development material in your mind and determine your readiness for the leadership and team-building process."

~ ~ ~

Rick didn't waste any time when he got back to his apartment to begin preparing for the leadership testing process. Excitement coursed through his body as he anticipated the outcome. Would he be recognized as a leader? He felt that the changes in his life had been significant and that he should be ready for leadership and team building; but would he be? And then again, was that the direction God wanted him to go?

DISCIPLESHIP/ LEADERSHIP TEST

QUESTIONS

> **Your *Paradigm***

- [ ] How do you know that there is a God?
- [ ] Why would God want to write your life story?
- [ ] Why would Satan want to destroy your life story?
- [ ] What are Satan's two major objectives?
- [ ] Can you destroy your life story? If yes, how? If no, why not?
- [ ] How should the picture of Communion (the Lord's Supper) help you live out your faith?
- [ ] Can a Christian lose his salvation? If yes, how? If no, why not?
- [ ] How should the picture of Baptism help you live out your faith and make needed changes in your life?
- [ ] Fill in the blank with the word "for" or "through." "*Only one life, it will soon be past; only what is done _____ Christ will last.*" Why did you choose the word that you did?
- [ ] What are the phases of the spiritual development process?
- [ ] What is spiritual maturity?
- [ ] Where are you in the spiritual development process?
- [ ] On a scale of 1-10 (1 = worst/10 = best), evaluate the healthiness of your *Paradigm*.

➤ **Your *Past***

☐ How do you handle God's use of negative situations to stimulate positive growth in your life?

☐ Describe the health of your relationship with your parents, siblings, spouse, children, and friends.

☐ Explain the impact of any traumatic experiences from your *Past* on your spiritual development. If you haven't experienced trauma, explain how you can identify with others who have.

☐ Do you have negative response patterns from your *Past* that are hindering your spiritual development process? If yes, how will you replace those response patterns with positive ones?

☐ How many relationships do you have where there is at least an 90% trust level between you?

☐ What are some relational limit violations that you have caused or endured?

☐ What is your skill level in creating and enforcing healthy limits on negative behavior?

☐ How well do you honor the limits others set for you?

☐ On a scale of 1-10 (1 = worst/10 = best), evaluate the health of your *Past*.

➤ **Your *Potential: Practices***

☐ What are the negative habits that have crippled your spiritual development process? How have (or should) you deal with those habits?

☐ Are you free from ALL addictions (alcohol, drugs, entertainment, financial, food, sexual, tobacco, work, other)?

❑ If you claim to be addiction-free now, and in the future an addiction surfaces that you did not disclose at this time, how should that situation be handled?

❑ What are your Bible intake habits?

❑ What tools do you have/use to accurately interpret and apply a passage of Scripture?

❑ What is the value of journaling your spiritual progress?

❑ What prayer habits have you developed? Are there any changes that you would like to make to your prayer habits? If yes, what are they?

❑ On a scale of 1-10 (1=unhealthy/10=totally healthy), where would you rate your emotional health (anger, bitterness, depression, fear, patience, peace, joy, trust)?

❑ Do you have any emotional triggers that could lead you to try reducing the resulting pain in illegitimate ways? If yes, what are they?

❑ Have you been, or are you currently, emotionally, physically, or verbally abusive to others?

➢ **Your *Potential: Partnership***

❑ On a scale of 1-10 (1 = worst/10 = best), evaluate how well you live out the *One Another* passages of the New Testament.

❑ On a scale of 1-10 (1 = not at all/10 = totally), evaluate how transparent you are with your Christian friends.

❑ On a scale of 1-10 (1 = not at all/10 = totally), evaluate how intentionally accountable you are with your Christian friends.

❑ What is your accountability plan?

❑ On a scale of 1-10 (1 = worst/10 = best), evaluate your communication skills.

- ❑ What challenges do you have in communicating with others?
- ❑ On a scale of 1-10 (1 = worst/10 = best), evaluate your conflict resolution skills.
- ❑ How do you resolve conflict?
- ❑ What is the most intense conflict you have ever been involved in?

➤ **Your *Potential: Personal Wiring***

- ❑ How well do you know yourself?
- ❑ What is your personal wiring combination?
- ❑ What are the greatest strengths of your personal wiring combination?
- ❑ What are the greatest challenges with your personal wiring combination?

➤ **Your *Potential: Passions (Spiritual Gifts)***

- ❑ What are you most passionate about?
- ❑ What is the God-given purpose of your life?
- ❑ How has God gifted you to live out His purpose and your passions?
- ❑ How do you share your faith with those who are lost?

➤ **Your *Potential: Perseverance***

- ❑ What are your time-management strategies and tools?
- ❑ What reflection practices do you use to keep yourself on track?
- ❑ How do you manage stress in your life?

❏ How do you prevent discouragement?

❏ How do you keep yourself replenished?

❏ Who are your heroes? How have they helped you live out your faith?

❏ What helps you to stay motivated to live your life story to its fullest *Potential?*

❏ What major spiritual memorials has God provided in your life to strengthen your faith and encourage you as you journey into the future?

❏ What are you doing to ensure that you will cross your life's finish line well?

➢ **Memorial Takeaway**

❏ **What was your biggest takeaway from this discipleship development process?**

INTERVIEWS

Garret, Vern and Vickie, and Maggie had all been interviewed. As Rick started through the process, Jared came uncorked. "I don't think Rick has what it takes to be a leader! Who's to say that he won't end up doing what his father did?" With hardened features, he looked directly at Rick and stated, "You'd be better off just going back to work in the woods where you couldn't hurt anyone by passing on your family's dysfunction."

"Jared! How could you say that?" The usually peaceful Ruth spoke with intensity and fire in her eyes. "You know that what's going on inside of you is because of your own family history!" And with that she left the room.

Rick sat there, stunned. Everything had been moving along smoothly. Those who had been interviewed experienced a blend of both positive and constructive feedback, but all had been approved for the *Adult* phase of training.

Rick had also done well until it came to the questions dealing with his *Past*, specifically his parents. Now, someone he considered to be a friend was throwing family heritage, which was beyond his control, in his face. And, truth be told, at low times, Rick felt exactly as Jared did.

As if he were in a dream, Rick felt Penny's tender hand move behind his neck and wrap around the side of his face pulling him toward her. She recalled Ruth's comment during their first visit in the Williams' home—"Jared doesn't really claim anyone for parents." Quietly, she whispered in Rick's ear, "Don't react. Remember to live in the truth you have learned. Take a few moments to quietly look at the facts and ask God for wisdom to apply the needed principles. Don't forget how far you've come. I love you, and I'm proud of you!" One part of Rick wanted to just shut down, but the other decided to follow Penny's advice.

While Rick was struggling to regroup, Lisa left to find Ruth; Peter asked Jared to go outside where they could talk. Garret and Maggie, along with several others, came over to pray with Rick and Penny.

When the prayers came to an end, Rick spoke the one thing he knew to be true; it was probably the most important lesson he had learned through the spiritual *Teen* development process. "I can't do this on my own. When I try to process things, they all get wadded up into one big, confusing mess. Will you guys help me work through this?"

"Absolutely," Garret responded. "What are you struggling with the most?"

Shaking his head, Rick answered, "Right now, I'm not sure."

Garret encouraged, "Emotions or facts?"

Rick was able to start vocalizing his thoughts. "Emotions probably. Jared is a good, solid guy; but, at times, he reminds me of my family. He stirs up wounds from my *Past* and makes me feel like I have no *Potential.*"

Maggie looked intently at Rick. "Is there any truth to what he said?"

Rick admitted, "Factually, he's right about my family having dysfunctional components. But he's wrong to assume that the dysfunction defines who I am or even who they are. Dysfunction doesn't disqualify people from being used by God; He can use negative situations to create positive results. My ability to help or hurt people is based on the choices that I make, not on the choices my family makes. If I have a God-centered *Paradigm* and a healthy view of my *Past*, then my *Potential* is just as good as anyone else's."

By the time Peter and Lisa walked back in with Jared and Ruth, Rick was amazingly calm and ready for the rest of the interview. Peter's comment was something Rick would always treasure. "Now this is something I wasn't sure I'd get to see when we first started interacting a year ago!"

Rick was so thankful for the skillful way Peter had walked him through the discipleship development process. ***From hell to health—there's not a better way for me to describe what has happened this past year.***

ADVENTURE 25 – CELEBRATION!!!

Gary and Kim offered to host the Memorial Celebration. Gary felt this would be the perfect opportunity to have a beef and pork roast. Vern volunteered to add clams and lobster to the menu. Gary had bought property that was in the demolition process and, during the week, he used his excavator to dig a large hole and fill it with bricks, slabs of concrete, and rocks. Using building debris, he and the guys built a huge fire over the bricks, concrete, and rocks to heat them up. Vern drove to the coast to pick up the seafood and a load of seaweed to cover the hot bed and cook the food in. What originally was meant to be an afternoon activity morphed into an entire weekend party with a bonfire, lots of food, music provided by Sam, games, and meaningful conversations.

Sunday afternoon was truly the highlight for everyone on the Team. When the time came to share memories of the past year, Sam reached for Michelle's hand and began.

"For Michelle and me, sharing our memorials from this past year will be challenging in a couple of ways. To start with, it involves a couple here who we have come to appreciate so much—Burt and Betty. Your painful experience this past year was the catalyst that God used to help us get to the bottom of our marital mistakes. Watching the way you handled your lives through your pain gave us the courage to deal with our baggage. We were tired of the dysfunction and the shallowness of our relationship."

"I was tired of living in a world where Sam never measured up to my ideals," Michelle inserted. "Sam used to be my dream, but his unfaithfulness shattered that. Slowly, I slipped into a fantasy world, wishing that someone would come and rescue me from my pain. Little did I realize that Sam was the only one God had designed to help rescue me. As we began to review some of the marriage materials we had received during previous counseling sessions, the Holy Spirit started to teach us how to put off the garbage and put on God's beautiful intentions for marriage. I know our marriage is stronger than ever because of what we have gone through."

Sam added, "We have enrolled in an online counseling program and hope to have a degree in marriage counseling in a few years. We're excited about God using us to help other couples find healing. I'm also convinced that my personal passion for evangelism will be exercised as we counsel couples."

Burt and Betty had their arms around each other, and their tears flowed freely as Sam and Michelle shared their story. Burt spoke with a mixture of joy and pain. "It's humbling to know that God can take such a traumatic experience and redeem it in so many ways. For the first time in my life, I have prioritized my time management and placed God and Betty at the top of the list. I've learned to become transparent with Betty and have started an accountability process with Garret. My biggest take-away from this past year is this—**knowing what you're supposed to do is never a substitute for obedience.** The joy I was always looking for came through my obedience."

Betty was too emotional to talk; but the way she was cradled in Burt's arm and the smile on her face let everyone know that the past year was transformational for her as well. Burt and Betty had resigned from their jobs and were planning to follow through with their decision to take a year off and explore how God wanted them to serve as a unified team.

"Burt's comment concerning obedience would by my biggest take-away," Vern shared. "Several months ago, I mentioned my ova'-eating habits, but even then, I did little about it. I've known fa' yea's that my health was at stake and that I wasn't glorifying God by using food fa' self-centa'ed gratification. Becoming accountable with the men on this Team has been one of the best things I've eva' done. Gary and I have established a workout routine that combines physical and spiritual exa'cise. My only regret is that I didn't sta't doing this earlia'. As I've gotten healthia', I've noticed that God has been givin' me moa'e chances to sha'a my faith."

"Watching the hard work Vern has been putting into exercise and seeing the changes in his life has motivated me to deal with my own baggage," Vickie interjected. "I finally got the courage to go and visit my father and step-mother and then my biological mother. The visit with my mother went about like Rick's did with his father, but several misunderstandings were cleared up with my father and step-mother. She actually hugged me for the first time and told me she loved me. We're planning on spending Thanksgiving together this year—another first. In the area of personal change, I've mostly quit nagging Vern about his tardiness. I've slowly realized that my nagging was like verbal diarrhea; once it got started, it was hard to stop."

"I can relate to verbal challenges," Misty added. "Through this spiritual development process, Kevin began to find his identity in what God thought of him, which then gave him the courage to share some things with me that he previously had been afraid to do. One of those things was the motherly way I communicated to him. Without realizing it, I was stripping him of the respect he deserved. Every time we got into an argument over our financial situation, I would insinuate that our entire circumstances were his fault. God is helping me learn how to communicate what I feel and think without letting it come across as an attack."

"How did you get to that point?" Vickie inquired.

"Mostly by asking open-ended questions. I try to think of what I would like to say, and then turn it into a *How* or *What* question."

Kevin affirmed, "When Misty asks me open-ended questions, she is still able to communicate what is bothering her; but I don't feel like she is a judge, a jury, and a Greek goddess on wheels."

"A judge, a jury, and a Greek goddess on wheels—I like that!" Jared chuckled. "Are you two gaining any ground with your finances?"

"I finally humbled myself and found a Christian organization that specializes in financial intervention," Kevin answered. "They have helped us come up with a plan which should get us back on solid ground in a few years. It's not going to be easy, but we have hope for the first time in a long time."

As Kevin was sharing, Gary looked at Kim and whispered something in her ear; she nodded "Yes."

Kevin continued, "I've also applied the same principles to my time management. Recently Sam told me about his educational decision, and that inspired me to reduce the time I've been spending in front of the television and replace it with online courses."

Jared responded with uncharacteristic encouragement, "I believe you're going to make it. If God can start to break my critical attitude toward people, then He can help you with your financial and time-management problems. Over this last year, God has led Ruth through a *Paradigm* shift which has enabled her to quit stuffing her feelings inside" Jared paused with a slight grin before adding, "as most of you got to see during the interview process."

"It was a beautiful sight," Sam teased.

"I'm sure it was," Jared chuckled before continuing. "With her opening up, I have begun to realize how my critical comments have hurt my marriage, my family, and, most recently, my friends. During the interview process, I had a reality check that I was still in the

Childhood phase of discipleship development. After a healthy one-on-one conversation with Peter, I will be repeating this training process; only this time, I will have the responsibility to teach it to a mixed group of guys—some *Powerful* like myself and some *Peaceful*—to create healthy tension."

Sam laughed, "That will be a beautiful sight, too. Peter, you are an amazing, but scary, dude!"

Rick subconsciously added one more piece of mentoring information to his discipleship/leadership toolbox.

Jared concluded, "On a positive note, I'm tobacco free; I haven't had a chew for almost two months now."

Applause and cheers broke out among the Team. As Maggie was clapping, Vickie caught a sparkling flash coming from a ring on her hand. When things had quieted down, Vickie commented, "Maybe Maggie should share next; from the looks of her left hand, she might have experienced more than one *Paradigm* shift this past year!"

Garret sprang to his feet, threw his right hand over his heart, and announced, "Last night, I asked Maggie if she would consider becoming my wife. She let me know that she had *already* considered it, and then she willingly accepted. And, yes, we have experienced more than one *Paradigm* shift!"

More applause and cheering broke out.

After things settled down again, Maggie added, "This process has helped us both individually and, lately, as a prospective couple. To develop our relationship while covering *Paradigm*, *Past*, and *Potential* issues has been wonderful for us. We are excited about our future together."

"Rick and Penny are getting married next summer. Is this going to be a double wedding?" Vickie asked half teasingly.

"We're planning on getting married New Year's Day," Maggie responded.

Rick quickly recalled the clash of expectations between him and Penny last New Year's Day; his mind rolled back still further to that spring day at Hell's Canyon when he had yelled questions to God out of pure frustration. Like scenes from a movie, he ran through memories of his discipleship development during the last year, marveling at how much had changed. All that really remained to discover was how to live out his God-given purpose.

Throughout the Memorial Celebration weekend, Rick had reviewed all his possible opportunities. There was the offer from Gary to use his creative building skills while focusing on mentoring others through the discipleship development process, the offer to pastor his home church in Enterprise, and the opportunity to partner with friends from this Team in a brand new ministry venture that Peter had been dreaming about for years.

Up until this morning, he had wrestled with question after question. *What should I do? Does it matter to God which choice I make? Will my decision affect Peter and Lisa's ability to experience the fulfillment of their dream? There is my family in Enterprise; will they ever find healing? How many people live out their faith effectively in the work place? Can I find personal fulfillment in each of these choices? Will I miss God's best if I fail to make the right choice?*

Today, worshipping with his friends and recalling the *Discipleship Adventure Truths* they had learned together, a smile broke out on his face like sun breaking through storm clouds. He was reasonably certain about what he was called to do—and why. God and the angels were smiling as he silently yelled a big "Thank You" to his Heavenly Dad.

As Rick stood to share his decision with the Team, he felt a soft squeeze from Penny's hand that filled him with warmth, and Pete's eye contact spoke volumes.

Rick's future was filled with promise.

EPILOGUE

I have always hated stories that had no conclusive ending. So, why would I choose to do the very thing that has caused me angst?

As you play out the possible endings to Rick's story, what decision do you think he made? And, what reasons would you give to support your answer? Your answers to those two questions will reveal the depth of how well you have processed the truths in this story.

The intent of this story is to be a help to believers who are serious about moving forward in their spiritual development process. Making it through this story, it is obvious you desire to grow spiritually. If you want to share your ending version of Rick's story and the reasons you chose that ending, I would love to hear from you. You can email me at tr.4sda@gmail.com.

ABOUT THE AUTHOR

In addition to extensive job experience in both the timber industry and the construction world, TR has pastored churches in New Hampshire, Alaska, and Nebraska. He possesses a rare combination of life experiences that have helped to shape his philosophy of ministry and to develop a deep passion for spiritual development of those around him. He specializes in mentoring disciples and equipping potential leaders who will build multiplying team cultures.

He was married to Marie (Patterson) for sixteen years before the Lord took her home. Together, they have three children—Jesse, Hannah, and Leah—all of whom are grown, married, and have provided the joy of nine grandchildren.

In 2001, TR experienced God's gracious gift of marrying Dee (Martelle). Together, they have two daughters—Celeste and Angela. They currently reside in Scottsbluff, Nebraska.

PRODUCTS & SERVICES

To learn more about TR's discipleship/leadership products and services, you are invited to visit us at www.spiritual developmentadventures.com

- ➢ From Hell to Health: Rick Thomson's Study (*Workbook*)
- ➢ Spiritual Development Workshop
- ➢ Spiritual Development Assessment and Growth Plans

FUTURE PRODUCTS

- ➢ *5 Phases of Spiritual Development*
- ➢ *From Hell to Health: Peter McCormick's Story*